A Hidden
Sicilian History

A Hidden Sicilian History

Ettore Grillo

Strategic Book Publishing and Rights Co.

Strategic Book Publishing and Rights Co., LLC
USA | Singapore
www.sbpra.com

For information about special discounts for bulk purchases, please contact Strategic Book Publishing and Rights Co., LLC. Special Sales, at bookorder@sbpra.net.

ISBN: 978-1-68181-112-3

To Sebastiano Cannizzo

Contents

The Find

Everyone has a unique history and a special life. Some people— prophets, great philosophers, musicians, artists, kings, heroes, and so on—have left a mark on the books of history. Good or evil, the ones who have stood out are remembered by posterity; people like Julius Caesar, Napoleon Bonaparte, Adolph Hitler, Josef Stalin, and others. At their demise, the lives of ordinary people are like dead leaves swept away by the wind when fall arrives. They sink into oblivion as history pays them no mind. In addition to the history of individuals, there is that of nations, but no book can include the biographies of all the people who formed the nations of the world.

In truth, if it were possible to write an enormous book of history, it should record the life stories of everyone who has populated the earth through the centuries and millennia, for each living being has something different and particular to say, often worthy of being handed down through the generations.

Each person follows their own special path; it is impossible to find two lives that match perfectly. Even members of the same family have different stories. It is like seeing birds in the sky. They may look identical, but they are all different in both shape and character. There are long and short lives, and the loss of someone young is like a bud cut by the gardener before it blooms fully.

In Greek mythology, the Fates, three ladies dressed in white, symbolized man's fate. The first of them, Clotho, spun the thread of life on her spindle; the second one, Lachesis, measured its length by her rod; the third, called Atropos, cut the thread of life at her will. Nobody was able to oppose them. Even almighty Zeus was powerless against them; he was unable to change the destiny of a person even if he firmly wished it.

Countless people over the years have wished to know their destiny and future. For that reason, there have been astrologers, magicians, wizards, and oracles to consult. In ancient Greece, the Oracle of Delphi was renowned, as was Cuma in Italy. Inside the temples, usually sacred to the god Apollo, there were virgin priestesses called sibyls who told people their future, and it seems that their predictions were always exact.

It is not only in mythology, but also in the Bible that there are many instances of the prediction of the future. In fact, the prophets were inspired people that told of future events. They predicted the destiny of Israel and events linked to Jesus's life, as in the case of the Prophet Isaiah, who lived around the eighth century BC.

Nowadays, horoscopes and astrological forecasts rage. Even disbelievers read their daily astrological forecast in the newspaper or on the Internet, or they listen to it on the radio or while watching television.

The issue about the existence of destiny more or less remains unsolved. People's lives look like numberless straight lines, each one a different color and nuance, which emanate from a common center. Like the rails of a railway, they never meet, and each of them follows its own predetermined course. According to many theologians, and even in some passages from Martin Luther and Saint Paul, the trajectories of our lives follow a route already set. They believed that God has prearranged everything.

Poets, philosophers, and writers think in the same way. Free will is just illusion; man cannot act apart from the events that drag him here and there like a flag, which changes direction according to the wind that is blowing. It is as if a great architect had already designed a path for every living being to follow, as a director does when giving the actors roles in a play.

When I was a high school student I asked my philosophy teacher this question: "If God is omnipotent and all-seeing, He knows what is going to happen in the future since He is beyond space and time. Therefore, where is our free will? If the life to come is already plotted and known, what can people do to change a scene already set up?"

My teacher was a beautiful lady from Catania. All the schoolboys had fallen in love with her. As for me, I was enchanted by her Junoesque bearing and the way she arranged her hair, which she gathered up and kept fast with a hair slide every day new. She had the habit of sitting at her desk and testing the students who stood by her. We schoolboys couldn't help watching her legs when she was sitting on her chair and her skirt was pulled up a little bit.

Despite her beauty and gracefulness, she was very strict. She gave me her answer by paraphrasing Saint Augustine. "If I see a man standing on the edge of a ravine, I know that he is going to throw himself down. Yet he is free to give up his resolution to die." She meant that despite the fact that the future is already known, our free will remains.

Her answer didn't convince me then, and I am still not convinced. In my opinion, if God knows our future and the events to come, it means that the railway tracks that we follow are already laid.

The length and quality of every person's life is different. Many lives are gloomy from the beginning, others are luckier. However, most lives are made of ups and downs—that is, continuous alternation of joys and sorrows. Many personal stories consist in struggle: to make a living, conquer the heart of a loved one, come to power, and attain freedom. However, each life is like a piece of a huge jigsaw puzzle in the sky. You cannot find two pieces that are identical.

I am fond of technology, but sometimes when I see youngsters looking at their smartphones all day long a question arises in my mind. Is this the goal of life? And whenever I see a self-employed worker or an employee working tirelessly on Sundays and public holidays, I ask myself again, "Is this what God wants from us?"

On that point, I cannot help thinking of a surveyor from my town who was married to a charming wife and had a daughter. He had a job at a state firm that did road maintenance. He was an indefatigable worker. His office was by the side of the Palermo-Catania freeway, and many times when I went to Catania on Sunday I spotted his car in the parking lot near his office. Obviously, his work was everything he had in his life, as he worked continuously, but it was probably just an escape from something he considered unbearable. Apparently, his family appeared to be close-knit in public, while in the privacy of their home things were quite different.

If you run away from situations that cause you stress, anxiety, or uneasiness, you have the illusion of ridding yourself of unbearable problems, but that is a false impression. You cannot resolve your troubles by escaping. You should cope with your issues and overcome them.

Later, the tireless surveyor was found dead in his chair with his head laid on the desk in his office, a revolver still gripped in his hand. That was evidence that his overzealousness was just an escape from his family problems.

I have seen many people who read books continuously. At first glance they look very learned, but if you observe them carefully, you'll see that their so-called love for books is just an escape from reality. In other words, any action that is repeated too often and which goes on without interruption for long periods of time is assured to be pathological.

Even going to Mass may be an escape. I once noticed a person that attended a 6 p.m. Mass and then headed for a 7 o'clock Mass in a different church. He had nothing to do, so he moved from one church to another just to kill time.

A dear friend of mine who was a Protestant pastor once confessed to me that he had had many arguments with members of his congregation and was on the verge of quitting his office, but he didn't because he didn't know what he would do without his church.

There was a shop seller who had a notions store, and even though he was too old to run his business and no customers bought anything from him, he continued to keep open his shop just to have a way to spend his time. Otherwise, he had no idea what he would do.

A trader of building materials used to struggle daily to manage his firm. He was always overwhelmed with debts, and had a lot of trouble honoring his bills of exchange. He finally went bankrupt and all his worries vanished. One day I stumbled across him. I didn't know he had quit his job, but he looked much too flabby; moreover, he was pale.

"How is business?" I asked.

"I don't work anymore!" he answered with a disconsolate air.

"You should be more relaxed now without anything to do. You have no worries!"

"No, it is not quite that easy. When I worked, I had lots of worries about my customers, my suppliers, the bills and taxes to pay, and I had many things to do. I had so many concerns that I couldn't sleep at night. But I felt alive and satisfied. Now, with nothing to do, I am like a dead man."

Some individuals seek shelter inside their family or get married to feel safe and stable. Often, people become engaged to someone who is a second-choice lover. They cannot get the person they truly desire, and resort to living with someone they don't love just for the sake of safety.

For some people, meeting friends seems to be a daily challenge. They go to dance schools, gyms, bars, and similar places in an attempt to meet friends. But the more friends they get the more they feel alone, because their search for friendship comes from the void they have inside. Running after friends might be considered as an escape from reality as well. People fear remaining alone. They dread having to look inside themselves, so they flee from their loneliness and try to fill their inner void through friends.

All the cases mentioned above are clear examples of escaping from reality, from life. Some people are unable to live as they want, and flee from their painful condition to take refuge in some activity that can give them the illusion of being alive and safe. I have always avoided watching too much TV or staying in front of my laptop too long, as it can also signify an escape from reality.

I don't set myself up as an expert. I am just a good observer of people and situations. I have realized that anything we get involved in so much that we become identified with it, takes us away from real and authentic life, which requests that we live it fully and in all its facets.

What is the meaning and goal of our lives? Over the years, everyone has tried to answer this dilemma. If our lives are predestined, we don't need a goal, as our aims and targets have already been laid out in heaven long before we were born. So why strive for a target? We can confine ourselves to living just as it happens naturally and follow the stream of life, as the migrant birds do when they follow the airstream. We don't need to improve ourselves to overcome our shortcomings that prevent us from reaching our target.

Not everyone has a goal, and many people live without aim. They just spend their lives with no purpose. Other people have short-term or long-term goals. There are innumerable variations in people's ends, for as I told above, every life and story is different from another.

As for me, I am not sure about the existence or nonexistence of destiny or predestination. Therefore, I want to do my best to deepen my quest to know more about life, death, and the end of life. To do that, I started collecting data and information, not only through my travels, but also by reading many different kinds of books, even those that are old and rare.

The public library in my hometown is located within a few rooms of an old palace that long ago belonged to Andrea Chiaramonte's family, who was one of the eminent noblemen in Sicily at the end of the fourteenth century. He fought against the Spanish, but was defeated by them and sentenced to death by beheading. He was executed in Palermo in front of the Steri Palace where he had established his court. Meanwhile, his family members forfeited all their assets in Sicily, including the prestigious palace in Enna, which later was split into three parts. One part was given to the Franciscan friars, one was used as a court of law, and the smallest part as a civic library.

The ancient and precious volumes are kept on the highest wooden shelves. To reach them you need a special ladder provided by the attendant. One day I was on the ladder looking for a book that told the history of my town, when something that looked like a scroll fell onto the floor after having slipped from a gap between two big volumes about the Spanish Inquisition in Sicily that were placed on the highest shelf. Therefore, the scroll was supposed to be a part of them, or was at least somehow connected to them.

I got down from the ladder and bent down to pick up the strange roll, which at first sight contained sheets of paper tied up with a string. Thinking they were precious rare writings, I headed for the director's office to hand in the yellowish bundle of sheets.

I knocked on the door of the office and a man with a stentorian voice prompted me to enter. As soon as I saw the manager, I recognized him. He was one meter and ninety centimeters tall, which is unusual in Enna, where the average height is a bit more than one meter and sixty-five centimeters. Whenever he walked in the streets with his German shepherd he stood out, but I didn't know he was the boss of the local library. His nose was quite red, with small hollows similar to those of a raspberry, a clear sign of his tendency to drink too much wine. However, he was very well mannered.

"Please, sit down. How may I help you?"

"I found this scroll on the highest shelf in the main reading room. I think it belongs to the library."

"When did you find it?"

"Just now, not more than five minutes ago."

The director untied the roll and unrolled it on his desk. Then he sneezed several times. "Sorry!" he said. "I am allergic to dust."

"That is no problem!" I answered.

The roll contained many handwritten pages. The paper was yellow with age and had a nauseating, moldy smell. The director examined the paper sheets very carefully. The writing was readable, even though some lines were discolored. However, from the expression on his face I got the sensation that he wanted to get rid of that bulk of old papers as soon as possible.

"These are not in the list of the things that belong to the library. However, I want to ask the attendant. He's worked at the library for almost forty years. He is near his retirement and knows everything about the old volumes in the library. Who knows, maybe he can give us some useful information. Abraham!" he called out.

Instantly, an old short man with greasy white hair and prominent jawbones came along.

"Have you ever seen these sheets?" asked the boss.

The attendant, who wore thick glasses for short-sightedness, came near the director's desk and bent his head forward to have a better look at the papers. He took off his spectacles to see clearly and eyed the bulk of stinky sheets narrowly, leafing through a few pages.

"No sir," he said. "This is the first time I've come across this kind of stuff in our library."

"Okay, that means that the shelves need better cleaning!" said the irritated director. "Tomorrow morning you must remind the cleaner to dust and mop all the shelves properly, starting with the upper ones. Now go toss this filthy stuff that is soiling my desk and my hands."

The attendant showed annoyance and replied, "The cleaner does her work irreproachably every morning. As soon as she comes she dusts off the volumes that are on the upper shelves. Then she sweeps and mops all the rooms."

I was so engrossed in the squabble between the two that I didn't pay attention to the attendant, who already was carrying the scroll under his arm. But I soon returned from my reverie and turned towards him when he was about to open the door to leave the room.

"No, please don't throw away those sheets of paper. I can use them," I said to the attendant.

The old man turned back and looked at the director, waiting for orders. "*Res derelictae, res nullius,*" said the director with his thundering voice.

"What does that mean?" asked the old man.

"It means that whoever finds a derelict thing has the right to take possession of it if it is not reclaimed by the rightful owner. This gentleman," continued the director, pointing at me, "has the right to keep what he has found. You can give him the material."

The elderly clerk stepped back and handed me the sheets. I folded and bound them with the string and left the library, rushing to my home.

Outwardly, they looked like very old and historical papers. I had the impression of having stumbled across a rare precious report about an *auto-da-fé*, which were held in great numbers throughout Sicily at the time of the Spanish Inquisition. According to some historians, 114 *autos-da-fé* were celebrated throughout Sicily from 1501 to 1748. The word *auto-da-fé* comes from the Portuguese *auto da fé*, meaning an act of faith.

An *auto-da-fé* consisted of a public ceremony where a sentence of the Spanish Inquisition was carried out. Before the enforcement of the judgment, the condemned person was made to file between two lines of people, their hair was shaved, and then they were dressed with a donkey cap and a sack on which were painted the grounds of the judgment. If it was painted with a full Saint Andrew's cross, it meant that the condemned person had repented in time to avert the execution; a half cross showed that he had been just fined, while the flames meant that he had been sentenced to death at the stake.

A solemn Mass attended by city authorities and a large gathering of the townspeople was celebrated where the *auto-da-fé* took place. People came together in great numbers as if there was a festival, and many street vendors flocked from the nearby towns and villages to sell cakes, carobs, licorice, and similar things.

In Enna, death sentences were enforced in the largest square, which is called Municipality Square. Near the scaffold was the small Church of the Lady of Sorrows, where the condemned person stayed and received the confession of sins and Holy Communion before filing towards the stake. Recent excavations in the Church of the Lady of Sorrows brought to light a niche where people sentenced to death spent the last hours of their life.

It was also possible that the old dusty scroll contained a report of one of the many capital sentences passed in Sicily against sodomites. It has been reported that at the time of the Spanish Inquisition, from 1547 to 1640, around a hundred capital punishments were enforced against homosexuals and people who had had "deviant" sexual intercourse, like oral or anal sex. Copulation with animals was also liable to bring a death sentence. In fact, any sexual activity not directed toward procreation was considered a capital sin. Sometimes the confession of those sins was wrung out by torture, even though at the time of the Spanish Inquisition it was not necessary to torture the suspect, because the mere sight of the instruments of torture was enough to persuade the alleged culprit to confess all their sins—or whatever else the inquisitor wanted them to confess, for that matter.

While heretics went directly to the stake to be burnt alive, homosexuals and sexually indecent people usually, as an act of mercy to make their death less agonizing, were strangled or hanged before being burned at the stake. In any case, those kinds of death sentences were enforced publicly to serve as a deterrent to others.

The main difference between the Medieval Inquisition and the Spanish Inquisition is that the former was directed by the Pope, while the latter was under the authority of the king of Spain, who enforced the Inquisition's rules not only in Spain but also in the Spanish possessions like Sicily, Sardinia, and Mexico. Spanish kings used the Inquisition not only to judge heretics and witches, but also to get rid of their political opponents, on the pretext they were heretics.

One of the most atrocious instruments of torture was that called "the mouse." The inquisitor inserted a live mouse into the vagina or the anus of the person suspected of heresy or witchcraft. The head of the small rodent was directed towards the inner organs of the prisoner. Sometimes the anus or the vagina was stitched closed. The little animal, striving to find a way out, penetrated the victim's body, scratching and biting it, provoking shooting pain.

I was so anxious to arrive home that, lost in my reverie as I was, I didn't even see the people in the street. I thought about how strange it was that one person's trash is another's treasure. I was sure of having found a document worth more than all the volumes in the library of Enna.

Once at home, I dusted off the sheets and laid them onto my desk, eager to decipher them. I wanted to know all the details of the trial against the heretic that had been sentenced to death and the exact protocol that was applied.

The handwriting was clear and readable. Nevertheless, the more I leafed through the pages the more I got disenchanted. Unfortunately, the papers didn't contain either a report of an *auto-da-fé*, as I had hoped, or a detailed account of a death sentence of the Spanish Inquisition against homosexuals.

The first page held the title "A Hidden Sicilian History," and about 300 numbered pages followed. The script was anonymous; its author could have been a man or a woman, young or old. There was no evidence to trace the author.

I read it line by line, day after day. To my surprise, the events told in the manuscript didn't belong to the remote past. How was it possible that such recent happenings were written on such old, filthy paper? One of the plausible answers was that the author had stocked a considerable amount of paper at home, which had then turned yellowish due to the dampness of the place where it was stored. That was not unusual in Enna, where the fog wrapped up the town very often and not many houses were fitted with a heating system.

I don't know why, but I doubted that the author knew what kind of research I was doing and had purposely put those sheets of paper on the top shelf so that I would stumble across them.

I also wondered why the author didn't try to publish their work. There were a few probable answers. First of all, it is not easy to be a published author, and if you want to publish a book yourself, you have to spend some money. Maybe the author didn't have the ability to do that. There was another likely explanation: maybe the author was so shy and introverted that they didn't feel comfortable asking anybody for help in getting the manuscript published.

Nevertheless, the writing denoted the presence of a person of action, someone strong and extroverted. The only explanation I thought acceptable was that somebody had told the events to the author, who then wrote a tale that didn't come from their own experience or imagination.

As soon as I finished reading the story, I was undecided as to what to do. In fact, in my opinion the tale was full of tortuous reasoning, and some passages were so absurd that nobody would believe them. It looked like a script for dead people. In fact, many of the characters seemed as if they had come back from their graves to tell their lives to a world in which they no longer belonged.

I thought that maybe the manager of the library, who intended to throw away the useless, yellowed old sheets of paper, was right. But after much mulling over what to do with the strange finding, I at last realized that it might be worth something. It was absolutely not trash, as it contained some useful information about life and the traditions in Enna, a mountain city in the center of Sicily. Moreover, it described the ways that religious searchers went along their spiritual path.

I was hesitant about typing the contents, and considered giving the work back to the library, but I was not sure that the manager would accept the gift. After ruminating for a while, I came to the decision to translate the story into English and have it published. I opted for the translation of the manuscript instead of maintaining the original Italian, because by doing so I thought it would fulfill the author's will. Indeed, he or she had intended to hand the tale down to whoever found it, in the same way somebody does when they fit a written message into a glass bottle and entrust it to the ocean. I thought by translating and publishing the story in English that it would be more likely to cross the ocean and reach faraway lands, as no country is devoid of English language readers.

A Hidden Sicilian History is not a great literary work. Its contents are very deep, and it is neither engaging nor gripping, but maybe it can be useful to somebody who wants to know something uncommon. It is quite boring at times, and contains many abrupt digressions, but some of the information is really unique.

I decided to publish the work because, in my opinion, chance events don't exist. In other words, if I stumbled across that script, it was not by chance but a superior will wanted it, and maybe the author chose me as a means to spread their thoughts. Furthermore, apart from its literary style, which is not lofty, the manuscript is worth reading because of the huge amount of information that it contains. It will definitely broaden the reader's mind.

Enna is a small town, but over the years it has fostered the hopes of great spirits and people that have devoted their lives to missions in faraway lands, like Blessed Girolamo De Angelis (1567-1623), a Jesuit friar who left his hometown to follow his spiritual path. At the beginning of the seventeenth century he went to Japan to spread the Gospel, but fell into fierce persecution against Christians and had his life ended by being burnt at the stake. Enna is the birthplace of good writers like Nino Savarese and Napoleone Colajanni—the latter was also an honest politician and sociologist—and musicians like Francesco Paolo Neglia. The spiritual path followed by the main character of this story is worthy of note, though minor in scale.

Not many towns in the world can boast so peculiar a lifestyle. It is possible that if I hadn't published *A Hidden Sicilian History* some of Enna's oral traditions would have been lost forever.

The events happen because they had to happen, not by accident. There is an invisible thread on Earth that links all people who have the same spiritual feelings, regardless of their race or skin color. They belong to the same spiritual race. The real races are not physical but spiritual, and you can feel it clearly whenever you have the chance to come across someone with similar feelings and nature. Through that scroll, the author wanted to create an invisible chain of spiritual beings, which he intended to become broader and broader.

Here is the translation . . .

Chapter One
The Church of Santa Croce

Ladies and gentlemen, let me introduce myself to the reading public. My name is Vincenzino, and I am one of the characters in a drama that was performed some time ago in Enna on the stage of the deconsecrated Church of Santa Croce.

All the sacred objects had been removed from the church: the wooden altar, vestments, and holy pictures. Where once there was the altar, now a stage had been erected. Of all the statues and holy paintings that crowded the walls, only one portraying the Virgin Mary on the crescent with a snake under her feet had been left, and now it stands on the far right of the stage.

Our director was Paolo, a middle-aged stout man with a limping walk due to an untreated fungal infection in his feet, who had been the sacristan of the small church and who had developed a deep passion for theatre and poetry through the years. He was unmarried and lived with his single sister, who was also the costume designer for our theatrical company. Their house was very old; it had been built at least a hundred years ago and was connected to the church.

As a sacristan, he'd had the task of keeping clean the place and locking the wooden chairs, which were stacked at the entrance. In fact, at that time all the churches in Enna were furnished with just a few rows of pews. People who wanted a seat during Mass or a religious function had to rent the chair from the sacristan, paying a fee. Nowadays, Mass is held every day in Catholic churches, but before the last ecumenical council it was celebrated only on Sundays and holy days. A benediction was performed every evening on the weekdays. After each function, Paolo took care of cleaning the hall; moreover, he restacked the chairs and fastened them with an iron chain that he padlocked.

After the church had been deconsecrated due to the shortage of priests, Paolo lost his job as a sacristan, but he still had money to live on. While remodeling his house some time ago, he had found an earthenware moneybox in a walled-up niche full of gold coins that were minted at the beginning of the Kingdom of Italy. On the other hand, his sister worked as a nurse at the local hospital and contributed towards the living expenses.

As for our play, Paolo had organized the work by making each actor perform his own life story on stage. According to him, life is just a play, or sometimes a tragedy, but never something real.

In the play, seven actors dressed in white sat astride on chairs with the audience behind their shoulders. When it was one's turn, the houselights were turned off and an usher, who wore a cloak fastened with a gilded buckle, lit a line of candles that formed a horizontal number eight, symbolizing infinite space and time. At the rear of the stage beside the candles, two musicians with a guitar and a violin constantly played their background music. Whenever it was their turn, one of the actors stood up, slowly turning their body towards the audience, and with a lofty tone started telling some episodes in their life.

Paolo used to say that this kind of play had a cathartic meaning, which is equivalent to inner cleansing, beneficial to the actors and the audience as well.

At the comment that the play would take a long time to get to the end constructed this way, Paolo answered that time doesn't exist; it is just human work. It is our limited mind that creates the concept of space and time, but in the universe it is always now and there are no distances between one side of it and another.

Every day we performed that play, and a few people alternated in the hall of the church, now turned into a theatre house. For Paolo, it was important to play with a loud voice without lowering the sound at the end of the words. For him, words had to be uttered in their wholeness.

It didn't matter if we moved along the stage or stood unmoving like statues. We were free to gesticulate as much as we liked. For our director, theatre meant freedom of expression. Life is freedom as well.

Someone objected that actors were not normally allowed to freely express themselves because they had to follow a script, but Paolo said that it was not like that in the beginning. Anyway, his job as a director was to restore the primeval freedom of expression, which was typical of the actors on stage. All the players alternated according to Paolo's direction. He was a kind person as well as a qualified director.

When my turn came, the lights in the church were put out. Everything became pitch black, except my white robe. The background was the starry sky and the candlelit number eight that was silhouetted against the sidereal space. As the musicians struck up their instruments, I got up from my chair and a stage floodlight followed all my movements. I headed for the center of the stage and started off by telling a few episodes from my childhood and adulthood. I confined myself just to telling what, in my opinion, was most significant. My aim was to pass something interesting and educational on to the audience, leaving aside whatever might sound trivial.

Chapter Two
The Estate in Pollicarini

Sebastiano was my father's uncle, although he was not much older. In fact, he was my grandmother's younger brother, and the difference in age between them spanned several years. He was born at the beginning of 1900 in the old neighborhood of Saint Peter, and he showed a disposition to acts of bravery from a young age. In 1917, despite being just seventeen, he volunteered for active service during the First World War.

Later, with the rise of Mussolini, he became a member of the Fascist action squads, taking part in the march on Rome. As the Fascist Party became established, he fit in first as one of the Blackshirts, and then got a job at the Fascist Federation of Enna. Apparently, he had an important role in the party. Thanks to him, my Uncle Salvatore got a contract as a hauler of military supplies in Ethiopia. Moreover, he was the one who helped my family's emerging business by ensuring the needed political support.

His wife, Annette, was ten years older than him. They were childless, and he considered his nephews and nieces as his own children. Angelina was the oldest, followed by Salvatore, Giuseppe, Francesco (my father), Mariano, and the youngest, Amelia. He loved all of them, but he was particularly fond of Salvatore. They were almost the same age and had an astonishing likeness, so much so that they looked like brothers. He admired Salvatore's heart, because he always put the family's well-being before his own.

My grandmother, Maria, died very young, when Amelia was still a little baby. When she fell ill with the disease that led her to death, she was so weak that she could not breastfeed Amelia, who was then in danger of dying as well. At that time, powdered milk was not available, and cow or goat milk was not always right to give to newborn babies. Some people used donkey milk, which was believed to be similar to human milk, to feed babies in extreme situations, but this kind of food was not always within reach.

No one in the family seemed able to save Amelia's life. My grandfather, Giovanni, was resigned to losing his wife and his daughter, but Salvatore didn't get discouraged and began frantically searching the streets and alleys, trying to find a wet nurse that could feed Amelia. He got information and knocked on many doors to find a woman with a baby that would take Amelia on her breast as well, but he was met with many refusals, as most of women had milk enough for only one baby. At last, just when his hope was about to die, he found a lady that had recently given birth and who would accept Amelia to her breast as well. He took his dying sister into his arms and rushed to the wet nurse. Thanks to her elder brother, Amelia is still alive. Every time Sebastiano recalled this episode, he got a lump in his throat and his eyes moistened with tears.

After Mussolini's death, the Fascist Party was suppressed and its reconstitution forbidden by the law. Of course, the Fascist Federation of Enna was also banished and Sebastiano lost his job.

What to do without a job? Sebastiano was in his forties, and the economic crisis after the war was biting the small town of Enna. Many people were starving, and if it hadn't been for food aid from the Americans, many townspeople would have died of starvation. As for me, even though my family was not poor, the food was not abundant. When I recall those times, I remember always being hungry.

To clothe us children, my mother reused things. I wore many woolen sweaters and underwear that had belonged to my elder brother, and my younger brother reused my clothes once they became too tight for me as I grew taller.

Fortunately, Uncle Salvatore had bought a plot of land for his family in a district called Virardi during the Second World War. When the war was over, he purchased another estate in an area called Pollicarini, so Sebastiano was employed to take care of his nephews' properties.

When I was eight years old I got typhus, and the next year I again got typhoid fever because I had eaten too many unwashed loquats. After fifteen days of fever, my body was heavily weakened and my weight went down. When I looked at my legs, I saw that they resembled two thin wires. My parents were very worried about my condition, so they decided to send me to the countryside for summer holidays and entrusted me to the care of Sebastiano.

The estate in Pollicarini, with its ancient house, had belonged to a knight named Greca. It was the first property that the nobleman had given away to finance his political campaigns. Greca was a rare example of a person who ruined himself by engaging in politics. He was born of rich parents and got married to a young woman named Caterina. Their union produced a daughter, but their marriage didn't last long. According to many, one day Caterina lost her balance while shaking a blanket on the balcony of her house and fell headlong onto the street. The truth was that she committed suicide.

Outwardly, his wife's suicide didn't affect Greca's behavior. He continued his political career as if nothing had happened. I still remember him with his big belly, wearing a grey suit and chatting with people in front of the town hall. Inwardly, he was not as unperturbed as he appeared. In fact, his wife's suicide had turned his life into hell. When a dear one commits suicide, the reactions of family members are often contrasting.

One day, I had the chance to meet a lady whose son had married a girl from Argentina. At first the husband and wife led a happy life, but as time passed their ties began to deteriorate. The husband's character got more and more gloomy until he put an end to his life.

His wife returned to her country, but his mother couldn't accept that her beloved son had passed away so suddenly. She was shaken to the extent that she couldn't even get rid of the furniture that had belonged to her beloved child. She wanted to buy an apartment in order to keep all her son's belongings inside. Finally, she bought the apartment and arranged her son's kitchen, bedroom, living room, laundry, and everything that had been in some way connected to him. She recreated the atmosphere of her son's home, thinking him still alive. Every evening she went to that empty apartment, prayed, and imagined talking with him. She also bought a garage to keep her son's car, and paid car insurance and taxes every year. For her, it was unthinkable to sell her son's car.

A twenty-year-old university student named Mario was engaged to an eighteen-year-old schoolgirl named Claudia. They dated for three years, but he felt that he was too young to be engaged. Furthermore, he couldn't bear the excessive influence the parents of both families had on their lives. He wanted to extricate himself from the commitment, but he didn't know how to get rid of the tie that he considered too tight for his age.

Nevertheless, Claudia's mother continued to press her daughter, who could do nothing to keep the engagement alive. The exasperating situation finally led Claudia to kill herself. Both families blamed Mario as being guilty of driving Claudia to suicide. The police even investigated him for allegedly inciting the suicide.

From that moment on Mario's life changed radically. He continued to feel guilty for the rest of his life, even though he had been discharged by the police and thought to remedy his wrongdoing by leading a life marked by his devotion to helping his fellow man as much as possible. Obviously, his propensity to do good deeds was not part of his character, but he suppressed all his natural shortcomings and bad instincts to become a good man to atone for his alleged sin.

Greca's reaction to his wife's suicide was the complete opposite. He wanted to forget whatever he could remember of his wife. He joined the political fray and began to sell his properties in Enna, one by one, to buy two hotels in Taormina, where he at last moved to spend the rest of his life. He left the furniture, pieces of cutlery, Chinese vases, and valuables in the house in Pollicarini. He wanted to erase the memory of the tragedy that had marked his life at any cost.

The house had been kept in good condition and had several rooms. Sebastiano took a small room with a bed for himself where he used to spend the night. When I came to stay with him in the house, he added a bed in his room for me.

The house had two stories, as well as a small room in the loft that we could enter through a winding wooden staircase. I only remember going to that room once or twice with Sebastiano. He used to keep his chicks there, as he figured that the magpies were not able to snatch them while they were in that room.

The person that worked the land lived in two rooms on the first floor. Other rooms were used as a stable and a wine cellar, as well as places for a wood-burning oven and a wine press. The henhouse was detached. There were two she-asses in the stable, which were co-owned by my family and the agricultural laborer.

A bit over the courtyard near the roost there was a cistern where the rainwater from the roofs was conveyed to be used to drink. Near the cistern there was a stone basin with some water for the bees to drink. The beehive was a bit further out and looked like a little house. Sebastiano had planted a long line of prickly pear cactuses to keep off the people from the bees, which were very vicious.

The house was ancient and still maintained the shape that it had from the time it was built. Everything had been kept intact: the black piano, the sofas, the tables, the chairs in the dining room, even the stonework kitchen with its fine, decorated tiles. The kitchen opened onto a wide terrace encircled by railings on three sides.

Many portraits on the walls revealed the figures of Greca's ancestors. All the portraits gave a sinister look to the house, but Sebastiano wanted to keep everything intact to respect the memory of those who had passed. At that time there was no electricity in the countryside, and we used an old oil lamp that had been left by the previous owner to provide some light.

The closets were still full of clothes. There were many evening dresses and suits. I remember seeing a black waistcoat with a vest pocket watch. I tried to imagine the atmosphere in the house and I could feel it was not happy. Many times, despite appearances, rich people are the most miserable of all.

Anyway, even the rich die, and now they are in another dimension, or maybe they have disappeared into thin air without leaving an imprint behind. What happens when we die? What happened to the Greca and his wife? Did they leave some imprints in the house, or at their death did they just slip away and vanish like snow under the sun?

While I lived in the house, we started our day with a cup of coffee made by Sebastiano. He didn't want me to call him Uncle Sebastiano, despite the fact he was old enough to be my grandfather, because if I did he would feel too old. In fact, his spirit was still young, and despite his white hair, he could run and jump like a little boy.

Usually after a cup of coffee and some slices of bread and biscuits we went hunting—or rather, he was the hunter; I just followed him. We set off around five in the morning when it was still dark and the air brisk. As we walked and the darkness of night gave way to the half-light of dawn, the air got a bit warmer.

To hunt we used our three white long-haired dogs, who were mongrels but who endowed with unerring noses. Obviously, I didn't have a weapon and confined myself to walking behind Sebastiano. He carried a double-barreled rifle, a cartridge belt around his waist, and a bunch of strings where he tied the animals he killed.

He was in the habit of making the cartridges himself, and for the purpose he used a kit made of a precision balance to weigh both the gunpowder and the pellets, and a tool to push the gunpowder and pellets inside the case. According to him, a good hunter must be able to make his cartridges himself, because a different kind of gunpowder and pellets are needed depending on the game you are going to hunt. The weather was also important in selecting the proper gunpowder. If the weather was dry he used the gunpowder of such and such brand; during moist or cold weather he employed a different brand.

Not many times in my life have I seen scenery comparable to that which I beheld when I went to hunting with Sebastiano. I'll never forget the sun rising from the flanks of the volcano on Mount Etna. The great mountain was still covered with snow, the sun was visible to the naked eye, and the morning star was silhouetted against the sky like a brooch on a blue, reddish mantle.

While we walked our dogs tried to rouse rabbits, Greek partridges, or hares. Suddenly, in the distance a rabbit moved quickly towards its burrow, but Sebastiano's unerring eye didn't give it a chance. I rejoiced over that rabbit's death, unaware that with passing time I would change my opinion about hunting, as I would become incapable of even hurting a fly. I would come to love all creatures. But at the time I was very cruel to animals and insects. In the upper level of the hen house at Pollicarini, Sebastiano had created a shelter where the domestic pigeons could nest and reproduce. When the young pigeons had grown enough to be eaten, we took them from the nest and killed them by drowning. I enjoyed drowning the small creatures, even though I didn't much like their meat.

Another cruelty I used to commit was killing the flies on the windowpanes by burning them little by little. First I burned their wings with a lighted match, and then when they couldn't fly I tortured them with the tip of my burning cigarette until they died.

Sometimes if I happened to catch a mouse its death would also be atrocious. I'd smear it with gasoline and then light a match and set fire to the tip of its tail. Then its whole body would catch fire and the mouse ran for a while until it died.

What I was not able to do was another cruelty that some people of my town committed. Whenever two dogs were making love, they remained stuck to each other for a while, sometimes for half an hour, because the male's penis could not withdraw from the female's vagina. Some stupid, dull people would fetch a shovel and strike a blow between the two dogs to get them separated. This appalling action usually resulted in the death of the male dog and sometimes that of the female as well.

Sebastiano used to say that hunting was a noble sport, and a good hunter must have his personal code of honor, which consisted of not killing more animals than you needed for eating, respect and love for nature, and never lighting a fire to drive out a wild animal. He never used a ferret to get a rabbit out of its burrow, because a ferret can kill many rabbits inside, giving rise to useless slaughter.

Moreover, he recommended I put prudence before greediness. "Never jeopardize the life of a dog when you shoot game," he used to say. "When you are shooting, the scope must be clear. Refrain from shooting near farm houses or in poor visibility."

Sebastiano taught me how wild animals live. The rabbit is an animal of fixed habits. It spends all his life in the same territory, while the hare lives in the flatlands and changes its territory continuously. There are animals that live long, like the crows, while there are insects like the mayflies that live just one day; they are born in the morning and die that night.

Sebastiano looked after me like a father, and every time I had a relapse and my fever rose he made me eat bread and honey. In his opinion, honey is rough and can remove the throat inflammation. However, thanks to him my health improved and my legs became fuller.

We usually hunted until 9 a.m. and then stopped because, according to Sebastiano, it was too hot for the dogs to smell the rabbits. Once at home, Sebastiano gutted the rabbit or the bird we had caught, and after a few hours he cooked it.

Once the sun was high in the sky it was impossible to hunt or work the land, so Sebastiano, the farm laborer, and I stayed in one of the rooms on the first floor waiting for lunch. It took several hours before we could have lunch, so we sat still on the bench and just waited. Nowadays, this kind of thing is inconceivable. People always have something to do—watch TV, listen to the radio, play on the Internet, or talk on the phone—but at that time we didn't have such devices. Television hadn't been invented yet, and we needed electricity to listen to the radio.

While we were waiting, my attention was caught by the singing of the cicadas that filled the silence of the countryside. I asked Sebastiano to show me one of them, but he said it was not possible because they lived on the high branches of the trees and it was not easy to spot them. Anyway, those long waits in the sunny summer mornings gave me the ability to endure waiting. We confined ourselves to waiting until lunchtime.

Sebastiano and I used to eat our meals on normal plates, but the farmhand ate more than we did and put his meals on his special dish called a *lemma*, which means "big bowl" in Sicilian.

The daily dish was pasta with cabbage and potatoes seasoned with olive oil. Meat was too expensive and not easy to get. Only when Sebastiano killed a rabbit or a bird did we have meat. On special occasions the farmhand wringed a chicken's neck. In any case, we couldn't preserve meat because we didn't have a fridge. To keep cool, we used to put a watermelon or a melon into a basket and put it down into the cistern where the water was quite cold. The only thing that could be preserved for a long time was cheese, which was yellow because of the use of saffron in its preparation, and stuffed with black pepper grains. In the evening our food was lighter and consisted of cheese or poached eggs that Sebastiano, in a kind manner, forced me to eat.

The table was laid by the farmhand who never shorted us good wine. I was too young to drink alcohol, but Sebastiano used to pour a little red wine into my glass, diluting it with water. In his opinion, good wine makes good blood.

In the afternoon when the air got cooler, we went around the land to check if everything was okay and that the farmhand had done an acceptable job. Sebastiano took particular care in the vineyard, which had to be dug often and sprayed with dry sulfur at the right time. A belated spraying could compromise the harvest.

Whenever he spotted some walnuts left on the soil, he picked them up. I thought that was quite strange.

"What are you going to do with those two walnuts in your pocket?" I once asked.

"I'll take the walnuts home and put them in the pile on the terrace to dry. I want to increase my nephews' finances!"

At night before going to bed we sat on the terrace gazing at the starlit sky. There was not much illumination in my town at the time, and in the countryside there was no power at all. We had an oil-fueled power supplier in the house in Pollicarini, but we used it only on special occasions. So we put our oil lamp on the marble top of the kitchen table, set two chairs on the terrace near the walnut heap, and sat, just watching the sky.

Moths thronging around the glass of the oil lamp cast their shadows on the walls of the kitchen. The moths' shadows projected on the walls looked much bigger than their actual size and made a pyrotechnic display that mesmerized me. From time to time our dogs barked at other roaming animals or passersby, and the sky seemed an immense blue space where every kind of heavenly body twinkled. There were so many spots of light that even counting to a billion would not be enough. Some sources of light were very bright, while others were barely visible. Sometimes meteors appeared and disappeared, streaking the vault of heaven.

Sebastiano taught me the constellations and the influence of the moon on the earth. "Whenever I sow a field with wheat," he said, "I consider the cycle of the moon. You cannot sow a field at random, but only when the moon is waxing. In that way the seeds absorb energy from the moon and the seedlings will be strong."

"Today is August fifteenth," Sebastiano said one night, "and in the neighborhood of Fundrisi in Enna they are celebrating the mid-August feast of the Madonna."

"What kind of celebration is it?"

"Tradition says that Mary, Jesus's mother, didn't die, unlike all other human creatures. She fell asleep and the angels took her to heaven."

"What is that long line of clouds in the sky?" I asked.

"Those are not clouds, Vincenzino. It is Saint James's Ladder, also called the Milky Way. Through it souls go up and down. They come from faraway stars, stay on the earth for a while, and then migrate towards new lands in the sky, always passing through Saint James's Ladder."

"Where are the sky boundaries, Sebastiano?"

"There are no boundaries in the sky. It is infinite, with neither beginning nor end."

"That's impossible! I cannot imagine anything without a limit. Everything has a boundary. For instance, our estate borders other neighboring properties."

"If you are convinced that there is a border in the sky, tell me what there is beyond the border, Vincenzino."

"Another universe, of course!"

"And where is the border of the second universe? And that of the third and so forth? As you see, we cannot find the last border, and we cannot understand the universe because our minds are limited. It is like trying to teach our dogs to read. You'll never succeed."

"When was the universe created, Sebastiano?"

"According to some scientists, it seems that the universe is expanding; in fact, both stars and planets run away from a center. In other words, there was a time when all the matter of the universe was concentrated in only one spot—like a storehouse where bricks are packed. Then suddenly the storehouse exploded and the bricks were cast into the space. They started moving in different directions and are still moving."

"Who made the storehouse explode?"

"I don't know, Vincenzino. Christians say that it was God who did it. Atheists, who are people that don't believe in God, think that the explosion happened naturally."

"What was there before the explosion? Has the storehouse always existed or was it made by someone?"

"I am not able to answer your question, Vincenzino, but I am sure that when you become an adult you'll study this subject and find the answer. Now, it is the time to go to bed."

"Do you know, Sebastiano, where all those souls are going that you say come up and down through Saint James's Ladder?"

"We'll talk about that tomorrow. It is too late now."

In the small room where we slept, before falling asleep under the light of the moon and stars that filtered through the shutters, Sebastiano used to tell me his war feats.

"You have to know, Vincenzino, that I was on the front line when I served in the army. During the Second World War, I was first sent to Croatia and then to Cyrenaica, and the sound of the bullets whistling close to my ears became familiar. One night in Croatia, our platoon was crawling towards the top of a hill, but the enemy was doing the same on the opposite slope. Suddenly, we heard the rat-tat-tat of enemy gunshots. Can you figure out what happened, Vincenzino?"

"I have no idea, Sebastiano."

"Well, the officer that commanded our platoon panicked, and instead of leading his troops to attack, he began to tremble with fear and was on the brink of having a nervous breakdown."

"What did you do without a commander, Sebastiano? Did you run away?"

"Not at all, Vincenzino! I scolded the commander. 'What kind of man are you? I will lead the troops to attack if you keep shivering in your shoes!' But he said, 'I don't want to die! I am still young!' I said, 'You have to die one day or another, but it is better to die and leave a scent behind you, instead of stinking if you escape as a coward.'

"The young first lieutenant was shaken by my words, and he gathered his strength and led our platoon to victory."

"Sebastiano, how is it possible that you went to war twice, always stayed on the front line, and never got even the tiniest injury?"

"It was not my destiny to die or be wounded in war. Remember, Vincenzino, even though you plan your future very carefully, you cannot succeed without God's will. Some people say that you can win your battles only if they are just and according to your destiny. Once there was a great commander called Napoleon who had planned his last battle at Waterloo very carefully. On paper he could not lose, but many unpredictable hindrances got in his way."

"What were those adverse conditions, Sebastiano?"

"Many! Above all the torrential rains that lasted two days and turned the battlefield into a quagmire. He was forced to delay the use of his most powerful arm, the artillery, which was not effective on a muddy ground. That day, some of his generals made mistakes as they had never done before."

"Do you mean we have to consult a fortune teller before doing anything, Sebastiano?"

"No, I don't mean that. But I want you to learn this principle: do your best in your life, but keep in mind that the earth is a tiny spot in the infinite universe governed by good energy. All actions must conform to the good, universal energy. In the end, only goodwill prevails. Therefore, keep a pure heart always. In this way, you will win all your battles."

As time passed, I often asked myself if the feats Sebastiano told me were true or the fruit of his imagination. Either way, he left the inclination toward dignity and bravery in me, and above all to be a good and honest person.

The condition of my body improved greatly while I stayed with Sebastiano. The healthy, natural food and the salubrious air of the countryside strengthened me both physically and emotionally. I was not the thin boy of two months earlier; now I was even stouter than many boys my age. My parents could hardly believe that I was their son, as even my mood was much more cheerful.

Nevertheless, staying in Enna didn't help me. I suffered from the strange atmosphere of my town, which was not very congenial to me.

Chapter Three
Enna Seventy Years Ago

When the Second World War was over, most women in Enna didn't work outside the home. They were housewives, dependent on their fathers, and once they got married they were submissive to their husbands. You often saw many ladies dressed in black in the streets, the symbol of sorrow. The close relatives of those who died wore black to show their grief. Every time a person died, the walls on the streets were covered with death notices as if the whole town was mourning.

The duration of mourning varied according to the kind of relationship with the dead person, but usually were observed the following criteria: if the dead person was an uncle, a cousin, or someone not a close relative, the woman dressed in black for three months. If a child had been lost, the woman dressed in black for five years. If a sibling passed away, his or her sister dressed in black for three years. If the dead person was the husband, the widow dressed in black the rest of her life. I never saw my grandmother dressed in anything but black. She lost two children and her husband.

As for men, the duration of mourning was shorter than that of women. They usually didn't dress in black suits for a long time, but confined themselves to wearing a black tie, an armband, a narrow band around their jacket collar, or sometimes they wore a black button on it.

In the afternoons, after having done their chores, the housewives used to sit on their chairs by the window and watch the people walking in the streets. At that time, Via Sant'Agata was unpaved, and in the early morning you could see the goats going along the street and the shepherd then selling their milk to the housewives. It was a very fresh product. The goats were white, long-haired, and quite tall with upright and coiled horns. Nowadays, there are people in the cities who have never even seen a goat!

One day, I was playing with other boys my age near the Church of San Cataldo, when one of my mother's cousins passed by. "How dare you play here!" she said with a stern face.

"Is it forbidden to play?" I asked.

"Don't you know that your grandfather died?"

It was the first time that I was touched by death. My parents hadn't told me about his death. Hearing those words, I immediately stopped playing. It was also the first time I experienced the feeling of guilt. I really felt guilty for not observing the mourning of my grandfather's death, and I immediately ran home. My parents were not there, just the maid.

"Is it true that my grandfather died?" I asked.

"Yes, it is."

"I want to go see him."

"Do as you like," answered the maid, "but children shouldn't go see corpses!"

"I am not a child! I want to go anyway. My grandfather is not a corpse!"

As I insisted, she washed me and dressed me up, and then I rushed to my grandparents' house. I was entering what had been my grandparents' bedroom when my ears were flooded by my Aunt Carolina's cries.

"Little Vincenzino, you haven't been here for a long time!"

She was right. I had not gone to my grandparents' house for two months. I felt even more guilty.

The dead body had been placed in the middle of the room. He wore white gloves and a grey suit. As soon as I arrived, I gave a quick look around the room full of people sitting on chairs that had been arranged along its perimeter. I spotted my mother and headed for her.

"Go kiss your grandfather's hand," she said.

I did as she had told me and then took a seat close to her. A man came in and cried desperately. He was not one of our relatives. Maybe he was a worker in the sulfur mine that my grandfather owned.

After the dead body had been kept in the room for two days, the moment of separation came. Two gravediggers entered carrying an empty coffin. At that moment, everybody cried and screamed with pain. My grandmother blocked one of the diggers and tried to prevent him from taking away her loved one, but unfortunately it was not possible.

The coffin was carried by my grandfather's friends on their shoulders to the Church of San Cataldo nearby, and after Mass it was set on a hearse dragged by two black horses. There were thousands of people at the funeral, and all of them followed the hearse to the cemetery. At that time there were not many cars in the streets, so whenever there was a funeral the streets were closed to traffic. Sometimes the municipal band played a funeral march for very rich or special people.

When the funeral was over, we returned to my grandmother's house. I was horrified to see a squabble between my Aunt Carolina and my mother. She accused her sister of having been absent during her father's disease. Actually, she was right. My mother said that she didn't know about the seriousness of his disease because my father had hidden it from her. My aunt's daughter cried desperately. As for me, I didn't cry, but that doesn't mean that I was not grieving over my grandfather's demise. Often we don't openly express our sorrow, or we suppress it while others show openly what they feel.

After the funeral we had a tasty dinner. For eight days we were served breakfast, lunch, and dinner by our close friends. All the families gathered around the table. In Enna, you could not make the time of mourning at your will. It had to last eight days. During this time, besides being served delicious food by our relatives and close friends, we received visits from our neighbors and acquaintances.

The food we received was more delicious than anything I had ever eaten before—so much so that a doubt arose in my mind: "Is this a time for mourning or a party?"

After eating, we returned to the double bedroom to show our grief as the visitors came in little by little. I sat close to my mother and observed the scene. The visitors entered the room and gave condolences to the family members, starting with my grandmother, and then they sat on the chairs scattered across the room and remained silent or talked with some of the family members.

Every family member was dressed in black. As soon as a new visitor came in, my mother and Aunt Carolina put a sad expression on their faces. Then they started chatting with the newcomers. While they chatted their faces were quite relaxed, but whenever a new visitor came in, they stopped chatting right away and reassumed a sorrowful look. In fact, it was mandatory to show a contrite face; otherwise folks might think that they didn't mourn the loss of their father.

Since then I understood the difference between "to be" and "to look like." The change in my relatives' faces in showing grief meant that appearances had great importance in people's eyes.

The custom of judging by appearances was widespread in Enna.

Even today we tend to judge by appearances and fail to see what is really hidden inside every human being.

Chapter Four

My Two Uncles

After my grandfather's death, his house had a sinister look for me.

There was no television at that time, and different families often came together to chat and spend their time. It was very cold during the winter in Enna, and people made use of braziers burning charcoal slack to warm up the rooms. It was customary to put some sausage or a potato wrapped with a yellow, thick paper of the kind used to wrap pasta inside the brazier. We children vied with one another to eat a small piece of that delicacy.

The climate was much colder than it is today and the roofs in Enna were white with snow all winter. Whenever I came home from school I had the bad habit of warming up my frozen feet and hands in front of the brazier. Because of this, I had chilblains on my feet. I don't know how this phenomenon happened. It was probably caused by the sudden contact of my frozen hands and feet with the hot brazier. My fingers and toes had purple hues and itched. To cure my chilblains, I wore thick woolen socks and gloves.

During one of my family meetings at my grandmother's home, I heard that many of my grandfather's friends had tried to discourage him from buying that house. They had said that the place was haunted by ghosts. My grandfather had been hesitant about purchasing the house after that, but then he decided to buy it after someone told him that the story about the ghosts was a trick plotted by the tenants, who wore white sheets at night to look like ghosts. They staged the show in an effort not to be evicted. As for me, since I was a child I was not convinced about the story of the tenants' trick. I suspected that the house really was haunted by ghosts.

One day I asked my mother to tell me the truth. "Is the story true about ghosts haunting your father's house?"

"I don't believe in ghosts, Vincenzino, but I was never happy when I stayed there. In fact, my father was too strict with his children, and my mother often beat my brothers until they bled. You have to know that your name is Vincenzino as a sign of respect to my brother Vincenzo. He was a great brother and I loved him more than my own eyes. Whenever my mother beat him, I interposed myself between them and often was beaten instead of him.

"My father had such a stern look that we couldn't meet his eyes. Furthermore, he couldn't stand it when children cried, and we had to stifle our crying even when my mother beat us. Laughing was not allowed in that house because it was considered imbecility. So all we could do was just study or work.

"At that time, only boys stayed in school, while girls stayed at home helping do chores, or in the best of cases they learned the art of embroidering. As for me, I went every day to the Franciscan nuns to learn embroidering. I liked life in convent very much, and I would have become a nun if it had been my choice, but without my father's permission I couldn't do anything. Therefore, I used the art of embroidering that I learned to embroider my trousseau.

"That house was really ill-fated. One of my younger brothers, Biagio, died of malaria at the age of thirteen. My brother Vincenzo died when he was nineteen. It was an awful experience for me. I would have given away one of my organs to save Vincenzo's life, but unfortunately nothing could be done for him."

"What disease killed Uncle Vincenzo, Mom? Was it malaria as well?"

My mother let out a deep sigh. She then looked around, uncertain what to say to me. Finally, she found inspiration and gave me an answer that seemed to be plausible. "No, it was another kind of disease. One day he went out with a ballerina and died."

"What is a ballerina, Mom?"

"She is a woman that dances on the stage of a theatre."

"How is it possible to die just by walking with a ballerina? Maybe somebody killed him."

My mother tried to change the subject. "Your Uncle Vincenzo was very handsome. His blond hair and green eyes were the envy of his friends. At school he was not—"

"I want to know how he died, Mom!" I insisted.

"You want to know too many things. You are very young now, but let me read a poem that I composed for my brother." My mother read a poem full of sorrow, and I listened until the end so as not to displease her.

"Now," she said, "I have to take back this poem to my mother's house. I keep all of them there with Vincenzo's scripts and his diary."

I felt really strange that Vincenzo had died because of walking with a ballerina, so I wanted to find out if it was a real story or just one of my mother's lies. I decided to ask Aunt Carolina, who knew the truth for sure.

Chapter Five

My Grandparents' House

My grandparents' house was an old Sicilian-style, four-story building. It had been made partly from building stones and partly by digging out the rock. The rocky part was the first floor, which was used as a stable, a storeroom where my Aunt Carolina's husband kept his builder's tools, and as a wine cellar. A bit further, a henhouse had been realized by digging out another side of the rock.

In front of the house there was a wide vegetable garden that we could access both from a gate that looked onto the public street or from the front door of the house. To go to the second floor, where my Aunt Carolina lived with her family, it was possible to go through a steep, dark staircase dug into the rock that swarmed with small rodents, or pass through another gate that was on the upper part of the street. I usually opted for the latter.

A courtyard was at the entrance of the upper part of the house. It was a common area for both Aunt Carolina and Grandma, and an external stone staircase linked the courtyard to the third and fourth floors where my grandmother lived. It was Aunt Carolina who took care of the henhouse and the vegetable garden. My grandma was too old to do that.

Every evening the hens came back from the garden to the poultry pen, and my Aunt Carolina then inserted her forefinger into the hens' vent to check if they were ready to lay their eggs the next day. Not all the hens used their straw nests; some preferred to lay their eggs in a recess in the vegetable garden. So it was very important to know how many eggs were expected, in order to find the ones that were in some corner in the garden.

On the third floor there was the landing, the lounge, and the wide double bedroom with a balcony that looked out onto the garden. After her husband's death, my grandma used to keep that part of the house dark. The blinds were always kept down, and it was pitch dark inside. I had the sensation that besides her personal grief, which she manifested by wearing black clothes, the third floor of the house was also in mourning, because of the darkness of the rooms. A narrow, dark staircase led to the fourth floor that had a very small bathroom, two small rooms, a kitchen, a dining room, and another balcony.

My Aunt Carolina was always busy making bread, cooking, or doing other chores. Whenever she saw me her eyes and lips conveyed her pleasure. That day she was in the courtyard. She had just wrung a chicken's neck and now was plucking it after having dipped it into hot water. Afterwards, she would pass the chicken over the fire for a few seconds to burn out the small feathers that were left.

Aunt Carolina was forty or so, and her hair was beginning to turn grey, but she still was a very beautiful lady, though a little bit plump. Her main feature was her smile, which she showed copiously, except for the rare circumstances when she was angry with somebody or something bad had happened.

These days, a subtle wrinkle crossed her forehead. She was worried because her husband didn't have a job and they might have to emigrate to northern Italy where it would be much easier for him to get a position as a builder.

"Hi, Vincenzino. Don't you want to go play with the other kids today?"

"I am not a kid anymore. I am a grownup!"

My aunt burst out laughing. "Okay, Vincenzino, I see that you are wearing long trousers. So you are an adult now, aren't you?"

Without making any comment, I went straight to the core of my inquiry. "Did you have two brothers, Aunt Carolina?"

"Yes, I had two brothers, but as you know both of them died young."

"Could you tell me something about them?"

"Why do you want to know this from me? You can ask your mother. She knows everything about them."

"Yes, I know, but my mother is not very talkative. She is always serious and thinks continuously about this and that. Her mind wanders in the clouds. She doesn't seem to care about talking with me much."

"Okay, as you like. I'll tell you something about my youngest brother. His name was Biagio. He looked like my mother. He was a good student, but whenever he had the opportunity to play football or other sports, he did, without caring much about studying. One day, my father presented him with a bicycle and he was happy. He covered long distances on it, and he even dared to cycle from the small town of Villarosa, which is on the plain, to Enna, which is on the top of the mountain.

"He had a strong likeness to my mother, to such an extent that he looked like Grandma with short hair."

Aunt Carolina went into her bedroom, and from one of the drawers took an envelope that contained many pictures of her beloved ones, including one of me riding a papier-mâché horse that the photographer kept in his studio to photograph children. At the sight of my Uncle Biagio's photo I was left speechless. He was standing at attention and wearing a black suit with children's trousers. His resemblance to my grandmother was astonishing.

"Sometimes," said Aunt Carolina, "he came home exhausted, and your mother, who was fond of him, washed him from his feet to his crown. Unfortunately, at the age of thirteen he got malaria and died."

"I didn't know that there was malaria in Enna, Aunt Carolina."

"At that time, malaria was widespread in our area. Later, Mussolini eradicated the disease from our territory through a massive anti-malarial campaign. Nevertheless, not many people died because of it. Biagio was unlucky because he contracted the pernicious malaria that had no cure.

"But let's change the subject!" continued Aunt Carolina. "I don't want to talk about sad topics. I have cried so much in my life that I don't have any more teardrops to shed. I want to show you my wedding photos."

She opened her album, which contained many pictures of her daughter receiving her First Communion with her mouth wide open and the priest in the act of putting the Host onto her tongue, her son riding a mule, her husband in a military uniform holding a sword, and herself with her husband on the day of their wedding. But at the sight of another picture portraying baby Biagio in her arms, her eyes got misty, and she closed the album and put it back into the drawer.

My aunt was almost crying at the thought of her brother when I, without giving her enough time to pull herself together, abruptly introduced my second question. "How did your brother Vincenzo die?"

My question took her completely aback. She stammered for a few moments and then lost her self-control. Her words got stuck in her mouth, her lips dried, and then she exploded.

"You bad little rascal! Every time you come here I get nervous. You should not come when I have a lot of work to do. Your mother has a maid, but I am alone in my house! I have to cook, bake, wash, hang out, and take in the washing. I have no time to chat with you. Go to your mother and let me work!"

I left her and rushed home. My aunt had behaved very oddly, and the feeling increased in me that something mysterious or unmentionable was linked to my Uncle Vincenzo's death. A few suspicions grew in my mind. One possibility was that my grandmother had beaten him with a stick so harshly that he died. Another possibility was that he had had a relationship with a married ballerina and that her husband had killed him out of jealousy. A third possibility was that he had been kidnapped, or the Mafia had killed him for revenge against my grandfather.

Many hypotheses were whirling through my head, and I often let my imagination wander about the possible causes of Uncle Vincenzo's death.

Maybe Vincenzo, by chance, was the eyewitness of some dirty crime and he was killed to hush him. There was another possibility: maybe he had killed himself. This last possibility was the most likely. My mother had told me that he died because of a ballerina, a dancer in the theatre, and that they were usually very beautiful. Yes, likely it was a matter of suicide. Uncle Vincenzo fell in love with a ballerina and she did not live up to his expectations. Or maybe they were in a relationship for a little while and then split up. Perhaps Uncle Vincenzo's pain at the loss of his beloved was so unbearable that he came to the point of putting an end to his young life.

The silence from my mother and Aunt Carolina would be understandable then. In Enna, suicide was considered an infamous action. Even the priest refused to officiate a funeral in the church for a person who had killed themselves, unless the close relatives of the dead person showed him a medical certificate that attested that the suicide had been from suffering from a nervous breakdown, and that they didn't have rational power at the moment of making the decision to put an end to their life.

Those were just conjectures in my mind. To know the truth I needed to get Vincenzo's diary. I was sure there was something written about the events that led to his death. I knew that the diary was kept inside a drawer in my grandmother's house along with my mother's poems. But where? The only way to solve the problem was to sneak into her home, get the diary, and then put it back into the drawer after reading it.

Quite often, my grandmother, who lived on the fourth floor, went downstairs with my Aunt Carolina to bake or wash or cook something together. I just had to find the right moment to enter my grandmother's house undetected. The only problem was that I was terrified at the thought of being alone in a place haunted by ghosts. Furthermore, my grandmother had the bad habit of keeping the shutters closed, which gave a dark, ghostly look to the third floor. But to know the truth, there was no other way. I had to overcome my fears.

One day, Grandma and Aunt Carolina were making bread, so thinking it would take a lot of time to bake it, I asked my grandmother permission to use her bathroom on the fourth floor. As soon as I entered that dark house, panic gripped me and I was on the verge of giving up my investigation, but curiosity and the love for truth prevailed. Nevertheless, I was seized by such a fear that I felt pain in my stomach, and now really I did need to go to the lavatory. So I closed the door behind me and went up directly to the fourth floor to the small bathroom, passing through the pitch darkness of the staircase.

While I was sitting on the toilet, I heard the crying of my grandfather's sisters while the coffin was being taken away by the gravediggers. Now I was visualizing the same scene. I could hear those cries as clearly as I had a few years before. Was it a hallucination? Who knows! Maybe ghosts really exist and were still haunting that house. Or maybe I was too shaken or an easily frightened boy who mistook the shouts of the children that were playing across the street for the shrieks of pain at my grandfather's death. However, I was too shaken to enter the bedroom where Vincenzo's diary was possibly kept. So I gave up on my quest that day, intending to continue it another time.

I only slept in that gloomy house a few times with my grandmother. She didn't use the double room after her husband's death. It was the biggest room in the house, and it was there that my grandfather's dead body had been exposed for two days. She had moved to the upper floor into a small room beside the kitchen. When I stayed with her we used to sleep in the same single bed. It was very uncomfortable for me, but that was my grandmother's will.

Before going to bed, my grandma and I checked the house to make sure that nobody was hidden under the beds, inside the closets, or behind the furniture. Once we finished checking every corner of the house, she put a chair close to the main door.

"What is the chair for?" I once asked.

"If a wrongdoer comes he will hear the sound of the chair and think that somebody is living in the house and he will give up trying to come in."

I found my grandmother's behavior odd at the time, but I am sure she was not the only person to have some kind of pet phobia.

She used to pray for long periods of time. She couldn't help saying her prayers before going to bed. Some prayers were the well-known Hail Mary and Our Father, and others were traditional prayers of my town. Other prayers were taken from the small holy pictures that contained written invocations to God, Mary, or the saints on the back.

My grandma taught me some traditional prayers, which I still say every night before sleeping, even now that I am old. One of these prayers is this:

I sleep in this bed
There is Mary over my chest
I sleep and she watches over me
If something bad is going to happen she will wake me.

The second prayer is:

I am with Jesus, I stay with Jesus.
As long as I am with Jesus I have no fears.
I know that I am going to sleep
But I don't know if I'll awake.
My soul be always commended (to Jesus).

Chapter Six
Aunt Filippa

In Enna, housewives believed that whenever a kid was seized with fear he grew parasites in his bowels. It was believed that parasites, if not treated in due time, could pass from the intestine to the stomach and then climb up along the esophagus, finally coming out through the mouth. In more serious cases, they could form a blockage in the throat, causing death by asphyxiation.

There are different kinds of intestinal parasites. The most common worms in children's bowels are pinworms and ascarids, but the latter are very dangerous because they can perforate the intestinal wall, slither into the bloodstream, and find their way into the lungs. The shape of the ascarid is wormlike. They can be 15 - 20 centimeters long, a few millimeters thick, and they have a reddish hue.

One day I found an ascarid, also known as a roundworm, in my underpants. Another day while I was in the toilet I noticed that an ascarid was striving to get out of my anus. Terrified, I cried out for my mother's help.

"Mom, Mom! Come quick, I have a worm! It wants to get out but I can't grab it!"

My mother rushed up the stairs to the bathroom and pulled out a thick worm from my anus that was almost twenty centimeters long. Obviously, when I had been at my grandmother's home trying to get Vincenzo's diary, I had built up so much fear that I weakened myself. Due to stress, I had lowered my immune system, giving rise to the growth of intestinal parasites.

"What to do?" I asked my mother with a worried face. "I don't want to live with these worms in my belly!"

My mother put her finger around her chin and pondered for a few moments. Then she faintly smiled and seemed to have found the solution. "We have to go to Aunt Filippa!"

Many years ago, most of the houses in Enna were detached. As time passed, single-family houses were demolished and replaced with big buildings full of apartments. Nowadays, people who live in apartments seldom meet one another, and many don't even know their next door neighbors.

When I was a child, I used to hang out on Via Sant'Agata. Aunt Filippa was not really a relative, but everybody called her "Aunt." Therefore, she was the aunt of all children in the neighborhood. She was particularly skillful in ridding children of their intestinal worms. To do that, some kind of small donation was needed I guess.

My mother had prearranged the meeting with her, and one afternoon we knocked on her door—or, more accurately, on her window. In fact, she used to sit behind the windows of her house to watch the passersby and the children that played in the street.

Her daughter came to welcome us and invited us to take a seat in the living room. While we were waiting, I took a look around the room. There was a cupboard that contained small decorated cups, glasses, and dishes, a table with a thick embroidered cloth on it, and a sofa.

My mother seemed very friendly with Aunt Filippa's daughter. In fact, they had been schoolmates at elementary school. Aunt Filippa arrived after a few minutes wearing a black dress—she was a widow—and thick glasses on her nose. Grey hair framed her white face. As soon as she saw me, she gently caressed my hair.

"I will help this cute boy with all my strength," she said. "First of all, we have to check if Vincenzino has some evil eye inside him."

I looked up at my mother with an inquiring look, but she seemed indifferent. "What does evil eye mean, Mom?" I asked.

"Let Aunt Filippa work and don't ask questions!" answered my mother with a harsh voice. So I just continued sitting on the chair, resigned to wait for whatever was going to happen.

Aunt Filippa opened the cupboard and took out a soup plate and a small cup. She put the plate on my head, asking my mother to hold it fast. Then, she poured some water into the plate and olive oil into the small cup. Finally, she dipped her finger into the small cup of olive oil and dripped some into the water.

I remained with that plate on my head for several minutes. Aunt Filippa was not convinced, and from time to time she dripped more olive oil. Then she scrutinized the shape of the drops.

The drops could take different forms. They could remain as they were, become wider, or even disappear completely. If the drop maintained the same shape it had when it was dripped, it meant that there was no hex on me. If the drop became wider, there was a real hex. Sometimes the drop disappeared completely, and that meant that there was a lot of hex. In my case, the drops disappeared, and for that reason Aunt Filippa dripped olive oil many times.

"This boy has a lot of hex," she said, "but I'll take it out of him. I swear!"

To do that she made special signs around the plate and said a special prayer, which she had learned from her mother on Christmas Eve. It was a secret prayer that had been handed down from generation to generation. She then concluded, saying that I was now hex free thanks to her prayer.

At the time I barely understood her method of removing the hex, but with passing time I realized that what Aunt Filippa had done probably had a scientific basis. Words, thoughts, and feelings have vibrations. Everything vibrates in the universe. It means that each kind of vibration affects both organic and inorganic matter, including the shape of the drops that Aunt

Filippa used to diagnose the hex. In other words, if my body vibrations were good the drops assumed a certain shape; otherwise they got broad or sometimes disappeared.

However, the real reason my mother and I had come to her was not to get rid of my evil eye, but for the intestinal worms.

I looked up at my mother again and shyly asked her, "What shall we do about my worms?" Once again my mother told me to keep silent and wait.

Aunt Filippa removed the plate from my head and put it, along with the small cup, on the near table. She then asked me to lift my T-shirt and bare my belly. Finally, she made certain arcane signs on my stomach, and at the same time said a special prayer, the words of which I could not understand because her voice was very low. The treatment lasted several minutes.

When her prayer was over, she recommended I drink a glass of olive oil with squeezed lemon and raw, mashed garlic the following day in the early morning. I followed her instructions, and I have to say that I actually excreted a lot of ascarids. Some of them were dead and some looked dazed.

Chapter Seven

Pietrino

I was very shaken by the voices I had heard at my grandmother's home. I also didn't appreciate my Aunt Carolina's reaction, who had offended me by giving me the epithet "bad little rascal" and kicking me out of her home. Therefore, I decided not to go to that haunted house for a while. As for my Uncle Vincenzo's diary, I opted for postponing my investigation indefinitely. Maybe when I was a few years older my boldness would increase and I would be able to enter the bedroom where my grandfather's dead body had been exposed and where Vincenzo's diary was likely kept. Who knows, perhaps Vincenzo had also died in that room!

I spent my teens hanging about on Via Sant'Agata where my family lived, going to school, studying at home, and whenever it was possible playing with other boys in the neighborhood. Across the street from my house was a carter, who used to work with his two-wheeled cart pulled by a draft horse. He had a shop where he sold building materials and he delivered them to the builders by his cart.

I was enchanted by that huge horse and the fantastic scenes depicted in bright colors on the cart, and whenever I had the chance in the afternoons I used to leap onto the cart and go around Enna with the carter. The horse was harnessed with a tall plume of feathers on its head and harness bells around its neck. The cart had multi-colored figures painted all over its sides that depicted the feats of paladins like Roland and Charles the Great. It was not a big cart, but it still could carry a fair amount of goods like gypsum, sand, cement, bricks, and tiles.

The carter was not able to read and write or count numbers beyond ten. He was just a good hard-working person, but his wife was very skilled in reading, writing, and doing arithmetic. Thanks to their children's help, today they are one of the richest families in Enna.

My playmates were my cousin Emanuele and my friends Carlo and Pietrino. I was the youngest; the others were two years older than me. We formed a group called "The Gang of the Horn," but we had nothing to do with a gang, despite the name. Our symbol was a white flag on which a horn had been drawn. I don't know who had made the flag, but it was probably Pietrino, who was endowed with manual skills like his father.

The town of Enna lies on a flat mountain a thousand meters above sea level. The main characteristic of the mountain is that it has deep cliffs on almost all sides. Enna has been inhabited since ancient times because of this peculiar feature, which made the city inexpugnable. The Arabs besieged Enna for a long time. They conquered a great part of Sicily, except my town, which was considered impregnable. They eventually were able to enter the city using a secret path that a traitor from Enna had taught them.

One day during the Second World War, a garrison of Italian troops came to Enna in the late afternoon. They camped in an area not far from the edge of a ravine. During the night, the Americans launched an airstrike. The soldiers tried to escape the bombs and ran away from their camp, but unfortunately they didn't know that my town lay on the edge of a cliff, and they all died when they plummeted into the chasm.

Basically, our Gang of the Horn devoted itself to exploring the territory. We used to run along the edges of the cliffs and search caves that were disseminated all around the area. In old times, people used to live in those caves, and it is still possible today to see evidence of some of the old dwellings. In a cave we saw a lot of juts that the owners had dug out to put lamps, food, and tools. Nobody lives in such caves today, but sometimes people use them to keep animals like goats, poultry, mules, horses, or donkeys.

One day we had just explored a cave on the edge of the ravine that had two entrances and four rooms. On our way back my cousin lost his footing and fell into the ravine. Only a tiny shrub prevented him from plummeting at least 200 meters down. He hung in midair between life and death. My cousin cried out and tears welled in his frightened eyes. We were all petrified with fear, unable to do anything to save Emanuele's life, but Pietrino summoned up his courage, put his legs astride a log that stuck out from the rock, bent his body, stretched his arms, and finally clutched Emanuele's hair. He lifted my cousin slowly until he could catch hold of the same log Pietrino was sitting on, and they finally both came up safe and sound.

I remember a Christmas when Pietrino's father had made a big Nativity scene at his home that occupied almost half of the entrance of the wide living room. His father had built cardboard castles, houses, and streets similar to those at the time of Jesus's birth. Christmas trees aren't part of Sicilian culture and tradition. Nowadays, many families dress Christmas trees, but at that time they made the Nativity scene and gathered around it to say their rosary.

Our Gang of the Horn was a united group and we loved one another. Carlo had been born with a harelip. He had been operated on, but he still had some difficulty speaking and it was not easy to understand him. Nowadays, people with physical imperfections are tolerated and helped to fit into society. Most countries have special classes for disabilities, but at the time of my childhood it was different. If you had a physical defect, the other boys mocked you and you felt humiliated.

I had some problems properly pronouncing the letter *R*, and I also stammered sometimes. In order to overcome this, I trained myself in pronunciation at home, lest my schoolmates mock me. I used to put a few little stones into my mouth and then tried to utter words that contained the letter *R*. That method worked, at least for my stammer.

You never saw people with disabilities in the streets of Enna in the old days. A weak person was an object of derision of other boys. The ideal person was strong, cunning, and cheerful. Therefore, many families secluded their members who had some kind of physical or psychical imperfection, lest they become an object of mockery.

Carlo was not able to pronounce words properly, and for that reason the other boys gave him the epithet "gnie-gnie." It was not easy to understand him, but our group could figure out his speech. Pietrino, who was the leader of the Gang of the Horn, gave orders to defend Carlo whenever other boys mocked him.

At that time in Enna, the quarter wars raged. Gangs of teens had formed dangerous gangs according to the area they belonged to. Their gangs were not peaceful like our Gang of the Horn. In fact, they used to attack anyone who didn't belong to the same neighborhood. They used stones, arrows, slings, and even chains. More than one boy had been blinded by pointed arrows made from the iron of umbrellas. Therefore, we couldn't go with our flag to explore quarters different than ours.

The oddity of life is that Pietrino, who had saved Emanuele's life, was not able to save his own. Cruel fate cut the thread of his life off prematurely.

There was a time when the Asian flu spread in Enna. Most of the children that contracted the virus got over it. Unfortunately for my friend Pietrino, the clock of his life was going to inexorably stop. As soon as he had taken ill with a high fever, his parents called their family doctor. He examined Pietrino and diagnosed him as suffering from the Asian flu. He prescribed some medicine to fight the virus.

As the days passed, Pietrino didn't recover. Fever hovered around high levels, and his body was reduced to skin and bone. When his parents realized that their son's health was getting worse and worse, they took him to the hospital. There, Pietrino had blood tests, and the doctors found out that he was not suffering from the Asian flu but from typhoid fever. They started the proper therapy, but it was too late. A complication arose; a tremendous hemorrhage occurred in his bowels and Pietrino's life was slipping away.

One afternoon, my cousin Emanuele informed me about Pietrino's bad condition and asked me to go to the hospital with him to visit.

"Of course!" I said. "Where is Pietrino? How can we find him in the big hospital?"

"I know where to go and how to find his room," answered Emanuele.

While we were walking to the hospital, my cousin informed me about the glaring mistake the doctor who had diagnosed Pietrino the first time made.

"How is that possible?" I asked.

My cousin and I meandered through the hallways of that big hospital until we finally found Pietrino's room. As soon as he saw us, his face beamed. He tried to get up from his bed to show us that he was still the leader of our Gang of the Horn, but he didn't have enough strength and fell back onto his bed. He didn't have the strength to talk. Seeing his pale face and dimmed eyes sunken into dark eye sockets, I realized that Pietrino was going to die.

A few days later it happened. The dead body, as was customary, was placed for two days in the living room where his father had once made the Nativity scene. Pietrino wore a grey suit with short trousers. When his mother saw me she cried desperately, tears streaming down her face.

"Vincenzino! Vincenzino! You will not come here anymore. Your playmate has left all of us forever."

I never did go to Pietrino's home again, but every year on the Commemoration of the Dead on November 2, I used to go to visit him at the graveyard.

His father had built a family chapel. At first, all the family members gathered around the tomb every year. However, within a few years, all five of their children died from diverse causes—some because of a car accident, others because of disease. It was a family marked by cruel fate. Eventually, Pietrino's mother also died.

Every year when I went to pray before Pietrino's tomb, I saw his father sitting in front of it. I have never seen such a strong man. His wife and children died before their time, but in spite of everything he stood up to his adverse fortunes. He looked as strong as the ancient gigantic cypress that stood near his chapel. He looked immortal, but at the age of ninety-eight he also gave up his ghost.

I have looked at doctors with suspicion my entire life, but who knows? Maybe fate exists and it decides regardless of human will.

"Who is the doctor that treated Pietrino the first time?" I asked my cousin Emanuele one day.

He told me the name of the doctor and, as I didn't know him, he pointed him out to me. He was very tall and enjoyed a good reputation. As for me, as soon as I spotted him I wanted to spit in his face. I pondered over and over how it was possible to mistake a diagnosis of typhus for the Asian flu. I decided that the stupid doctor should be struck off the professional register! Every time I met him in the street I was tempted to slap him, but unfortunately that was not possible. Over the years, I reexamined the concept of guilt. In fact, in my life I made some mistakes similar to that of the doctor. Everybody can make a mistake. No one is infallible.

Anyway, when Pietrino died it was the second time I had been touched by death in my life. With Pietrino's death, our Gang of the Horn came to an end. He was the leader of our group and no one else was in a position to lead us. Meanwhile, from time to time Vincenzo's diary crept into my mind. I had given up detecting it because of my cowardice. Now I decided to confront situations instead of fleeing every time I was seized with fear. I had to figure out a strategy to enter my grandmother's double room. To overcome my fears, I decided not to think about ghosts and dead people. My anxiety would not help me. Therefore, once I entered my grandmother's house I should stop thinking and go directly to my goal. So, I did.

One day, my grandma left the front door ajar. She was at Aunt Carolina's to bake bread. I took advantage of the favorable situation and sneaked into the house. Then, instead of thinking about anything, I went straight to the double bedroom. I was determined to overcome my fear and thought, *If I can succeed now, I'll also be a winner in life. But if I give up now, I'll be a loser and a quitter all my life.*

I opened the door of the lounge and then the bedroom, but I made the mistake of not completely closing the doors. The bedroom was pitch black because my grandmother used to keep the shutters completely closed. I groped my way to the shutter in the bedroom and raised it a little bit to see more clearly. Once there was enough light, I headed for the big closet. I opened the door and saw a hunting rifle in the back that was similar to Sebastiano's. On the shelf there was a big revolver that I had never seen before. Curious, I took the handgun and unsheathed it.

I was scrutinizing that big revolver when my grandmother's voice resounded in the hollow house. She was sure of having closed the door to the lounge, and the light that filtered through the shutters of the bedroom made her certain that a wrongdoer was inside.

"Who is there?" she spoke out with quivering voice. Obviously, she feared having an unpleasant encounter with a thief.

I was paralyzed by fear and feelings of guilt for entering the bedroom without permission. As my grandma flung open the door of the bedroom she saw me with the revolver in my hand. She screamed so loudly that even the neighbors could hear her. Aunt Carolina, worried by my grandma's shrieks, stormed into the bedroom where I was still frozen by my feelings of guilt.

Aunt Carolina got close to me and calmly took the revolver from my hand. Then, feeling more relaxed, she started railing at me. "You little monster! How many times have I had to warn you not to come here? You should stay with your mother and let us live in peace. I can't look after you. Next time you come here I'll beat you!"

I left the house with my tail between my legs. Due to stress, I wet my trousers and underwear. I decided to give up trying to find Vincenzo's diary.

Chapter Eight
My Mother's Poems

I started middle school in my town. My parents were so eager to make me a good student that they also provided me with afterschool teachers. I was at school and afterschool all day long. Studying had become an obsession for me. Also, the relationship with my new schoolmates was different than in elementary school, where I had felt my friends more spontaneous and naïve.

I remember a dream that I often had at that period in my life. I saw the earth like a big rocky ball; then the end of the world came and I was crushed by that huge rocky sphere. Obviously, my grandfather's and Pietrino's deaths had made a strong impression on me. Someday death would knock on my door as well, and I would not be able to send it back as an unwelcome guest.

Later, I no longer had those kinds of nightmares, but death would remain the most important theme in my life. I constantly asked myself things like: If God doesn't exist, what is going to happen when we die? Is it possible that we are the ones who create God in order to have the illusion of not disappearing into thin air forever when we die? Maybe God is just a projection of our insecure minds to give us a footing to live our lives without anxiety and care about the hereafter.

I kept mulling over death without ever finding a definite answer. With Pietrino's death, I had lost the only real friend I had. I didn't consider my schoolmates trustworthy friends. I used to spend some time with a few of them, but they had little sympathy for my problems. They couldn't understand why I was worrying about death instead of enjoying life.

Now the only friend I had left was Sebastiano. He had found a temporary job as a foreman at a building site. The job lasted a year, and then he found another job as a mink breeder. On Saturday afternoon I used to meet him at his workplace. I liked to watch him while he prepared mince for the minks. While he worked he never stopped talking politics, which was his great passion. His hair was completely white by now, but he was still a strong man. He kept his hair short and crewcut, according to military style. His beard was shaved as deeply as if he was going to undergo a review by his commander.

"Vincenzino, you have to know that the actual Italian ruling class is made of the same type of people that were in the ranks of the Fascist Party."

Then he showed me a newspaper, whose ideas were similar to his. "In this newspaper, there is evidence that the Fascist Party leaders have turned themselves into champions of democracy.

"There was more democracy under Mussolini than there is today!" he continued, getting worked up. "Nowadays, to get a job—any kind of job—you need your political connections. The different parties pretend to fight against one another, but that is just a farce. In fact, both the party in power and the opposition each run a slice of the power. Do you believe that it was Mussolini who led Italy to the Second World War? Not at all! Vincenzino, you have to know that behind the shoulders of every politician there are hidden powers who actually decide the destinies of nations."

"Who are these hidden powers, Sebastiano?"

"First of all there are the lobbies. There are many lobbies in Italy, as there are in all the nations of the world. One of the most dangerous lobbies is made of the magnates of industry. They sell most of their output to the states, and whenever there is a war they take the opportunity to sell more goods. The weapon industry is based just on war. The more wars there are, the more weapons that are made. Mussolini paid with his life for his faults, but no one who belonged to the hidden power paid anything. They are still rich, produce weapons, and increase their earnings more and more."

Then he took a picture from his shoulder bag and showed it to me. "Do you recognize this man?"

"It looks like the mayor of Enna," I answered.

"You are right. That is our mayor, but this picture was taken in Mussolini's time when he wore the Fascist uniform, which included the black shirt. Now he's turned himself into an antifascist, but the truth is that he seized the opportunity offered by the new pseudo-democratic regime to continue his political business in the same way he did under Mussolini.

"When Mussolini was alive, there was no Mafia. He stamped out it almost completely. Almost all mafiosi were arrested or sent to prison. I say almost because he arrested only the so-called small fry. He couldn't catch the big shots, because they belonged to the economic and political power. Both the political and economic class formed lobbies, otherwise called Mafia organizations, to control the economy of the country. In other words, the big Mafia was within the Fascist Party, and for that reason he couldn't eradicate it completely."

"May I ask you for advice, Sebastiano?"

"Yes, of course. You can ask me whatever you want and I'll be happy to help you."

"I want to get my Uncle Vincenzo's diary that is kept with my mother's poems."

"Why do you want that diary?"

"I want to know how Uncle Vincenzo died. Both my mother and Aunt Carolina have been reticent to talk about his death. I am sure that in his diary I can find a few clues to trace the cause."

"Do you know where the diary is kept?"

"Yes, of course. It is in my grandmother's house in one of the drawers of the closet in the bedroom, along with my mother's poems."

"Well, that means that it is very easy to get the diary. All you have to do is ask your grandmother for permission to see your mother's poems. Once you have spotted them you can pick up the diary."

It was the most natural and straightforward way to get Vincenzo's diary. Why didn't I think about that before? Why did I run all those subterfuges to get into the bedroom surreptitiously? Indeed, I had the habit of walking along blind alleys without seeing that there was an avenue in front of me with all the doors flung open. Now Sebastiano was opening my mind, teaching me not to complicate my life with useless reasoning. I had to act in a more straightforward and simple way to hit my targets.

"Thank you, Sebastiano! I'll do as you have suggested, and this time everything will be all right."

One day I went to my grandmother's house and nonchalantly asked her, "Can I see my mother's poems?"

"Yes, of course, Vincenzino. They are in the lower drawer of the bedroom closet. You can go there to see the poems, but don't touch the guns!"

Sebastiano was right! He had paved my way to get finally Uncle Vincenzo's diary. I headed for the bedroom and opened the windows one by one. The light entered the room and those ghostly presences seemed to fade away.

I opened the lower drawer, which was filled to the brink with slips of neatly folded paper. I dipped my hands in to find a notebook or something similar and fathomed with my fingers here and there until at last I felt something that seemed like a notebook. I took it out very carefully and found that it was a black exercise book. It was exactly in the middle of the drawer, as if my mother's poems were the bed and the blanket for it. I leafed through the pages, and felt sure that it was Vincenzo's diary. My heart was pounding as never before, but I kept calm and gently put the diary inside my T-shirt to take it home.

Meanwhile, I wanted to have a look at some of my mother's poems. A quick look showed me that they were prayers for her brother. According to my mother, Vincenzo was not dead, for he continued to live in another dimension. I picked one of the folded pieces of paper and inside it was written this poem:

FLOWERS

My beloved brother,
when you cross the river of eternal life
may the angels strew your way with flowers.
Your heart is pure and stainless
and your soul never will die.
You are now in a faraway land
where the moon always shines
and the sun never sets.
Before long we will hold hands again,
to walk together until the end of space and time!

I didn't know that my mother had such an unschooled talent! I unfolded two more small sheets to read two more poems:

THE MOON

O moon! Over the eras
you have been giving inspiration
to poets, artists, and philosophers.
I know the reason. Because
our dears' souls live on your surface.
We cannot see them, but they are
still alive and watch over us and teach us

and love us.
Someday I will abide on your bright face too,
along with my brother Vincenzo and together
we'll protect and guide to the straight path
our beloved offspring.

RIVER

The river has emerald-green waters.
It flows calm and marks the border between life and death.
If I could, I would have built a bridge to unite the two worlds,
but I cannot. I am too frail, too powerless. I am a human being and
only the gods can make up such a bridge.
For now we are separated, O my beloved brother,
and Charon keeps ferrying souls across the river.
One day a new light will guide me to you,
and we will stay together in our star, which is the same
as that from where we came.

I kept reading poems, but almost all of them had the same nostalgic tone for her beloved brother Vincenzo.

I refolded the sheets very precisely and tidily, so as not to arouse suspicion about Vincenzo's missing diary. I closed the windows one by one, lowered the blinds, and the darkness again took over that part of the house.

With the diary well hidden between my belt and T-shirt, I sneaked out, homeward bound. I closed my grandmother's main door behind me and was coming down the stone staircase when my Aunt Carolina came out from her house and beckoned me to join her.

A complication! If she sees the diary, I am ruined! I thought. *What to do? I have to make up an excuse!*

"I cannot come to you, Aunt Carolina, because my mother is waiting for me."

"Please come over here, Vincenzino, just a few minutes. I have something special for you."

I had been raised to obey my elder relatives, so I couldn't refuse my aunt's invitation.

"I have just made some bread. I'll take it out from the wood-burning oven in a few minutes, and for you there is a special surprise. I have prepared some buns just for you."

We went downstairs where my aunt used to bake her bread, and she took out a few buns from the oven. They smelled of fresh Sicilian flour, and their color was between white and yellow. My aunt sliced one of the buns with her long knife and seasoned it with olive oil, ground garlic, salt, and black pepper. Then she offered it to me.

While I was eating with gusto, she noticed something sticking out from my chest. "What is that? What did you do at Grandma's?" she asked.

This time I didn't want to raise any suspicion about something I had stolen. So I answered without thinking much. "This is my armor, Aunt Carolina!"

"Armor? What is it for? Are you leaving for the war?"

"No, the problem is that some friends of mine mock me and try to attack me, so I have to protect myself."

"I knew you were a little strange, but not to such an extent."

Anyway, I swallowed the bun in two or three mouthfuls and then rushed home.

Chapter Nine
Vincenzo's Diary, Part One

Now I had to find a safe place to keep the diary and read it peacefully. I thought about putting it into my school bag so nobody could find it. Moreover, the diary was always with me and I could read it whenever I wished. It was not a long journal. Vincenzo had started writing it in 1933, about six years before he died. The beginning of the diary coincided with the time that Vincenzo began being attracted by the opposite sex.

At the Church of Santa Croce, I showed our director, Paolo, Vincenzo's journal. He selected the most significant pages and slightly rearranged the style and the times when the events took place, so as to make an orderly and flowing account.

October 1, 1933

Today was my first day of school. I am twelve years old and I attend the second class of the middle school. My class is composed of boys only. There are no mixed classes in Enna. Maybe it is possible to have mixed classes in more open-minded countries like those in Scandinavia, but in Enna, a town impregnated with deep-rooted sex prejudice, this is unthinkable.

The girls have their class close to ours, but we spend recreation time in the same schoolyard. I noticed that all the girls have flat breasts, except one, who is grown and has two round, attractive breasts. Her name is Maria. Today at recess she was talking with a friend of mine about her class interrogation in Latin. Once again I looked at her breasts and fell in love. I realized for the first time in my life that love and physical attraction coincide. Love is like an animal instinct.

However, I am too young for her. She prefers boys older than her, and that makes me terribly jealous. I have no hope to conquer her heart.

October 10, 1933

My progress at school is not good, because I think of Maria all the time instead of studying. I talk about her with my sisters and friends. I cannot suppress my emotions. Sometimes I think that I cannot live without her.

October 12, 1933

I don't know how, but my mother knows about my crush on Maria. Today she scolded me harshly and forbade me to think of her, threatening to beat me hard.

October 22, 1933

Maria has disappeared from my dreams, not due to my mother's reprimand, but because she has fallen in love with another boy. This morning I saw them in the grove near the cemetery. They were walking hand in hand, when all of a sudden he kissed and hugged her. Maria flushed and shivered. Maybe it was her first kiss.

October 23, 1933

My mother was at my school this afternoon to ask the teachers about my progress.

"Your son doesn't study enough. He always has his head in the clouds. If he continues to go wrong, we will fail him for sure." That was the teachers' unanimous verdict.

When my mother came home, she cried out, "Vincenzo!" Hearing her voice, my blood ran cold. I knew that she had been at school, so I figured that my teachers had not talked well about me, and now my mother was ready to beat me harshly.

She reached me while I was reading a book at the table in the dining room. As soon as I saw her, I got up while she tried to get hold of me. We both moved around the table, I fleeing and my mother pursuing me. At last she gave up.

"I'll tell your father that you're not making any progress at school, and that will be worse than my beating."

Actually, I fear my father more than my mother. He is very strict, but I hope that my mother has just threatened to tell him I am not a good student. She probably will tell him nothing.

October 25, 1933

Two days have elapsed and my father has not been at home. He works at his sulfur mine all week, but today is Sunday and he enjoys staying at home. At the thought that he knows what my teachers said, my legs quake.

At lunch we were sitting around the table. My sister Carolina and my mother took places close to him, and my sister Rosa Maria and I sat facing each other. My father sat at the head of the table. He said nothing to me, so I thought that the worst had passed. After eating, he stared at me from my crown to my feet. I had the feeling that he knew something. Then abruptly he spoke.

"Tomorrow you must get up at four o' clock in the morning. You must help me saddle my mare and then we will go together to a certain place."

October 26, 1933

It was 3:30 in the morning when my mother woke me up. "Get dressed within ten minutes, because your father is waiting for you!" she said.

I looked at my mother with my eyes wide open and obeyed her without saying any word. I got dressed and *went down to my parents' bedroom where my father was waiting for me. As soon as I entered the room he took his revolver from the closet and loaded it with six bullets. Then he fastened his cartridge belt around his waist. Then he put on his blue hooded cloak and buckled it near his neck. At last, he took his double-barreled gun from the closet and slung it over his shoulder.*

"Now we are ready to go," he said with his grim face.

I was breathless. I couldn't imagine what was going to happen. I had a bad feeling, but I didn't have the courage to ask my father what he was going to do with those arms. I followed him down the inner stairs that led to the stable. The light of the lamp was feeble, but here and there I saw some mice running through the straw. My father took the packsaddle that was hung on the wall and put it on the mare, which was startled. Finally, he pulled the girth tightly.

"Take the reins and the saddlebags," he said.

I did as he asked, and then he ordered me to get a small barrel of wine, a bottle of water, and an acetylene lantern. We would use the lamp on the road.

He lifted me with his strong arms and put me on the front of the packsaddle and walked the mare up to the exit of the vegetable garden. He closed the gate and leapt back into the saddle.

Our mare walked briskly through the empty streets of Enna. The streets were illuminated until we reached the Janniscuru Gate, but little by little as we advanced along the country road it became darker and darker.

My father took the acetylene lamp and lit it. "Hold it!" he said.

I grabbed the lantern from the hook, and I have to say that it actually lit the road in front of us very well. It wasn't very heavy, but the smell that it gave off was disgusting!

I had heard from my mother that there were bandits along the roads who mugged passersby, but I blindly trusted my father. He is very strong and nobody dared confront him. My only worry was what my father would do to me. I was sure that my mother had told him that I was a bad student, so I expected punishment, but I couldn't figure out what kind. At last, I summoned up my courage to ask him.

"Where are we going, Father?"

"Shut up!" he said with a voice so firm that it made me shiver with fear. We kept going through the pitch-black night, while I kept holding the lantern.

After an hour of riding, I saw a long line of men, young men, boys, and ragged children walking slowly on the road with their lanterns in their hands. They looked as if they were souls that were heading for the Valley of Jehoshaphat near Jerusalem on the day of the Last Judgement.

Where are all those people going at night? *I thought.* I could never have imagined so eerie a scenario. It was as if I was dreaming, but the lantern in my hand, which was now getting heavy, dispelled all my doubts. I was awake, as were all those people walking along the edge of the road.

It was almost dawn when we arrived at a place with many cylinder-shaped stone mounds that gave off smoke on the top, while below a yellow liquid leaked through a crack in the stones. We had arrived at a sulfur mine.

As soon as they saw my father, three mine laborers headed for us. They all bowed to my father and kissed his hand. One of them took the reins of the mare, while another laborer took my father's cloak. A third workman was waiting for my father's orders.

"This is my son, Vincenzo. I want you to show him the mine, both inside and out," my father said with a commanding tone.

The laborer nodded. "It will be done!" Meanwhile, he helped me dismount. Holding my hand, he led me to the smoking stones that I had seen at the entrance.

"These are furnaces," he said. "We put the sulfur ore inside and smelt it. At least two-thirds of the molten sulfur is lost in the air as sulfur dioxide. The remaining third flows into wooden casts. We wait until the sulfur is cold, then we take it out of the wooden casts and load it into trucks. We export sulfur all over the world. It is used in agriculture as a fertilizer, to make gunpowder, as an insecticide, a fungicide, and so on. Nevertheless, I have to say that all the people that work here breathe toxic fumes due to high levels of sulfur dioxide in the air. Sooner or later we all get sick. We are doomed to die young. Therefore, I advise you to stay as far away from this sulfur mine as you can."

We kept walking around the area until we finally arrived at an entrance that had been dug into the ground. The upper part of the tunnel and the walls were propped up by wooden piles and beams, and a narrow staircase led underground.

"Is it not dangerous to go underground? I don't think these wooden posts are stable enough," I said.

"Actually, accidents happen every now and then, but we must go down, otherwise your father will reprimand me. Anyway, don't be anxious. You are safe with me," he said, holding my hand tightly.

We went downstairs for about a hundred meters. Then the stairs became steeper and slippery. Little by little, as we went down it got hotter. We kept going until we arrived at a wide area from where many tunnels branched off. They were propped up precariously.

Along the stairs and the galleries I saw an uninterrupted line of children who were carrying that nauseating acetylene lamp in one hand and a heavy weight on their shoulder. The ore was stuffed into canvas bags or baskets. The children wore small bags stuffed with rags on their *shoulders and heads to soften the harshness of the ore. Stooping under the weight and with labored breathing, they went upstairs slowly, giving out a painful moan with every step. I had the impression of seeing human-shaped moles which didn't like to come out in the daylight.*

"What is the average age of those children?" I asked.

"Their age ranges from seven to eighteen years. They cannot grow well because the air here is too rarefied and humid. Moreover, they carry weights that are too much for their young age. They cannot stop on the stairs to take a rest or the entire long train of carriers would stop. Their bodies are misshapen and they will never grow taller."

We kept going down, and finally arrived at the end of one of the galleries. The air there was hot and unbearable. I saw that a few men were completely naked because of the stifling heat. With picks in their hands, they dug out the ore. Near them, a few children filled baskets and canvas bags with the ore, while other little laborers helped other children put the loads on their shoulders.

"Every pick man has at least three children at his disposal. He cannot do his work without children that carry out the material that he digs out. For this reason, he makes an agreement with children's parents. The pick man gives the parents money in exchange for their children's work."

I was itching to leave that goddamn, underground place. I wanted to breathe freely in daylight, but the laborer, who had to follow my father's orders, took me all around the mine to see more naked laborers and misshapen children.

"One last thing," the laborer said. "You have to know that accidents are not infrequent in this mine. Some are caused by the accidental collapse of the props, but the most serious tragedies happen when the laborers come across firedamp, which explodes when it comes in contact with the flame from the lanterns. A considerable number of both pick men and children, sometimes dozens, are left trapped

in the bowels of the mine. Their deaths are appalling. The oxygen runs out little by little and they die of suffocation."

When I got out of that infernal mine, my legs were quaking. My mouth was dry and my face was pale. The hand gave me some water and we both sat down on a bench near my father's office. From there I could see the people who set fire to big logs below the furnaces, while other laborers loaded the blocks of melted sulfur into wheelbarrows and then carried them to the trucks.

My father didn't allow me to enter his office, so I had to wait outside on the bench. Two hours later a hand came with our mare. It was the sign that we could go home.

On the way back home my father broke his silence. "Did you visit the mine?"

"Yes, I did."

"Did you see all those children working hard?"

"Yes, I did."

"Well, now I'll give you an option—you either make progress in your studies, or you will come and work inside the mine like those children you just saw. You can be sure that if you fail as a student I will take you to work in the mine!

"You can consider yourself a privileged boy," my father continued, "because you are given an option, while those unlucky children have no choice. They belong to large families with six, seven, sometimes twelve children. Their parents cannot afford to support them, so they entrust them to the pick men for a handful of money."

"Okay, Father, I promise from now on I'll be a good schoolboy!" I said.

October 27, 1933

Today I went to school with my tail between my legs, firmly resolved to study hard and not fail, otherwise the mine's doors would be wide open to me.

During recess I saw Maria. My heart had a start, in spite of the fact that she was now in a relationship with another boy. In order not to think of her, I envisioned working along with those misshapen children in the bowels of the sulfur mine. I turned my back on her and headed for a group of schoolmates that were chatting cheerfully.

November 6, 1933

I have struck up a friendship with the son of the police chief in Enna. His name is Roberto and he is a few years older than me. The police station is near my home, and the officers' quarters are next to the station. We wrestle quite often. He should be law-abiding, seeing that he is the son of a policeman, but he spurs me to perform illegal acts.

November 10, 1933

Roberto told me I had to steal an apple from a market stall. "It is very easy! Don't be shy! You just have to go near the stall, and when the greengrocer is inattentive, grasp an apple and run away at lightning speed."

I don't know why, but I have the tendency to blindly do what my friends tell me. If a friend of mine tells me, "Look! There is a donkey that is flying," I believe him. I am one of the most gullible people in the world.

In the late afternoon while my friend was waiting for me at Garibaldi Square, I headed for the fruit stall. My heart was pounding like a drum, but I finally grabbed an apple and ran away as fast as I could. Once I joined my playmate, I gave him the apple, because I don't like their taste much. He ate the apple with gusto and then congratulated me.

"Now you are a real strong man," he said.

November 18, 1933

Roberto incited me to commit another act of bravado. "If you want to be a real man, you have to go to Saint Francis Square, and whenever you see a kid who is playing or walking there, you have to slap him and then run away."

I did as he had told me. So now every evening at the time when the square swarmed with kids, I got near a little kid, gave him a slap in the face, and then ran away.

My bullying lasted only a few days, because this evening after I had slapped a little kid, his father ran after me and caught me. When I was in his hands he spanked me harshly. His face expressed rage and his words were fiery.

"I'll teach you how to behave in society. Next time I catch you slapping a kid I'll send you directly to jail!" His words terrified me and he didn't want to release me. I was so frightened that I wet my underwear and my trousers.

Obviously, from now on I will take care not to slap children anymore.

November 21, 1933

After that regrettable episode, my playmate has disappeared mysteriously. I don't see him in the streets anymore. Maybe his father has been transferred to another city.

I looked for him at Belvedere and Piazza Mazzini where he used to hang about, but there was no trace of him. Even though his company is not good for me, he is still my friend. I finally decided to go to the police station and ask for him.

At the entrance, a policeman stopped me. "Where are you going?" he asked.

"I am looking for Roberto, the police chief's son. He is my friend."

"Roberto is not here anymore," the policeman answered.

"Where is he?"

"He is in Bronte now. It is a town at the foot of Mount Etna. There is a big seminary there. His father has enrolled him in that school so that he becomes a priest."

A priest? I can't imagine Roberto as a priest. He likes to live as a gangster. Who knows, maybe he can better himself and become a good man by studying and living in the seminary. Many people change their inclination in the course of their lives. I hope Roberto is one of them.

November 25, 1933

Since Roberto has disappeared from my life, I have made friends with a boy three years older than me. His name is Giovanni. He is very tall for his age, and when we stroll together he looks like my father—or at least like my uncle. We like to walk in the high street and along Belvedere.

This evening he got an idea. "What about having a bet?" he asked.

"What kind of bet?" I replied.

"In Enna, to start a relationship between a boy and a girl, we stop a girl who is walking in the street and make a declaration of love."

"What does a declaration of love mean?" I asked.

"It means that you have to propose to her."

"I have never done that! I don't know how to talk with a girl about love."

"Don't worry!" Giovanni said. "Our bet is not about which of us is able to conquer the heart of a girl. Our bet is about how many refusals each of us collects. The one of us that scores fifty refusals will win a free beer at the tavern."

"Okay, I agree. Let's start tomorrow," I said.

November 26, 1933

This evening I stopped three girls. The first one walked with me for a few minutes. I proposed to her, but I was too *crude and was met with a kind refusal. The other two girls I stopped didn't want to walk with me and almost ran away.*

November 27, 1933

I kept courting girls, but no one wanted to start a relationship with me. On the other hand, I just now noticed that Giovanni doesn't stop any girls. He just wants to make fun of me!

November 28, 1933

I decided to put an end to this harmful companionship. In fact, by constantly being mocked by Giovanni and being met with all those refusals from the girls, I am losing my self-esteem and becoming the laughingstock of the entire town.

December 20, 1933

Last night I slept in the bedroom with my parents. They slept in their big bed and I in the smaller one. Suddenly, I heard my father's voice say, "Is Vincenzo sleeping?" My mother didn't answer, but I answered yes. My parents didn't know that it was me who had answered. Obviously they were too excited.

After a few seconds I heard my mother gasping. I was worried about her. I thought she couldn't breathe. I was about to get up from my bed to run to help her, but I didn't because I had the sensation that my parents were doing something dirty. I couldn't sleep all night, and when I woke up I had a feeling of disgust for their bad actions.

January 10, 1934

Last night I didn't sleep in my bed, but in the double bed with my parents. I didn't sleep in the middle between them. I set myself at my mother's side. I was sleeping well when I was awakened by my mother's body, which swung towards me. She kept swinging up and down for a long time and I couldn't sleep. I got the same sensation of nausea and disgust about my parents, who were having sex in the same bed where I was sleeping.

March 6, 1934

Today a friend of mine told me about his sexual activity. He said that he used to masturbate several times a day. He explained to me how to do that.

"It is very easy!" he said. "Just hold your penis with your hand and then shake it up and down. After a while you will have a sensation of pleasure and some white fluid will well from the mouth of your penis."

I went to the bathroom and did as my friend had taught me.

May 10, 1934

I went to the bathroom too often and aroused my father's suspicion. Today he looked through the keyhole and saw me while I was masturbating.

"Who taught you to do that?" he asked with his terrifying voice. I didn't have the strength to answer him, but the blood ran cold in my veins.

When I got out of the bathroom, my father grabbed me by my arm. "Give me your hand! Give me your hand!"

He struck me on my hand so many times that it became red. "Don't do that dirty thing anymore! Otherwise I will chop off your hand!" he shouted.

From now on I will not hide in the bathroom to masturbate. I will do it when I am in my bed. Even though I will wet my underpants, they will dry soon and my mother will wash them.

June 2, 1934

Today my mother asked me, "I have seen a few unsightly yellow stains on your underpants. Are you sick?"

I was terribly embarrassed and couldn't answer.

"Answer me!" continued my mother. "If you have any disease we will call the doctor or take you to the hospital."

"No, there is no problem, Mom. The fact is that yesterday I ate too much yellow cheese," I lied. "That is why my urine is yellowish, but now I will eat more vegetables and it will become normal again."

My mother swallowed my lie and didn't seem to suspect anything. As for me, I swear that I will not masturbate again, even though I predict that I will break my oath frequently.

December 8, 1934

Today was the Feast of the Immaculate Conception. It marks the beginning of the Christmas holidays. The feast is celebrated in the Church of Saint Francis, also called the Church of the Immaculate Conception.

My mother, my sisters, and I went to the church for Mass; the bishop of Piazza Armerina officiated. It is a great event, because the bishop seldom comes to Enna, except to confirm the boys and girls who have already received their First Communion.

My mother, who is an earnest Catholic, wanted all of us to be blessed by the bishop. "When you come close to the bishop," she told us, "remember to kneel and kiss the ring that he wears on his finger."

There was a long line to see the bishop. When I arrived by him, I was seized by awe and my legs were shaking, but I finally kissed his ring, and he repaid me with a smile and a loving caress.

My father is not with us, because he is working at his sulfur mine. He has many workers under him and cannot leave the mine unattended. He usually comes home once a week on horseback.

In front of the church there was a long line of market stalls. They sell lupines, bilberries, and another tasty fruit called holy oil. In the square, which we citizens of Enna call Saint Francis Square, even though its real name is Piazza Vittorio Emanuele II, the city band played their wind instruments, drums, and cymbals nonstop. Then a litter with the statue of the Virgin Mary on it came out from the church. At least fifty brethren dressed in white robes and blue mantillas bore the heavy litter on their shoulders. The city band followed the litter and we got into the procession behind the band.

The number of processions during the year in Enna is considerable. Every quarter has its own patron saint, who is taken in procession along the streets on the day of his or her feast.

When the procession was over, my mother bought four small paper bags of lupines, one for each of us.

December 13, 1934

Today is the feast of Santa Lucia, a saint from Syracuse who was martyred under the emperor Diocletian. She is the patron saint of the blind and people with limited eyesight.

As usual, there are processions on her day, and the statue of the saint is carried on a litter along the streets of Enna. On this day, many families in Enna make a special meal called cuccìa. It is a ritual meal that was made in ancient Greece on the day of the commemoration of the dead. Nowadays in Sicily, the cuccìa is cooked on the day of the Feast of Santa Lucia. It is made from boiled wheat seasoned with chocolate or sweet ricotta, honey, and pieces of candied fruit. My sister Carolina used to cook cuccìa in a big cauldron and then invite all our neighbors to taste it. Even though I don't like cuccìa, I really enjoy the coming and going of our neighbors who crowd my home all day long.

December 21, 1934

There was a joyful atmosphere at home today. My aunts and cousins joined my mother to prepare buccellati. They are typical Christmas sweets made from pastry filled with mashed almonds or figs. I was really happy to see all of the relatives gathering at my home. My mother looked delighted while she was making the buccellati and chatting with her relatives.

February 8, 1935

I wanted to become a Catholic priest and devote my life to God and Jesus, but after pondering my decision for a long time I opted not to go to seminary. What prevents me from dedicating my life to Jesus is the fact that I don't feel that I am able to suppress my sexual activity and my feelings for people of the opposite sex.

Being a Catholic priest means accepting a life of depriving oneself of sexual impulses. How can priests do that? In my opinion, many of them are homosexual. You can recognize a gay priest by the way he talks and acts. The inflection of his voice and his gestures clearly denote that he is a gay. Other priests are not gay but have some kind of secret relationship with women. Sometimes when their illicit love is unveiled it is cause for scandal and they leave their ordained life to marry their lover. That has happened a few times in Enna.

As for me, I am not able to take the vow of celibacy and suppress my sexual instincts, and above all I don't want to give up my ordinary worldly life. Therefore, I have decided to follow Jesus in my daily life by doing my best to be a good person that follows the precepts contained in the Gospels. It is not necessary to be a priest to be a good Christian!

The Catholic religion considers masturbation a great sin. Therefore, every time I masturbate I rush to the priest to confess my sin. The priest doesn't tell me the reason why masturbation is a sin, but he confines himself to giving me absolution. I have decided to stop confessing, because I feel that it is absurd to confess a sin and promise not to sin anymore when I know in advance that I will masturbate again and again.

June 20, 1935

My afterschool teacher is quite strange. On the one hand she beats me, but on the other she has the habit of lifting up her skirt and pulling her nylon stockings up. When she does, she shows her thighs almost up to her groin. I am very embarrassed and I try not to look at her. Her thighs are nice, but my awe of her is too great to think of her when I masturbate.

November 1, 1935

I am a high school student now. I got good grades in the entrance examinations. I am happy about getting rid of my afterschool teacher who used to beat me and show me her naked thighs, but now I am out of the frying pan and into the fire.

My new afterschool teacher is a man. He has the habit of beating me too. When he gives his lessons at his home, he wears a bathrobe and slippers. His bare feet stink so much that sometimes I get a headache.

December 10, 1935

Today I was with another student, a girl, at the afterschool teacher's house. He was not in the room where we get his lessons, but his sister was sitting in front of us. I started to play with the other student and touched her breast. The sister informed the teacher, who came in the study room and asked me to follow him to another room. Once there, without saying a word, he beat me more harshly than ever before. He punched me in the face and other parts of my body. Then he hit me with a hail of blows.

I will never forgive that teacher for that. He should have explained to me in words that my behavior was wrong—but he didn't. He just used his brutal power against a defenseless student. I also cannot inform my parents, because they trust the teacher more than me. They would say that I am wrong.

March 7, 1936

I have two close friends at the high school. One, Renato, has the reputation of being a very good student. He is short, square-built, with a dark complexion. His hair and eyes are as black as a block of coal. The other, Fabrizio, is just a friend of his and doesn't belong to our class. He is always stuck to Renato, and as a consequence he is also my friend. He studies at the technical high school. He is a boy of medium build. In spite of his shoulders stooping a little, he is strong, and his brown, deep eyes show aggressiveness and defiance.

March 8, 1936

Today Fabrizio said to me, "Why don't you sit close to Renato in the class so you can copy his work and be a successful student?"

I answered, "I don't need to crib off him, because I am able to do my work by myself."

When I arrived home, I told my mother about the episode. I was proud of having turned down the proposal of copying Renato's work, but instead of praising me because I wanted to be independent and diligent at school, my mother rebuked me.

"You are stupid and silly," she spoke out. "Renato is a good student and can help you be successful. You should accept his proposal. Sit close to him at school and copy his work!"

I was astounded. I could never have imagined my mother acting that way. Obviously, what mattered to her was that I pass the final exam; it didn't matter how. It was important to her that at the end of my school career I got my certificate of degree, even if I didn't deserve it.

That way of thinking is widespread in Enna. A certificate of degree is considered more important than actual good grounding. In fact, by having a doctor's degree you can get a job in the civil service through good political connections.

Nowadays, the competitive state examinations in Italy are all fixed. Membership in the Fascist Party or the closeness to this or that Fascist Party leader is a prerequisite to getting a good job or making progress in your career.

March 9, 1936

I followed my mother's orders and sat at the same desk with Renato. The consequences were disastrous. I stopped thinking with my mind and slavishly followed what Renato suggested to me. In the afternoons, when I didn't go to my afterschool teacher, I studied with Renato. Our way of studying was that he read the school books and then repeated to me what he had read, and then I repeated to him what he had said to me. In other words, I didn't read books anymore, but confined myself to memorizing what he explained to me.

October 23, 1936

Fabrizio bullies me. He is very arrogant and mocks me continuously. Today I tried to fight back, but he punched me. He is stronger than me and more aggressive. What to do? He is Renato's friend and it's important I follow my mother's orders: Follow Renato all the way, because he is a good student!

I cannot breakup the friendship between Fabrizio and Renato, and now it is too late for me to be an independent student. In fact, I depend on Renato for my school progress. I am used to copying his work, and now I am unable to do my work by myself. Renato has become indispensable, and cribbing off him is a habit, or worse, an addiction for me.

By enduring Fabrizio's bullying, little by little I have quenched my natural sense of boldness. I get desperate whenever he mocks me. This morning he called me queer. I felt humiliated and my pride was wounded. This time I attacked him, but he soon reversed our positions and hit me very hard.

I cannot help recognizing his superiority. In fact, he is stout, stronger, and above all more aggressive than me. Every time he calls me queer I pretend not to hear him, but inside I am devastated. By acting this way I have learned to be a victim of somebody else's power, and I will surely be a loser in life.

November 4, 1936

Fabrizio and Renato are proud of getting money from the pederasts. They even boasted that a rich pederast used to give them two lire if they allowed him to masturbate them.

"Where did you meet that pederast? I want to get money from him as well!" I said.

"Usually," they answered, "we meet him at the cinema. If you go to the cinema in the early afternoon, you can meet pederasts as well. As a rule, they hang about on Belvedere in the evening or they go to the cinema in the early afternoon."

November 5, 1936

Today I went to the cinema at around four in the afternoon and took a seat in the middle of the balcony, waiting for a pederast to come.

At a distance, in the same row, a distinguished gentleman was sitting pretending to watch the movie, but apparently he had different ideas in his mind. He wore a jacket and a tie. He had the air of belonging to a high class. He moved from the end of the row towards me, and sat down two or three seats away. I watched him out of the corner of my eye. I thought he might be a pederast and he would give me some money.

All of a sudden he moved close to me. It was evident that he intended to do something with me. In fact, the balcony was almost empty and there were many seats available. Nevertheless, he seemingly was not interested in me and kept watching the movie. He was sweating profusely and looked uneasy and tense. It seemed that a tremendous struggle was happening inside him. He unbuttoned his shirt and loosened his black tie. It was too hot for him, so he took off his jacket and put it on his legs.

Little by little, he moved the jacket towards me and slipped his hand onto my genital area. Then he lowered my zipper, put his hand into my underpants, and took out my penis. I was not interested in his masturbation, but I didn't want to disappoint him, so he kept touching my penis. After around ten minutes he left. Apparently, he had already satisfied his perverted sexual need.

I didn't get money from him. Maybe I should have asked him for money when he got close to me before allowing him to masturbate me. If I had Renato's or Fabrizio's boldness I would have acted differently, but I was too sheepish to have the strength of coping with that pederast.

I don't know if I will tell Fabrizio and Renato tomorrow about my meeting with the pederast. I will probably say nothing, because they will think that I am a really stupid boy and will mock me for not being able to get money from him.

January 8, 1937

Today Renato and Fabrizio convinced me to play hooky. Renato claimed that he was able to perfectly forge the headmaster's signature. He showed me the faked signature, which did actually look identical to the headmaster's.

In my school, every time you miss a class, a note written by one of your parents needs to be shown to the headmaster, who generally accepts the excuse and admits the student to class. Then the student has to show the note signed by the headmaster to the teacher in the classroom.

"It is very easy!" resounded Fabrizio. "The teacher in the classroom only checks the headmaster's signature, not your parents' note. Therefore, you can write the excuse note by yourself and Renato will forge the headmaster's signature."

"That is absurd!" I answered. "The teachers know my handwriting and they will smell the trick."

"That's no problem!" answered Renato. "Fabrizio doesn't belong to our school, and no teacher knows his handwriting. So he can write the excuse note and teachers will not suspect the swindle. Then I can forge the headmaster's signature. It's so easy and simple!"

I was so gullible that they convinced me to skip school. I had never done a fraud in my life. My parents are very strict, and if I don't tell them the truth they beat me harshly. Above all, my mother doesn't endure me lying to her. Whenever she discovers that I have told her a lie, she hits me wildly, sometimes even on my head.

We spent our hooky time at Lombardia Castle. It is a stronghold whose origins are lost in the dim and distant past. It stands on the highest place in Enna and dominates the valley, which in the springtime has a green color, while in the summertime it takes on a yellow hue due to the withering of the herbs from the scorching sun and the lack of rain. The castle is very old and stands on a rocky spur. You could say that the rock itself is a natural stronghold. In some stretches, the nearly sheer rock face is around twenty meters high.

Of the six towers left, the one in better condition is the Pisana tower, which takes its name from the Roman consul Lucio Pisone, who took the stronghold by storm at the time of the slave revolt. Tourists from all over the world come to the top of the tower to see the scenery that encompasses a great part of Sicily.

Fabrizio wanted to show Renato and me how fearless he was. "Are you able to climb the rock face?"

"That is impossible!" we both answered. "It is sheer!"

"I'll do it!" he said, looking firm while his voice betrayed a hint of worry.

Renato and I tried to dissuade him from his mad idea, but he was stubborn. He took off his shoes in order to adhere better to the rock, and then started his crazy climbing. I was sure that he would fall headlong, but to my surprise, little by little he climbed the rock face and then climbed down from another side where the cliff was less steep.

We spent the morning around the castle area. From time to time, Renato approached some tourists to practice his English. At the time, we studied French as a foreign language at school, but Renato had taught himself English.

Finally, Fabrizio wrote the excuse notes for Renato and me, while Renato wrote a note for Fabrizio and forged the headmasters' signatures. Around the time our parents expected us to come home from school, we parted.

Oddly, today my father came home unexpectedly from the sulfur mine and questioned me about what I had done at school.

"Did the teacher test you today?" he asked.

At his question I blushed throughout my face.

"Why are you blushing? What happened to you?" continued my father.

I didn't know how to justify my blush, so I gave him the first answer I thought of. "Yes, today I was tested in Latin."

"How did you do? Was your teacher satisfied?"

"The test went so-so," I answered.

"Tell me what your teacher asked you and what your answers were."

What stressed me most was the fact that my father, who had studied only at the elementary school, wanted me to tell him Latin. Anyway, after my continuous refusal to talk Latin, he finally gave up.

January 9, 1937

Today I had to enter class with a forged excuse note. My legs were quaking continuously from the time I left home, my heart was in my mouth, and a wave of blush pervaded my whole face. What would I do if the teacher suspected the scam?

In the past, students had been suspended from school throughout Italy for disciplinary offenses. That happened in Enna at the classic school. One day, a student that was unsatisfied with his final grades tore all the notices off of the school board where the names and marks of the successful and failed students were posted.

That was a serious offence, while my mistake was, in some way, forgivable. But who knows! Sometimes criteria to assess students' behavior vary according to the person who is doing the judging. So a venial fault may be considered a capital sin by a person that observes the rules strictly. As for me, the worst would happen if the headmaster informed my family of my hooky.

I met Renato at the school entrance. He looked quite calm and was going to show the teacher his fake excuse note with nonchalance. But I was not calm at all, and my legs shook as if I had a vibrator under my feet. It was impossible to show the teacher that excuse note, because I was sure that my hands would also be trembling when I handed the note to the teacher. It is absolutely impossible for me to lie.

What to do? I decided not to go to school and play hooky for the second time. This time I didn't go to the castle as I had done with Renato and Fabrizio, because somebody seeing me alone in that place at school time might have informed my parents. Therefore, I opted to go to the billiard room. I am not a good billiards player. Furthermore, I was not in the right mood to play. I confined myself to watching the others shoot pool, but the thick cloud of cigarette smoke that permeated the room made my eyes water.

After noon I headed for my home.

January 10, 1937

I couldn't sleep well last night. The headmaster appeared to me in a dream and pointed the way out of the school to me. At the thought that I should tell my parents the truth, I woke up panting, my body damp with sweat.

I had to confront my ordeal, but I didn't have the boldness to show the teacher that goddamn forged excuse note. Furthermore, it referred to only one day of absence from school, but now I had been out for two.

I spent my third day away from school at the billiard room.

I went home at the usual time. As soon as I crossed the threshold I saw my mother, who oddly was standing in the landing. She came close to me and then landed a punch on my eye, using all her might. If she had had the strength of a man, she would have sent me to the hospital. However, her fury was so high that she continued to beat me so badly that I reeled under her blows.

Then she started shouting. "I met Renato's mother by chance this morning! She told me that you didn't go to school for three consecutive days!"

She screamed as if she were possessed, and meantime she kept dealing blows and kicking me. I couldn't react. I had been brought up as an obedient child. Furthermore, my mother had inculcated in me a sense of passive obedience to her by linking religious punishments to my acts of disobedience.

One day I was about to fight back against her, but her words made my blood run cold. "If you beat your mom, you will be excommunicated!" she said.

"What does that mean?" I asked.

"It means not to be recognized by God."

Now, while she was screaming and beating me, my sisters ran down the stairs and rushed into the vestibule to make a wall between my mother and me. Then they took me under their protection until my mother's fury cooled down.

January 11, 1937

My mother wrote an excuse for me. To justify my absence, she wrote that I had been unwell. Now I could enter school without a problem. It was the first and last time that I played hooky.

January 15, 1937

I saw three girls at the bus stop today. Two of them were the same height, but the third was quite tall. Of the shorter ones, the one with blue eyes and brown hair attracted me. The other two had both brown eyes and hair.

I noticed that every day they waited for the bus at the same stop after leaving the school.

January 16, 1937

I pretended I was nonchalantly walking today when I passed the three at the bus stop, and had a quick look at them. Abruptly, I changed my mind. Seeing her polished features, I fell in love with the one who is not very tall and has brown eyes. I want her to become my girlfriend, but I don't know how to approach her.

January 17, 1937

After long thinking, I finally approached the girl I liked and asked her to become my girlfriend. She refused and I felt her refusal like a wound in my stomach.

April 4, 1937

While I was walking to the Belvedere, I fixed my eyes on a green-eyed girl. I liked her and decided to woo her. I approached and asked her to become my girlfriend. She said that she would think about it.

April 9, 1937

I met the green-eyed girl again this evening. This time she accepted my proposal to become my girlfriend. Once at home, I was happy that she had accepted, but I also asked myself if this new relationship was not a makeshift solution. In fact, if the previous girl had not refused me, surely I wouldn't have approached the green-eyed girl. The body and polished manners of the previous girl had attracted me, but what to do! I cannot stay away from girls, so I accepted this stopgap.

October 8, 1937

The relationship with my girlfriend lasted a few months, but today I told her that I didn't want to continue our relationship, so we split up.

February 10, 1938

I met an older friend of mine outside the school. He is passionately fond of hunting. He owns a sporting gun and two greyhounds from Etna.

"Why don't you come with me this afternoon? I'll show you how to hunt," he said. I told him I had to go to my private teacher for afterschool activities that afternoon and couldn't.

"He is just a private teacher! Nothing happens if you skip one lesson!"

My friend insisted so much that he at last convinced me to go. Besides, my afterschool teacher didn't require written excuse notes whenever I missed a lesson.

It was not a great day for my friend and he didn't catch any prey. At sunset, we went to our homes with empty hands.

As soon as I entered the vestibule of my house, I met my parents' angry stares. They looked like two guards that were there to carry out an arrest warrant. Obviously the teacher had informed them of my absence. Now they were ready to punish me harshly.

I had the sensation that something terrible was going to happen, so I ran headlong to my room while my parents ran after me. I entered my room just in time to lock the door, leaving my parents outside. I felt safe and just hoped that my parents' fury would cool down within a few hours.

Unfortunately, events took a different direction that I never expected.

My father kept pushing on the door, but the lock held. Despite his efforts, he was not able to force it. Abruptly, he started planting kicks to the door. His rage grew more and more while he continued shouting, "Open the door! Open the door!" But I took good care not to open it.

Suddenly a blow more violent than the previous made a breach in the door, but the lock held. My father kept kicking the door until the breach was wide enough to let a person get through. When the entire door had almost collapsed, my parents stormed into the room like soldiers who had conquered an enemy's position. They rushed at me. I lay on my bed unmoving, resigned to my fate like prey under the predator's claws, unable to wriggle free from it and just waiting to be devoured.

My parents' violence was unprecedented. They both punched and beat me as if they were beating a drum. I was silent and passively bore their ferocity.

My sisters couldn't do anything to rescue me. They feared my father too much, but finally their love for me prevailed. They left and asked one of our neighbors to come because I was in danger.

At the sight of my sisters, who were visibly upset, our neighbor rushed to my aid and grabbed my father by the arm. "Stop beating your son or you'll kill him!" he yelled.

At his words, my father came to his senses and his ferocity diminished. His choleric dark eyes took on a light hue. Calm seemed to return to my grim house after the raging storm. My parents finally released their grip.

I overcame the terrible predicament thanks to my beloved sisters. I am sure that if I commit a serious fault one more time my father will shoot me with his revolver.

I must be obedient in all ways. Now I want to immerse myself in studying. I am itching to finish my last year at the classical high school of Enna. Then I will move to the University of Catania, free from my parents' haunting presence.

February 11, 1938

The carpenter came to take out the broken door. He couldn't fix it because the frame cannot be repaired. A new door is needed. While he was measuring the door opening, I sat on the bed pretending to read a book. Now and then he gave me a pitiful look. I am sure that he knows, or at least he can figure out, what happened to me yesterday.

I will stay at home for three days. I cannot show myself to my teachers and schoolmates in such bad condition. My body is covered with bruises.

July 2, 1938

Today was the first day of final school examinations all over Italy, which started with the written Italian test.

Even though this is the day of the most important feast in Enna, since it is a local feast, schools, public offices, and banks were open. Today, the town was woken by a hundred-and-one gun salute, and the city band went through the streets. Everybody got dressed up, and the farmers left the countryside and came to Enna. They are not well-off people and only own one formal dress, which they keep in the closet all year and wear on July 2 for the celebrations in honor of Our Lady of Visitation.

I was sitting at my desk writing the Italian essay, the subject of which was "Describe nature as seen by Foscolo, Manzoni, and Leopardi" (three important Italian writers and poets). While I was absorbed in writing the essay, I heard the sound of the town band, and hoped that today might be the feast of my liberation from Enna and my oppressive parents. It took six hours to write the essay, but in the end I was satisfied that I had done good work.

In the evening I went out to see the procession. Barefooted brethren bore three litters in the procession with the statues of Our Lady, Saint Joseph, and the archangel Saint Michael along the street from the cathedral to the Franciscan monastery of Montesalvo.

July 20, 1938

I passed my final examinations and can now enter the University of Catania. I got through thanks to Renato, who helped me in the written work, and thanks to my father, who fixed my oral examination with the examining board.

Chapter Ten

The Public Whorehouse in Enna

There was a public whorehouse in Enna until 1958. Afterwards, all brothels were suppressed throughout Italy by an act of the national parliament. Enna's public whorehouse was located in the upper town, which looks onto the nearby town of Calascibetta, but it was not far from downtown. Of course, Enna is a small city lying on a plateau, and the distances between one side and another are not long.

To go to the public brothel from Saint Francis Square, which is the heart of the city, you had to go down the main street called Via Roma. When Mussolini came to power, he decreed that the main street in every Italian city, town, and village should be named Roma, which he considered not just the capital of Italy, but also the symbol of the Italian power, history, and traditions.

Walking a short distance down Via Roma, there is another small square called Piazza Balata, named by the Arabs who had conquered Sicily around the tenth century AD, and who remained here for two centuries until they were defeated by the Normans.

Four streets branch off from Piazza Balata. One of them that goes uphill is called Via Sant'Agata. The main business centers of Enna are on this street. The small Church of Santa Croce was located on Via Sant'Agata as well. The street that branches off downhill is called Via Pergusa. It leads towards mythological Lake Pergusa. Of the other two streets, one is the continuation of Via Roma, while the other leads to the area where the public whorehouse once was. That street is called Via Vittorio Emanuele II, who was the king when the unification of Italy took place.

Walking uphill on Via Vittorio Emanuele II, on the right there is a square that is raised about one meter above the street, which at harvest time once swarmed with folk from all over Sicily. Those people were farm workers who hoped to get hired to reap the wheat, which is abundant in the fields around Enna.

Further on is the impressive Church of San Cataldo with its wooden-trussed roof. According to a friend of mine who is an archeologist, this church overlapped the old Temple of Persephone, named for Demeter's daughter. He could be right, because through a glass floor inside the church it is possible to see old remains that likely denote a preexisting place of worship.

Walking along the external wall of the church, the street gets narrower for a few meters and then leads to the area called Popolo (the common people). In this area, the street takes the form of a backbone from where, like ribs, a series of alleyways branch off. As we keep walking, we find the Church of Santa Maria del Popolo (Saint Mary of the People) on the left, the origin of which was the chapel of a convent of cloistered nuns.

Long ago, a great part of the city of Enna consisted of churches, convents, and monasteries. After the unification of Italy, the convent attached to the Church of Santa Maria del Popolo shared the lot of much of the ecclesiastic real estate. It was expropriated by the Italian liberal government. The nuns were asked to leave, and the Italian army turned the convent into a military garrison.

The ex-convent, the square in front of it, and the bordering houses took the appellation of *Colombaia* (dovecote), due to the fact that, before the telegraph was invented, the military detachment used to communicate with other outposts by carrier pigeons that were kept in the state-owned dovecote. The carrier pigeons had the task of delivering messages from one place to another, and it seems that they never got lost. In fact, they were able to cover a distance of a thousand kilometers at the speed of 100 kilometers per hour, bearing the message to be delivered stuck on their claw.

If you keep walking uphill on Via Vittorio Emanuele II, it leads to another street called Via San Francesco d'Assisi. Almost at the end of Via Vittorio Emanuele II, on the right, there is Via Aspromonte, a narrow alley that just leads to the building that once was the public whorehouse.

The brothel was run by a brothel keeper, but the building belonged to a wealthy Enna family and had been leased to an ex-prostitute who had made enough money from her "work." Brothel keepers were often called queens, and were usually unmarried. If it happened that one of them was married, her husband was called the "king."

One room of the whorehouse was left for a police officer, who had the task of keeping order and checking the personal documents, above all the ones regarding the customer's age. In fact, entrance was forbidden to young men under eighteen years of age. Nevertheless, the brothel keeper controlled everything in advance and kept order. She was always present at the entrance, and was very strict with both the prostitutes and the customers.

The brothel's main door was kept ajar till late into the night. A wide red curtain separated the entrance from the rest of the house. Over the curtain there was a hall. The queen's room was on the right, and on the left two steps led to a corridor. At the bottom was the room for the policeman; on the left there were two wide bedrooms, and on the right two waiting rooms.

The bedrooms were equipped with a washbasin, a bidet, an irrigator, and a small closet where tubes containing calomel ointment, thymol, and silver mercury for the treatment that had to be done after every intercourse were kept, and obviously there was a bed. It was a big double bed covered with a bedspread and a simple white cotton sheet.

The whorehouse was not furnished with a heating system, so every room had a wood stove with a saucepan full of water on it, which served the purpose of keeping moisture in the air. The hot water was also used to fill hot-water bottles that warmed up the girls and also the chilly customers, who put them on their genitals. Some girls obliged their customers by taking a hip bath, using the bidet, before having sex.

In the waiting rooms, where the customers sat on wooden sofas, there were placards that listed the dangers of sexually transmitted diseases, the preventive treatments to apply, the location of the prevention and treatment dispensaries, and where to go for clinical tests.

In one of the lounges that the girls used to talk with the customers, there was a desk where the queen kept the accounts. One drawer held the tokens and in the other she stashed the money. After the customer had paid the fee, the girl got a token, which was the equivalent of a simple sexual intercourse, and at the end of the day the tokens that each girl collected were counted and exchanged into ready money by the brothel keeper.

Behind the desk, stuck on the wall, there was the price list pinned on a wooden board:

- Simple service £ 1
- Double £ 1.8
- Fifteen minutes £ 2.20
- Half an hour £ 3.50
- One hour £ 5
- Towel and soap £ 0.50

From the hall, a staircase led upstairs where there were three more rooms for the girls, the medical room, and another waiting room reserved only for high-class people or someone that wanted to hide his identity, like a priest, a monk, or a married person. The entrance to this waiting room was regulated by the queen, who ordered the doors to all rooms shut, except the one reserved for the police, in order to let in the person that had asked to remain anonymous.

Another staircase led to the basement, which was comprised of the kitchen, the laundry, and the dining room.

The meeting between the girls and their customers took place in the waiting rooms. It was not as easy as you might imagine to find a mutual attraction, because everyone has different tastes. Some people liked a thin girl, and others a plump one, or one with a great pair of tits. Some preferred blondes and others the dark-haired ones. Once the choice had been made, the couple headed for the bedroom, and within about ten minutes the meeting was over. It was possible to stay in the bedroom for a longer time, but in that case the customer obviously had to pay more.

Before having intercourse, the girls examined their customers very carefully, and sometimes they were able to diagnose some of the sexually transmitted diseases.

Some customers used to take two girls, and sometimes a couple of men went into a bedroom with only one girl. Sexual activities varied widely. Some men liked to have anal intercourse with the girl, some enjoyed the girl sucking or moving her tongue around his penis, while others preferred to move their tongue across the female sexual organs.

A friend of mine, who had been a great haunter of the brothel, told me that before having sex he used to lick the whore all over her body, from the tip of her toes to her crown. He told me that the time he spent there had been the most beautiful in his life. The charming atmosphere of the girls sitting in the lounge was unforgettable. He enjoyed talking and joking with them for long periods of time before going to the room to have sex.

In 1958, when public whorehouses were suppressed by law, he stuck a death notice on the walls of the buildings in Enna: "The public whorehouse of Enna is dead and an era is ended. All the men who used to go to that house mourn the loss of their beloved meeting place."

The prostitutes in the whorehouse shifted every fifteen days. The fortnight shift happened by bilateral agreement between the brothel keeper and the prostitutes. The girls were brought there by a recruiter. Once in the brothel they had to give half of their earnings to the queen. They also had to pay their board and lodging.

Once in the brothel, the girls took nicknames, which usually reflected the place of their origin or the peculiar "skills" they had. For instance, if one was good at giving a man oral pleasure, she was called the blow jobber.

The girls used to be able to sleep or rest however they pleased in the mornings; only one of them was on duty and available in case a customer had the pressing need to have sex. In the evenings, all the girls sat scantily dressed in the lounge where the meetings with their customers took place. Some men quite often went to the whorehouse just to chat with the girls. They didn't want to have sex, but just to loaf about. In this case, the queen intervened and asked the person to leave. However, as Enna is a small town where almost everyone knows one another, the queen was able to spot the dawdlers in advance and wouldn't allow them to enter.

The chat with the girls went on for a while in the lounge. Some people used to grope the girls before making their choice. Once the customer had opted for one of the girls, she couldn't refuse, even if he was ugly, dirty, or had a penis out of proportion. She had to follow him to the room and satisfy him according to his will.

A friend of mine, who had lived in Enna during the Second World War, told me that when the American troops conquered the town, most of the soldiers were looking for brothels or prostitutes that ran their business at home.

One of the freelance whores lived in Colombaia Quarter not far from my friend's home. He told me that whenever he passed by her house, he heard her crying out with pain.

Obviously there were some problems with the penis size of those soldiers, or the way they wanted to have sex. Whorehouses in Italy had different standards. There was a classification similar to that of hotels, ranging from five-star to one star. The whorehouse in Enna was listed at three-star. The difference of the standards of brothels was given not only by the more luxurious environment, but above all by the quality of the female "material." Girls in a four- or five- star brothel had to meet certain criteria: beauty, age, and above all buxomness.

All girls in any brothel had to have their health certificate to work. Apparently, the society of that time was openly male chauvinist, because health certificates were required only for girls, not for men that entered the whorehouse. The fact is, that after one year of work, almost all prostitutes fell ill with a venereal disease, especially syphilis. When the queen had the tiniest suspicion that a girl had contracted a venereal disease, she asked her to leave the house right away.

In Enna's whorehouse, the new girls all had to undergo health examinations. The outpatient clinic was on the other side of the city, so the new prostitutes were paraded by the queen through Via Vittorio Emanuele II, Saint Francis Square, and Via Roma to go to the doctor. It was a good opportunity for them to be seen by the townspeople and to publicize themselves.

The medical examination consisted of an overall body check-up, but above all genitals and mucosae needed to be examined. Then the doctor had to check if gonococcus, the etiological agent of gonorrhea, was present.

Even though the examination was very thorough, it didn't guarantee with absolute certainty that the prostitute didn't have a contagious venereal disease. In fact, all infectious diseases have an incubation period of a few days. During that time it is impossible to make an accurate diagnosis, and a sick prostitute could still infect her customers.

My friend who lived during the brothel era told me that an outstanding professional man, who was married to a noblewoman, once contracted syphilis when he had sex with a prostitute in a five-star brothel in Catania. Then he infected his wife, who was pregnant. The twins that she delivered were both born syphilitic. It was a real tragedy at that time. Syphilis could not be cured completely and it affected many organs like the liver, the kidneys, and the central nervous system.

Besides the activity that was run in public whorehouses, there was a kind of underground prostitution. Those prostitutes used to take a seat in front of their homes—usually located on the ground floor and looking onto the street—and lured passersby. Sometimes the oldest prostitutes took in some young girls.

Those whores were not as beautiful as the ones in public brothels. They were often getting on in years. Their average age was around forty or fifty, but they were the only way for teenagers to have sex. At that time, morals were very strict and it was even considered improper for unmarried couples to merely stroll on the street. Whenever two engaged people wanted to go together to some place, to the cinema for instance, or just wanted to take a walk, they needed to be escorted by another woman of the family, who remained stuck to them all the way.

For teenagers, there was no other opportunity to have sex except with a whore. Most of the teenagers in Enna had their entry into the sex world through prostitutes that ran their business at home. While whores in brothels didn't need a pimp, for street prostitutes a kind of protection was necessary. Usually the pimp was her lover who had started her off on the career as a prostitute.

The greatest danger whenever a boy had sex with a whore was contracting a contagious disease. Some sexually transmitted diseases were not very serious, like pediculosis and candidiasis, while others like syphilis were very dangerous. Gonorrhea was considered much less serious than syphilis, and if no complications arose, it was cured without any lasting effects.

Chapter Eleven
Vincenzo's Diary, Part Two

November 3, 1938

I decided to enter the University of Catania. I had been quite hesitant about which school to choose. I would have liked to be a diplomat, but I thought that I would not pass the competitive state examination to be a diplomat without good political connections. I was about to enroll in law school, but after long rumination I gave up, because in my opinion it was not right for me. In fact, to be a lawyer or a judge you must be endowed with a strong personality. I was hesitant and too anxious whenever I had a close confrontation with my opponents. I would have liked to study the classic languages and literature, but I had become accustomed to copying the schoolwork on translations from Latin and ancient Greek into Italian from Renato, and now I didn't have enough confidence in myself to continue classical studies. Finally, I opted to enter the school of medicine, which would allow me to help others and relieve people's sufferings.

Catania is quite far from Enna, so I must live there if I want to attend lectures and seminars.

November 5, 1938

My father has found accommodations for me at the boys' boarding school that is run by Catholic priests. The room is wide and full of light, but the bathroom is shared with the other students. It was my father who chose the room. I would have preferred another room that overlooked the playground, but my father said no because he thought it would take my mind off my studying.

My parents entrusted me to the warden and presented him with one cheese typical of Enna called "Piacentino." My father wanted to know how much freedom I would have. The warden told him that students are free from seven in the morning until ten in the evening. If a student gets home late, he is automatically expelled from the boarding school.

My father and mother finally left for Enna, and at long last I was alone in Catania. For the first time in my life I savor the taste of freedom. In fact, here I will be far away from my overbearing parents!

November 6, 1938

The beginning of my university experience is a time for taking stock of my life. I want to radically change my way of living. What I wouldn't do if it was possible to go back in time! First of all, I wouldn't copy Renato's work at school. That was one of the biggest mistakes of my life. By cribbing off Renato I lost my self-esteem, which is one of the most important features of a human. Without it, a human being is like a ship adrift at the mercy of the waves.

Another mistake I wouldn't repeat would be accepting Fabrizio's bullying. Everything is linked in human behavior. If I had not copied Renato's work I wouldn't have lost my self-esteem, and therefore I would have been stronger and more sure of myself, able to cope with Fabrizio. Surely I would have found a way to oppose his bullying.

A third thing I wouldn't repeat is the mistake of judging by appearances. So far, I've only approached girls on the basis of the features of their face and the voluptuousness of their body. From now on I will value the inward side of women much more.

November 10, 1938

I have been approached by other students who are very pleased to have me as a friend. Here, I want to change the way I behave with my companions. I was bullied by Fabrizio in Enna; here I want to appear as if I am a stout boy, endowed with courage, dignity, and strength. Unfortunately, that is not my real character, and sooner or later my weakness will come to the surface.

November 18, 1938

A friend of mine advised me to buy a toy pistol. "With such a weapon," he says, "you can appear stronger than you are. All the students will fear you and your personality will be strengthened."

I did as my friend advised. I bought the toy pistol and plan to show it to my new friends.

November 19, 1938

Today I showed my toy pistol to the other students, but apparently nobody cares about my gun. Even though I have a revolver, I don't look like an aggressive or dangerous boy. After showing it a few more times, I finally opted to throw it away. I still cannot rid myself of the bad habit of doing whatever my friends suggest.

November 22, 1938

Today was my first day of school. In the morning the lecturer held a lesson about human anatomy. I am enthusiastic about my career and feel that I can become a good doctor.

In the afternoon, I read my textbooks eagerly and I was sure that I would pass my exams without help from anybody. I feel strong, sure of myself, and I don't need my father to fix my exams for me to pass them, as it has happened in the past.

December 15, 1938

I have good relationship with the other students in the boarding school. I don't accept it when other students try to bully me. I look quite strong and nobody dares to defy me.

December 16, 1938

My tendency to follow others blindly is not always negative. Staying in Catania at the boarding school, I have struck up a friendship with two very good friends. One of them, Ugo, is from a village at the foot of the Madonie Mountains. He is so shy that he doesn't allow anybody to enter his room. He looks a little bit strange, but he has a good classical education. He reads continuously, all kinds of books, because for him culture is all-embracing.

Seeing him so inclined, I started reading books too. So far, I have only read books that were necessary to make headway at school. Now I want to broaden my cultural scope.

I have to thank Ugo, because he put me on the amazing path of books. I will owe it all to him if my cultural horizons broaden.

December 17, 1938

My other good friend at the university is Mario. He is from a town near Syracuse called Noto. He studies at the School of Mathematics. He is a close friend of the warden of the boarding school. He has got the keys to the warden's room, and from time to time he invites me to go there. We sit on the armchairs and listen to classical music.

He also teaches me the history of music. "This overture is by Rossini!" Mario explained. "He is famous for his crescendos. This is the 'Moonlight Sonata' by Beethoven. He is a great composer. Did you know that he couldn't listen to his masterpiece, 'The Ninth Symphony,' because he was deaf?"

Mario helped me enter a new world unknown to me. We didn't listen to music at home in Enna. We had a radio with a gramophone, but we confined ourselves to listening just to the news bulletin. The only kind of music I had heard before was the Italian national anthem and Fascist songs like "Giovinezza."

February 5, 1939

Today, the celebrations in honor of Saint Agata, the patron saint of Catania, reached their peak. Townspeople wore white habits and ashen-black headdresses. For ten days, twelve gigantic candles on baroque-style litters were borne on the shoulders of guild members as they went along the streets. Today, the litters went ahead of the statue of Saint Agata to light up the street. The patron saint stood on a wagon dragged by hundreds of devotees.

People crowded round the statue and lit big wax candles, which they then handed a man on the wagon. There were so many candles that the wagon couldn't hold them all. Every now and then, it was emptied of all the candles and they were tossed into a truck.

The wagon was dragged along the places where Saint Agata suffered martyrdom. According to history, the saint belonged to a noble family and wished to be a Christian, but the Roman governor wanted to possess her. She refused, and for that she was imprisoned and later executed.

I saw the procession from the sidewalk of Via Etnea. The streets were so crowded that it was impossible for me to get near the wagon. So I watched the bust of Saint Agata from a distance.

There were also many street vendors. I saw an unusual, beautiful red apple in one of the stalls. I asked the vendor what it was, and he told me it was an apple mixed with sugar, the traditional fruit of the Feast of Saint Agata. I couldn't help purchasing and eating that apple before I headed for my lodging house.

I would like to write down more things about Saint Agata and the celebrations in her honor, but I have to stop and study hard. I really want to pass the exams on my own, unlike in the past. I want to show I don't need Renato's support.

June 22, 1939

I got up this morning telling myself I had to pass my first exam. I knew if I passed my test in anatomy all the doors of my career would be flung open. As soon as I got out of bed, my heart was beating fast. I knew I had to strive to keep my nerves and emotions calm or all my studying would have been useless. I asked Saint Agata to help me. Above all, I am eager to pass my examination to make my father happy and so he will be proud of me.

There were three professors sitting behind a desk inside the exam room. On the opposite side were many students sitting and watching the interrogations. As soon as I sat down, I gave the professor sitting in the middle my undergraduate record book. He asked me to sign both that and another register. To my surprise, I noticed that all my anxiety had disappeared and I was ready to face my ordeal.

The three professors tested me orally for an hour. With my nervousness gone, I felt ready to continue the test indefinitely. Finally, the professor sitting in the middle gave me back my record book and they all shook my hand.

I felt like I'd passed the exam. Mario and Ugo, who had come to encourage me, felt that the test had gone not badly. We left the room and I opened my record book to see the mark I'd been given. To my surprise, and to the great delight of Mario and Ugo, I passed the exam with full marks!

I called my parents to give them the good news. They were as happy as me.

June 28, 1938

My mother called me on the phone this afternoon. She is always worried about me, and told me to eat good food and go to a restaurant from time to time. She asked me if I had seen Renato and Fabrizio, who are studying in Catania as well. She overheard that their marks were not as good as mine, and they had even failed a test.

June 29, 1939

It is a very hot day in Catania. Ugo, Mario, and I decided to go to the beach. I had never seen the sea until I came to study in Catania. The color of the sea is fantastic. It looks like an infinite space and it takes on the same hues as the sky. The water is deep, and many people enjoy swimming. Mario and Ugo don't know how to swim and remained under the beach umbrella, while I had no problems floating in the deep water because I had learned to swim at Lake Pergusa near Enna.

July 1, 1939

I go back to Enna once a month to see my family, but tomorrow is a special day for my hometown. We celebrate the feast in honor of Our Lady of Visitation, the patron saint of Enna. Last year I could not enjoy the festival because I was worried about my final examinations in school, but now I am free from school commitments. Moreover, I consider myself a winner because I passed my anatomy exam.

I headed for Theatre Square in Catania early in the morning to take the bus back to Enna. This time I want to stay home for a week, and spend my time cheerfully, even though there are not many things to do in Enna. I usually confine myself to strolling along Via Roma.

July 2, 1939

I was awakened at seven o' clock by the sound of the one-hundred-one gun salute that announces the feast. I got dressed, and at nine o' clock my mother, sisters, and I went to Mass celebrated at the cathedral. When the Mass was over, my mother and sisters went home to prepare lunch, while I remained in the street to have a look at the stalls on Via Roma and Belvedere.

While I was strolling I stumbled across Renato and Fabrizio. They are still inseparable friends. I pretended not to have seen them, but Fabrizio called me in a loud voice so I couldn't escape them.

"Hi Vincenzo!" Renato said, smiling from ear to ear.

"Hi Renato and Fabrizio," I said in return.

"I heard that you got good marks on your exams. Is it true?"

"Yes, it is true. I don't need your help anymore. I can manage my studying by myself," I answered with a sneering smile.

Renato tried to show happiness for my success, but a wince on his face showed that he was green with envy.

"Fabrizio and I intend to go to the brothel. Would you like to join us?"

"Are you crazy? If my father found out that I had sex with a whore he'd immediately shoot me with his revolver. He's a hothead! Do you want me to die?"

"Don't be a stupid, silly boy!" he replied. "How would your father know? We go to the brothel, have our intercourse with a beautiful girl, and then everything is over. Nobody, except Fabrizio and me, will know that you had sex with a prostitute."

"Somebody might see me while I am entering the whorehouse. Enna is full of nosey people who enjoy reporting what they've seen. One of them could tell my father that I knocked on the brothel's door."

"That's impossible!" said Fabrizio. "The front door of the whorehouse is kept ajar all the time. So we're not noticed, we will pretend to stroll in the street and then we will suddenly turn left and step into the brothel."

"I have to think about that," I answered. "Are you going there now?"

"Not right away," Renato said, "because in the morning the doors of the brothel are kept shut. This evening, after seven o' clock, is a good time to go."

"Tomorrow there is the fortnight shift!" Fabrizio said. "New whores will arrive in Enna from northern Italy. I overheard that one of them is very beautiful and also works with her mouth."

"Thank you very much, but I cannot come with you. It's very dangerous. We could get a disease. And if that happened, what would I do to cure myself? I cannot tell my father that I got a sexually transmitted disease at the brothel!"

"That is impossible!" replied Renato.

"Why is it impossible?"

"Because the whorehouse is a public establishment run by a brothel keeper who has a license from the government. The prostitutes are checked and tested nonstop by a doctor, who is a specialist in venereal diseases, so it's impossible to get one!"

"Let's meet tomorrow at Saint Francis Square at seven o' clock and then we'll go together. You will have an unforgettable experience," Fabrizio and Renato said with one voice.

"I am not sure whether or not I can come," I answered.

When I arrived home, my entire family was enjoying the merry atmosphere of the feast. My father had shot several wild rabbits and one hare. My mother had cooked exquisite food. On the table were plates full to the rim with steaming spaghetti seasoned with hare gravy. Moreover, there were *a lot of side dishes. As for my sisters, they had baked a big fruit cake, set the table, and filled the glasses with red wine.*

Very few times had I enjoyed the peace and the gaiety that pervaded my family today. We all sat around the table, and before eating my father proposed a toast to me. He is proud and happy to have a son who passed his anatomy exam with full marks.

In the evening, we all went to see the procession. My mother and my sisters followed it in bare feet. They had promised Our Lady that they would do so if she granted them the gift of me passing my exam.

July 3, 1939

At seven o' clock in the evening I was in my room holding one of the books that Ugo advised me to read. It is The Leopard *by Giuseppe di Lampedusa. I was reading to myself when my mother entered my room.*

"Renato and Fabrizio are waiting for you in the landing. They have asked me to call you. If you don't want to see them I can come up with an excuse. What do you want me to do?"

At my mother's words I snorted, closed the book, and got up from my bed. I was quite hesitant about what to do. I was not enthusiastic about them being there, but I am too well-mannered to send them away. So I got dressed and met them in the landing.

As soon as I saw them I stopped short. "I have no intention of going to the brothel. If that's why you've come, you are free to go while I remain at home reading my book," I said in a harsh tone.

"Vincenzo! Don't forget that we are your best friends. We just want to go for a walk together like the old days." Seeing their insistence, I gave in.

We were strolling along Via Roma and Belvedere when Fabrizio abruptly burst out, "If you don't come to the brothel, it means that you are a gay."

"I am not a gay! I told you why I cannot go. If my father finds out I went to the brothel he'll shoot me for sure."

They then slipped their hands under my arms and pushed me forward. "Come on, Vincenzo! We are your best friends. Trust us! You will enjoy it. You will have the most exciting experience of your life. It will be like being in paradise!"

I had promised myself that I would only consider girls based on their spiritual qualities from now on. Having sex without love is, for me, like drinking a bottle of cheap wine. However, I put up with Fabrizio's bullying and Renato's boldness for too long time, and I am still too weak to oppose them.

We kept walking along Belvedere for a while, but little by little Fabrizio and Renato walked me towards Piazza Balata and then to Via Vittorio Emanuele II. I followed them passively, because I am still dominated by their baleful influence over me. We walked across Popolo Quarter until we arrived at Via Aspromonte, which leads directly to the brothel.

The façade looked grim. All the shutters were closed to prevent anyone from the outside seeing in. Between the whorehouse and the edge of the cliff there is a pathway that overlooks the valley and the town of Calascibetta.

Before crossing the threshold I had a moment's indecision. I walked to the edge of the cliff and had a look at the valley, which was embroidered with the feeble lights of the scattered farmhouses. Calascibetta looked like a Nativity scene, while in the distance Mount Etna was erupting. It was a silent night and I could even hear the sound of the cowbells coming from the countryside. The landscape reminded me about the simplicity and spontaneity of nature. Making love with a prostitute sounded artificial and unnatural, the exact opposite of the wonderful scenery that spread out before my eyes.

I had a bad feeling about the whole thing. My legs were shaking and my hands were sweating. I thought of my father who, with his revolver in his hand, is ready to shoot at me. I was on the brink of giving up the idea of entering the brothel, but my natural curiosity and tendency to try new experiences prevailed.

Fabrizio passed the red curtain and a lady dressed in a short silk skirt and a stole made of ostrich feathers welcomed us. She took us to a big lounge where six or seven whores were lazing and chatting while waiting for their customers. As soon as we entered the hall, the girls smiled at us. I could see that they were vying for the customers' attention. Obviously, the more sexual encounters they had, the more they made.

The queen was sitting behind the desk. She asked me to show her my identity card to make sure that I was over eighteen. She already knew Renato and Fabrizio, who went directly to the sofa and sat close to the girls. They chatted and laughed with the girls as if they'd known one another for a long time. Two girls leapt on Renato's and Fabrizio's legs, who for their part groped their thighs, breasts, and buttocks.

"Where is that girl from northern Italy who is attractive and works with her mouth?" I whispered in Renato's ear.

"Ask the queen!" Renato answered with a vulgar laugh.

"The girl is not in the lounge," the queen answered. "She is entertaining another person, but she will be here in a little while. Her customer has paid for a simple service, so it will not take much time."

I turned to the staircase and saw a tall, slender, peroxide-blonde girl coming down. She looked beautiful at a distance, but as she came near the queen's desk, I spotted many imperfections that ruined her pale face.

The queen beckoned the whore to join me. What I especially dislike in a lady is a lack of refinement. A gracefulness of bearing and a delicacy of features are essential to me when I approach a girl. I cannot have sex with a girl whose features and manners are coarse.

I was on the verge of upsetting everything—the brothel, my two friends, the queen, the whore—and running away home, but I was much too polite to let the girl down, who in any case was just doing her job.

"Did you ask for me?" she said, holding my hand.

"Yes, I did."

"Let's go up to my room!"

I had a look around and didn't see Renato and Fabrizio. Apparently, they had gone to the rooms with the girls they had chosen. In the lounge, the other girls, the queen, and two customers looked at me, curious about my hesitation.

I saw that the customers chatted with the girls for a while before heading to a room, but I had nothing to say to the whore that was waiting for me. I was in the place just to have sex. Besides, I am not a good talker, and I sometimes have the sensation that my heart is as cold and hard as a piece of metal. I prefer not to talk when I have nothing to say, because everything I say then is as if it comes from a robot and not a human being. I kept watching the girls and their customers, and asked myself what they were talking about. And why didn't I have anything to say? My mouth seemed sealed. I had the sensation that my inner soul was already dead and unable to express itself.

After a while of looking at each other without saying a word, the whore that I had chosen broke the silence and said, "Let's go!"

"Yes, we can go," I answered.

I followed her up the stairs and then into her room. The environment smelled like loose face powder. The furnishings were a console table with an upright mirror, a small closet, a sink, and a double bed. In one of the corners of the room there was a wood stove with a pot full of hot water on it. She obviously used the water to wash her vagina after each encounter.

She stripped bare and lay down on the bed. Seeing that I was standing motionless by the bed, she got up and slowly undressed me. She finally took off my underpants and started working on my penis with her mouth. Not one word was exchanged between us. I was about to leave the room and pay my fee in vain, but when she sucked my penis I couldn't resist and I soon became very excited.

Then she lay down on her bed again. "Come to me, don't be shy. Is this the first time you've made love with a girl?"

"Yes, it is," I answered with a trembling voice. She had taken off all my clothes except my socks, so I took them off as well.

"What are you doing?" she said, laughing loudly. "Do you think you are going to bed to sleep?"

I climbed on top of her, but I couldn't find the entrance to her vagina. So she grabbed my penis and inserted it into her. The intercourse lasted a few minutes. When it was over, I felt disgusted. The sex without love left an acrid taste in my mouth, as if I had drunk bitter medicine.

After we finished, she washed my genitals and her vagina. We got dressed and went downstairs. Once in the lounge, she got a token from the queen, who was sitting at her desk. I took a seat on an armchair and waited for Renato and Fabrizio.

They came fifteen minutes later, beaming with joy.

"I climaxed twice!" Renato said.

"Me too!" Fabrizio replied.

We paid our fees and left the brothel. They both kept boasting of their sexual potency.

"Why don't we go to the tavern and drink some wine?" proposed Fabrizio.

The subtle thread that had kept my friendship with them alive was broken. I felt a heavy burden walking with them and passively following their whims.

"No thank you," I replied. "I'm going to walk along Belvedere for a little while and then go home."

When I returned home my parents were talking about me. I felt guilty of a great sin and I think my eyes revealed that I was trying to hide something.

"Are you okay?" my mother asked. "Your face is pale!"

"No, I am okay. I just took a walk with Renato and Fabrizio."

"You need to forget them! You are a good university student now and need new and different friends. Those two are not right for you!"

I cannot understand my mother. Years ago she spurred me to strike up a friendship with Renato and copy his work. Now she was suggesting I do the opposite. "You must strike up a friendship with new students at the university, Vincenzo!"

While my mother gave her advice, I wondered why I had to look for new friends. Friendship just happens. Bonds of friendship are not something to look for. In fact, friendship is a feeling, and you cannot look for something immaterial like feelings or emotions in the same way you look for an item to buy. Friendship and love are feelings that grow inside you when the conditions are the right. I have to confine myself to just living my life and new friends will naturally arrive. No need to look for them.

July 12, 1939

I'm back in Catania at my boarding school. I have to study hard, because I have to pass another exam at the end of the month.

Last night something unusual happened to me. I couldn't urinate easily. In fact, I got up and went to the bathroom three or four times trying to go. I did it with difficulty, but I couldn't empty my bladder.

July 13, 1939

This morning I woke up with a sore throat. Now, besides my trouble urinating I have to cope with my throat. What is happening to my body? Maybe I've caught flu and am experiencing its symptoms. I'm sure I'll get over it in a few days!

July 14, 1939

The difficulty urinating and my sore throat persist. I have also noticed that my underpants are soiled with a yellowish, greenish, evil-smelling liquid. My testicles are a little bit swollen and my eyes have taken on a reddish color.

July 15, 1939

I woke up with a pain in my testicles, my eyes were watering, and the light of the day irritated them. I am worried about my condition. I need to do something. There is a medical student at the school who is about to graduate. I'll ask him for advice.

July, 16, 1939

This morning I approached Vittorio, the sixth year medical student. He told me I looked a little bit strange in the face when he saw me. He said I was pale and my eyes seemed to be suffering from conjunctivitis.

"You are right, Vittorio," I said. "I am not well. Could you examine me, please?"

He brought me to his room and I lay down on his bed. He examined my throat and eyes, and then I took down my trousers and underpants. As soon as he smelled the stench and saw the yellowish hue of the blotches on my underpants, any doubt vanished from his mind.

"Did you have sex with a whore?" he asked.

"Yes, in the whorehouse in Enna two weeks ago."

"I hope it isn't too late!" he said with a worried expression. "We have to talk with a friend of mine who is graduated and works at the venereal disease unit in the hospital."

July, 17, 1939

Vittorio took me to an appointment with his friend at the hospital. He was very friendly and looked like a competent doctor. He examined me meticulously and then expressed his diagnosis.

"You are suffering from a sexually transmitted disease called gonorrhea. This disease is caused by a bacterium called Neisseria gonorrhoeae. To treat it we use a bactericide called silver nitrate. It has bactericide and disinfectant properties. It is injected through the orifice in the glans.

"There is a very powerful antibiotic called penicillin, but it is under testing and not available yet. Maybe it will be on the market next year. When you go to Enna, go to the hospital right away to have your disease treated. Don't lose time! Treat your disease as soon as possible, before it is too late."

I left the hospital confused. I didn't know what to do. I should go to the hospital in Enna, but that would mean that I have to tell my parents the truth. When my father finds out that I contracted the illness in the whorehouse he will kill me. Knowing my father, I have no doubt about that.

I cannot go to Enna and tell my father that I need to go to the hospital. I fear him too much. What to do?

July 20, 1939

I have heard that lemon has disinfectant properties. So I thought that if I injected a few drops of lemon into the orifice in my penis, the citric acid would kill the bacteria and I'd get over my gonorrhea, and maybe I wouldn't need to go to the hospital.

I cut a lemon in half and squeezed it into the mouth of my penis. When the drops got into my orifice, the pain was the worst I had ever felt. I couldn't endure such terrible pain, and I rolled all over the ground. I thought about banging my head against the wall.

July 30, 1939

My condition is getting worse. The lemon didn't work. I am very weak and feel the urgent need to talk with my parents and go to the hospital in Enna as soon as possible. It is the end of the month and time I normally go home to see my parents.

July 31, 1939

I took the bus at Theatre Square and three hours later I arrived in Enna. I got off, took my baggage from the roof, and I headed for my house.

As soon as my mother saw me when I walked in, she put her hands on her head. She didn't have the strength to speak. "What happened to you, my son!" she said in a whisper.

"Nothing bad, Mom, but I feel very weak. Maybe I need to go to the hospital."

"Your dad will be home this evening. We'll talk with him and decide together what to do."

I couldn't stand the light. My eyes were too sensitive. I went to lie down and asked my mom to wake me when my father got home. I was terribly embarrassed thinking about my father knowing the truth about my disease. What would he do? Would he shoot me with his revolver? Or would he punish me in a different way?

In the evening, my father came home and, seeing my bloodshot eyes, he had no doubt. "Vincenzo, don't worry. You will recover your health, but we have to go to the hospital immediately."

August 1, 1939

I went to the hospital and was put in a single room. After visiting me, the general practitioner called for a consultation with the specialist in sexually transmitted diseases. I was terrified that my father would know the truth now.

When the specialist came, he examined me thoroughly and then went out of the room with my father. Obviously, he was informing him about the kind of disease I was suffering from. My father is a very strict and harsh person, but he is endowed with a heart as great as the entire universe. I knew he would try everything possible to save my life.

When he came back into my room, he kissed me on the forehead and then whispered in my ear, "Vincenzo, we must go to Catania. The hospitals there are more advanced. We'll leave tomorrow in the early morning."

Apparently, the doctors in Enna had given up hope of saving my life.

August 2, 1939

My parents and I took a bus to Catania. We went to the venereal disease unit in the general hospital. The doctors there agreed with their colleagues in Enna. It was not possible to treat me because the bacterial infection was widespread now, and there was no broad-spectrum antibacterial medicine available. Penicillin is under testing.

August 3, 1939

The report that I am doomed to die is a great blow to my father. He wants to try more, so he decided to call a professor from Paris who is a specialist in treating bacterial infections.

August 7, 1939

Today, I received a visit from the luminary at the University of Paris. He entered my room followed by a train of other doctors. He didn't speak Italian.

He carefully examined my tests, talked with the other physicians, and then began a close examination of my whole body. At last, he whispered in French, "C'est la fin!" It's the end!

I studied French at school, so I could understand that the end of my life was drawing near. All my hopes to survive were dashed.

Suddenly, cold sweat ran down my forehead and I felt as if I was having heart failure. All my dreams were fading away. It is as if all the sand castles that I have been building have been razed by a huge wave.

When I enrolled in the University of Catania I dreamed about becoming a great physician, a scientist, and an outstanding person in society. I often dreamt of finding my soulmate, who in my imagination was chestnut-haired, curly-headed, with a never-ending smile on her lips. Now the fictitious figure of a woman was vanishing in my mind along with all those sand castles.

August 8, 1939

Renato and Fabrizio came to the hospital to see me. Entering the room, they glanced at my parents and sisters, and then came close to my bed. Hot tears welled in their eyes. At the end they are not bad friends. They love me in their way.

Fabrizio took hold of my hands, but he couldn't control his emotions, and his tears dripped copiously onto my arm. My sisters stood motionless, watching them.

Whose fault is the tragedy that has happened to me? The main culprits are not Renato and Fabrizio. The only person accountable for what has happened is me. I was not able to say no to them, and now it is too late and useless to regret what happened.

August 9, 1939

I don't have the strength to get up from my bed. I remain lying in my bed daydreaming and staring at the ceiling. It is said that the person who is about to die has the tendency to look at the ceiling continuously. Maybe it is true, as now I feel an urge to direct my eyes upwards.

I wished to be a traveler across the world, to meet new people, see new religions, and experience different ways of intending and living life. Now everything has collapsed!

While my body deteriorates hour by hour, I can understand that even though I had very carefully planned my life, I forgot about the imponderable force that no human being is able to control. This force may be named destiny, circumstances of life, fate, or God, who undoubtedly knows when our earthy marathon reaches the finish line.

What of all my dreams? In the past I have fantasized so much that sometimes I even asked myself whether mine was a real life in a state of wakefulness or if I was living in the dream world. My head has always been in the clouds. I used to spend great parts of the day thinking about my future and the achievements to come, but human dreams, plans, and the great things we have in mind are doomed to fail against a power bigger than us, like large waves that impact the cliff but are unable to crest over it.

Even though we carefully organize our lives and futures, there is no guarantee of success, because God has the last word.

August 10, 1939

Now that my fate is sealed, I recall a parable from the Gospel of Luke, which I heard many times during Sunday Mass.

Once upon a time, there was a rich farmer who had a very good crop one year. The wheat harvest was so abundant that his many barns couldn't contain it. "What to do with all this wheat?" he thought. Then he found the answer to his dilemma.

"I will demolish all my barns, and instead build a very big barn that will hold the entire crop. In this way I'll be safe and peaceful for the rest of my life and won't need to worry about my old age." This was the farmer's reasoning, but his plan failed against a force bigger than him. In spite of all his plans and riches, he died that same day.

Now that I am going to die, I can see the futility of my daily struggles to build a better future.

August 10, 1939

I remember when a friend of mine, who is a painter and a sculptor, invited me to visit his workshop one day. At the entrance I saw a wall covered with his paintings. He was not a representational painter, but a surrealist. I couldn't understand his pictures, which for me had no meaning. His sculptures showed the same incomprehensive style.

Then I saw one of the sculptures with a huge figure hovering over a globe that seemed to be the earth.

"The title of this sculpture is 'The Dominion,'" he said. "The ball represents the earth, and on its surface are many small figures who symbolize human beings.

"I have sculpted a bigger man suspended over the ball, holding a scepter in his hand that I have given the form of a war club. This man was able to subdue all other men on earth, but as you see, there's another, bigger figure that holds a bigger mace and hovers over everybody and everything. The man that has succeeded in subduing all cannot do anything against that figure who is more powerful than him."

"What does this human figure devoid of face who dominates all others represent?" I asked.

"You can call it God if you like. As for me, I prefer calling it destiny, which is the only force that dominates human beings."

August 11, 1939

It's four o' clock in the afternoon. My body is weaker and weaker, and now my feet feel cold, as if they were frozen.

While I am dying I have only one regret: not to have lived my life in my way. The main mistake I made was following advice and recommendations given by others, and that blunder led me to the end of my life. If I didn't listen to Renato and Fabrizio, who spurred me to go to the whorehouse that day, I wouldn't have contracted the horrible venereal disease and I would now be full of life instead of having one foot in the grave.

If there were another life after death, I would act a different way. I would use my brain not another's. But who knows, maybe there is no life after death, and my existence will end here in this goddamn hospital. In this difficult instance, only faith can sustain me—my faith in Jesus, who was the one who beat death. Thinking about my grave, I am seized by claustrophobia. I am not quite sure whether all vital functions cease to work at the same time when the heart stops beating. I am seized by terror at the thought that I might be still aware at the moment my coffin is let *down into the womb of the cold earth and the gravediggers shovel ground to cover my grave.*

I was tempted to ask my father to cremate me, but I quickly gave up that idea, because cremation isn't part of our culture and he wouldn't understand me.

My parents and two sisters were in the room. I wanted to ask them to take me home, but I didn't have the strength.

I dozed for a few minutes, and in that time I got the impression of seeing a clear light in front of me and some figures moving here and there. I could see a golden river and a man with a hat standing on a boat who took souls across the river. I rubbed my eyes to see better, and was about to ask the boatman to take me to the other side when the light, the figures, and the boat disappeared, and then I was back in my hospital room.

I could still spot the silhouettes of my family members, but they looked blurred. My legs are getting frozen. It seems that a vital force is deserting me. I don't have the strength to write anymore. I'm going to hand my diary to my sister Rosa Maria, because this time is really the end of my life.

Vincenzo's heart stopped beating at midnight the following day among the piercing shrieks of his mother and sisters. His father, even though was racked with grief, stayed outwardly composed.

Now I understand why my mother and Aunt Carolina kept the real cause of Vincenzo's death hidden. For them, a disease caused by sex brought dishonor to the family. At that time, sex was a religious and social taboo. That was why my aunt and mother couldn't talk with me, still a little boy, of brothels, sex, and the sexually transmitted disease that led to the death of their brother Vincenzo.

The dead body was taken to Enna and buried in the family vault. My grandfather enlarged a picture that portrayed Vincenzo. It is two meters high and one meter and a half in width. It is framed with fine wood, and stands in front of the family mortuary chapel. This was the last gift for his beloved son Vincenzo.

When I finished reading the diary, a teardrop ran down my cheek and fell on the diary, leaving a stain on the words "end of my life."

I kept the diary with me for five or six years. I didn't want to part with it, but I finally thought that I had better put it back in the drawer of the closet, along with my mother's poems, at Vincenzo's home.

In the meantime, the situation in my grandparents' house had changed. My grandmother had died of a heart attack and my Aunt Carolina and her family had migrated to Milan, a city in northern Italy, to find a job for herself and her husband. That haunted house remained empty. The blinds were all shut and gloom hovered over the rooms. The keys had been handed down to my mother by my aunt, and were kept along with all the other keys in a drawer in the dining room.

One day I took the keys and went to the house to leave Vincenzo's diary in the place where it should stay. I opened first the entrance gate, then climbed the stone stairs in the courtyard and went upstairs. The wooden front door had swollen due to the humid climate and disuse. I had to push it hard to enter the landing.

Once inside, I could feel a musty smell. That house smelled of death. I had the sensation of having presences at my side. I couldn't wait to leave. I headed for the double bedroom, lifted the blind, opened the drawer, and set the diary in the midst of my mother's poems.

Suddenly, I heard footfalls coming from the upper floor. Maybe it was another hallucination, as had happened to me when I was just a boy. However, I thought well to leave the house right away. I shut the blinds and ran away, slamming the main door with all my strength to shut it.

It was the fifth time that I had come in touch with death. My grandfather, Biagio, Pietrino, Vincenzo, and my grandmother had all passed away. What had happened to them? Had they disappeared into thin air forever, or were they still alive in another dimension? What will become of me once I am dead?

The terror of my annihilation grips me day and night. What if there is no life after death? What to do? At the mere thought that I will simply be sleeping forever, I fall into desperation. Is it just delusion to believe in life after death? Does the immaterial world exist? I mused upon my fear of death, and finally decided that I had to do something to better understand the topic. In my opinion, human beings put aside the issue of death and life after death, even though it may be the most important subject to learn more about.

Time flies very fast, and sooner or later we will die. We have to leave our possessions to our heirs. We have to part from the people we love, and we have to quit our identity, our name, and our role in society.

I had no other means to do this kind of research except by using my mind and reasoning, and collecting information from learned people and books. I wanted to know whether or not there is some kind of immaterial entity or energy inside our body. Where does the inner energy go when it leaves the body?

Chapter Twelve
Saint Francis Of Assisi

The official biography of Saint Francis was written by Saint Bonaventura, who was appointed this task by the Franciscan general chapter in 1260, thirty-four years after Saint Francis's death.

Saint Francis was born in the city of Assisi on September 26, 1182 and died on October 3, 1226. His father was a prosperous merchant and his mother a noblewoman. He was given the name John by his mother, but when his father returned from France, he changed the name to Francis, in honor of France, the country where he had made his wealth. Coming from a well-to-do family, Francis had the opportunity to study Latin, poetry, music, Italian, French, the Provencal dialect, and literature. It seemed that Francis was destined to follow in his father's footsteps.

Around the age of twenty, Francis joined up with the Assisi army and fought against the city of Perugia, but he was taken prisoner and remained in prison for one year. The time he spent in jail was very hard, so much so that he contracted a serious illness when he returned home. His sickness was the turning point in his life. He decided to radically change his lifestyle. To that point he had lived a worldly life, but now he chose to dedicate himself to following Jesus's model. He began to give money to help the lepers, the poor, and the needy.

Francis's new life and prodigality were not appreciated by his father, who eventually disinherited him. From then on, Francis lived a life of poverty and absolute simplicity. Soon other young people joined him, giving rise to the monastic

Franciscan order. His soul was so pure that he talked with birds, and one day he even tamed a wolf. An example of the pureness of his heart can be found in the "Canticle of the Creatures," which he composed in 1225.

Saint Francis's life was short; in fact, he lived only forty-four years. After his death, many authors started writing his biography. Some biographies had a hagiographic aim, while others were straightforward accounts, but some data is common to all of them:

Saint Francis was a great traveler. Around the age of thirty he left his hometown to go to Syria. Unfortunately, his journey was interrupted in Dalmatia for an unknown reason, but probably because he couldn't find a ship to Syria, so he was forced to return to Italy.

In spite of the failure of his first attempted trip to a Muslim country, he set off on another journey to Islamic lands, this time Morocco. To go to Morocco, he crossed France and Spain. Again he failed to succeed in his plan, because he contracted a serious disease in Spain and once more had to return to Assisi.

His third endeavor to get to an Arab country finally succeeded. He boarded a ship at Ancona in the year 1219, seven years before his death, at the same time the fifth crusade was under way. Once in Egypt, Saint Francis wanted to meet Sultan Malic al-Kamil. Their meeting really happened, and as far as we know, he was treated kindly by the sultan as a guest, and not as an enemy. He received safe conduct and was invited to return to visit Egypt anytime.

From Egypt he travelled to the Holy Land. About two years before his death, he received the stigmata on Mount Verna.

Later, his health worsened and he died in a small church near Assisi called Porziuncola. At his death, his body was taken to Assisi and a basilica was later built in the place where he was buried.

I had the opportunity of going to Assisi three times in my life. The first time was with my parents on a travel to north

Italy. It happened many years ago. Even though I was very young and not in a condition to appreciate Saint Francis's message to humanity, a few things remained etched in my mind. One was the sight of the cilice, which Saint Francis wore to mortify his body.

The cilice was a special garment made of goat hair, which caused considerable suffering to the person who wore it. The flesh was considered a kind of contamination of the soul; therefore, through the mortification of the body, the soul would be purified.

Hearing the story of Saint Francis from my parents, I was struck by the strength of character of this great man who rebelled against his father in order to follow the aspirations of his heart.

The second time I visited Assisi was while I was traveling on a trip organized by the parish priest from the Church of San Cataldo. We visited the basilica, which is divided into three parts: the upstairs basilica, the walls of which are covered with gorgeous frescoes by Giotto; the downstairs basilica, which contains other works of art; and finally the crypt where Saint Francis's mortal remains are kept.

The tomb is placed in a raised position over the altar, and is made without frills of grey square and rectangular stones. As soon as I knelt to say some prayers and make a wish, I had the sensation that a kind of energy was radiating from his tomb, and then I asked Saint Francis to hear my prayer.

"Please, Saint Francis, grant me a gift! You are a very powerful saint and can easily make my wish come true. I love Elisabetta more than life, and I want her to become my wife. There are many hindrances that prevent us from getting married. Please, Saint Francis, remove all the hindrances and help us get married as soon as possible."

At that time I had fallen in love with a young lady named Elisabetta. She was from Enna as well, and taught Latin and Greek at the high school. I courted her for two years and wanted to get engaged to her. We used to stroll along Via Roma and Belvedere and talk religion. In fact, she was an earnest Catholic, to such an extent that she was once on the verge of quitting her job to become a Carmelite cloistered nun.

One day while we were walking around the Lombardia Castle, she told me of her pilgrimage to Assisi. "I have been struck by Saint Francis's burial place. I felt a special energy coming from his tomb," she said.

Now, I don't know whether or not it was due to autosuggestion because Elisabetta had told me her feelings, but the same strange sensation was now happening to me. While I repeatedly asked San Francis to grant my wish, I felt as if powerful energy was radiating from his tomb and talking to me.

"I have spent all my life searching for God," Saint Francis's energy seemed to say, "and now you arrive at my tomb and ask me to grant you a trivial wish, Vincenzino!"

I wondered why Saint Francis would consider my wish to get married to my beloved trivial. As time passed, I realized that I had actually requested something really trivial. In fact, human affairs like love, business, careers, and so on are trifles in comparison to the search and love for God, who is the giver of life.

Meanwhile, Elisabetta got married to another man, and I understood that what I had considered a great love was nothing more than an infatuation doomed to dissolve like the fog dispersed by the wind.

True love is not related to a woman or a person. Love is something that you must have inside you. Love comes from your heart and mind, and it stands apart from the appearance and character of the people who you come across and the happenings of life.

Later, I married a lady from Greece, and we now live together in Enna. In the evenings after dinner, my wife and I usually stroll along Via Roma and Saint Francis Square, which is surrounded by old palaces on three sides and by the stately Church of Saint Francis on the fourth.

A small green area had recently been attached to the church, with an olive tree and a statue of Saint Francis surrounded by white doves inside it. While my wife and I were going back home and passed by that green, we noticed a fragrance emanating from the area. We turned in all directions but couldn't spot a flower or a tree from where that subtle scent might be emanating. The following days we passed by the same place again, but we couldn't smell anything.

A subtle thread was leading me to Assisi for the third time. My Greek wife and I decided to take a car trip across northern and central Italy. We embarked on a ferry in Palermo and landed in Genoa. From there we travelled to Pisa, Florence, and San Gimignano.

While we were admiring the numerous towers of the last town, my wife suddenly cried out, "What about going to Assisi? Is it far from here? Do you remember the fragrance we smelt in Enna near the Church of Saint Francis?"

"No, it is not far away. We can go to Perugia first, and Assisi is a stone's throw from there," I replied.

We arrived at Saint Francis's hometown around midday and found lodging in a monastery run by Filipino nuns. We strolled for a while around the medieval city and then arrived at the basilica. My wife was surprised at the sight of the frescoes both upstairs and downstairs.

"Even though I am not a Christian," she said, "and don't follow any religion, I cannot help being astonished by the religious ardor that was behind these great masterpieces."

Then we went to the crypt and sat on a pew facing Saint Francis's tomb. As soon as I sat down, I had the sensation that the same energy that had talked to me many years ago was now speaking again, suggesting the path I should follow to find out who really I was.

Purify your heart, mind, body, and actions, and then you'll see God inside you!

What was Saint Francis telling me this time? I inferred that he meant that the real kingdom of God is inside every living being, but we cannot find it if our mind is contaminated by too many materialistic desires or our actions are not directed towards the wellbeing of our fellow creatures. I also inferred that prayer and meditation are a good way to purify the mind and get close to God, as long as my actions aim not towards an egoistic goal, but to the love of all creatures.

While I was meditating on what Saint Francis was suggesting to me at that moment, my wife suddenly turned to me. "I have a pain in my heart, and my heart is pounding! I shed tears and I don't know why. I don't feel sad and I don't know why I am crying!"

My wife is not Catholic, and actually doesn't practice any religion. So we couldn't understand why such a phenomenon befell her. Maybe the same energy that had talked to me was revealing itself to her in some way.

I left Assisi with a strong devotion to Saint Francis. Every time I had trouble in my life after that, I thought of him and reminded myself that my worldly misfortunes are a mere trifle. What really matters in life is the search and love for God and all His creatures.

Reviewing my encounter with Saint Francis, I reconsidered what my law teacher had taught me a long time ago. She had stressed the importance of the difference between a piece of evidence and a clue. A piece of evidence is a fact that you have seen or heard, or a way that an event can be proved with absolute certainty—evidence that can direct the judge to return his verdict. A clue doesn't have the strength of evidence, and a mere clue is usually not enough to bring in a judge's verdict, but if the clues are numerous, unambiguous, precise, and concordant with one another, they can be taken into consideration by the judge in order to pass judgment.

In the case of my encounter with Saint Francis, there are five clues that can be admitted as evidence of the existence of another spiritual level that is beyond our ordinary worldly life:

1. The energy that Elisabetta felt while she was praying before the tomb of Saint Francis;

2. The fragrance that my wife and I smelt near his statue while we were strolling in Enna;

3. The energy coming from his tomb that talked to me about the true goals of my life, which were not a mere love of a woman, money, or some other worldly pleasure. Searching for God is the real goal;

4. The energy that I felt when I went to Assisi for the third time. I realized that the kingdom of God is really inside me. I just need purify my mind, my heart, and my actions, and then I can be on the path that leads to the spiritual world;

5. The unusual sensation of pain in my wife's chest and the tears in her eyes while she was sitting with me in front of Saint Francis's tomb.

These days, Saint Francis is the master in my daily life. Whenever I am too worried because my business didn't go well, I remind myself of the teachings he gave me in the crypt in Assisi. The ups and downs of life are mere trifles when compared to meeting God, who stays in the heart of every human.

By minding Saint Francis's teachings, I live my life in a more relaxed way. I am less anxious. I just juggle the events of life as soccer players do when playing a friendly match.

Chapter Thirteen
The Path of Sufferers

By researching Saint Francis's life, I discovered that one of the first things he did when he left his family home to start a new life was to help the lepers, the poor, and the needy. Musing about that, I found that the way to God for most saints is marked by the help they gave to marginalized people.

A friend of mine, who is an atheist writer, once wrote a pamphlet in which he came to the conclusion that if poverty was eradicated from the earth, the Catholic Church would have nothing to do, because all its teachings are focused on alleviating others' suffering. According to my friend, if there was no suffering in the world, the Catholic Church—and all religions, for that matter—wouldn't have meaning. He stressed that the Catholic Church needs the poor, or the priests and monks would be out of work.

In that pamphlet, he maintained that the creation of a new religion-free humanism, where people with no social class could live in togetherness, was still possible. He often emphasized the old saying, "Religion is the opium of people." He said that even the Vedas, which are the holy books of an ancient religion, were written by people under the effect of drugs.

One day I said to him, putting my arm on his shoulder, "My dear friend, what you talk about is impossible. You cannot realize paradise on earth by eradicating suffering. Every person who has depicted an ideal society, like Plato, Saint Augustine, Tommaso Campanella, and many other philosophers, has just made a utopian work. Karl Marx, Lenin, and Stalin, whom you quote continuously, also couldn't realize their utopian ideal society ruled only by the working class."

He and I are no longer friends. There was too much difference and misunderstanding between us.

As for me, even though I am not an atheist, I want to use my brain as much as possible rather than believing blindly in religions. Therefore, like my friend, I doubted that the saints who had given up their worldly lives to help the marginalized classes were themselves marginalized, maladjusted people who were unable to fit into their social classes. They escaped from normal lives to find shelter in environments more congenial to them.

Anyway, I had chosen Saint Francis as my spiritual guide by now. Based on the extraordinary, miraculous events that had happened to me whenever I had been near his tomb in Assisi, or when I passed by his statue in Enna, I considered him a great master. By following his teachings, I wanted the experience of helping sick people as he had done to see what would happen to me on my way to God.

I gathered some information and then decided to go to Scotland to a center where people with major physical health problems were assisted by specialized staff and volunteers. It was Christmas time, and my wife and I decided to spend our winter holidays individually for the first time after many years of being together. She flew to Athens to stay with her old mother for two weeks, while I went to Scotland to spend my winter holidays at a center for disabled people.

The manager gave me instructions about the use of wheelchairs, both manual and electric, and the functioning of the hoist. Ninety percent of the disabled people living there were completely paralyzed and needed to be lifted by a hoist to be put to bed from the wheelchair and vice versa. To have their shower, they had to be hoisted and moved to the bathroom through a linking track in the ceiling.

At lunch I was asked to feed a young man named Chris. He was completely paralyzed and was not even able to stay upright in his wheelchair. From time to time I pushed him and inserted a cushion over the handrail of his wheelchair so he could assume an almost upright position, but his muscular strength was completely lacking, and his neck was unable to carry the weight of his head, which was constantly bent over his chest.

Despite my efforts, he couldn't keep his trunk and head upright. It didn't appear he was able to raise his head, but whenever a nice girl passed by, he summoned all the strength he had in the innermost recesses of his paralyzed body and found the strength to raise his head a little bit and look at her furtively. That figure of the opposite sex had the power to light up his face and give vital strength to a body that otherwise didn't have the power to react to external stimuli.

It was impossible for him to have sex because his body was a mass of flesh without any muscular strength, but his sexual urge had not faded. Nevertheless, he was deluding himself at the thought that the girl would return his love.

From then on I stopped feeding Chris and asked a volunteer girl to do that in my place. I was aware that, for at least a few moments of his troubled life, Chris would be happy. By observing Chris several times, I came to the conclusion that sex is the most powerful ruler of living creatures. It seems that even geldings give a start when a mare in heat comes close.

If my utopist ex-friend had been with me in Scotland at the center for disabled people, I would have said to him, "Your theory about the possibility of creating a heavenly, religion-free world is unattainable!"

"Why?" he would have asked with a commanding tone.

"Because as long as sex appeal rules living beings' behavior, there will be suffering on Earth."

He would have rebutted, "Sex is a positive emotion. The fact that sex is considered a sin is an invention of the Catholic priests, all of whom I would send to the stake."

"Be careful before sending Catholic priests to the scaffold," I would answer. "All religions have some kind of reservation about sex. In fact, many require purification before the person who has copulated enters holy places.

"Sex," I would continue, "always triggers suffering in human creatures. Look at animals! They fight fiercely against one another in order to copulate. There will be a loser that will suffer, and a winner that will enjoy its victory. But its triumph will not last long, because sooner or later it will be defeated by a stronger animal, and its life will turn into suffering.

"Look at how lions kill one another to prevail over their opponents. Look at a pack of dogs or wolves and see how they fight and are heavy injured and sometimes die for the sake of mating. I can quote thousands of cases where sex gives rise to suffering. Freud is probably right when he says that most of human behavior is conditioned by sexual energy."

I figured that if my uncle Vincenzo had not had sex at that goddamn whorehouse he would still be alive.

"What you are saying is valid for the animal kingdom," my friend would refute, "but human beings are different, because for them sex is sublimated by love."

I would answer that love has nothing to do with sex. True love is totally independent from sex. Human love is tainted by sex drive, therefore it is not true love. Family is not a natural institution but a by-product of sex. For that reason, most families turn into prisons after a while, and what was supposed to be a great real love between the husband and wife sooner or later changes into hate. In paradise, supposing it exists, there are neither families nor couples, and nobody gets married. Jesus himself teaches us this concept.

Related to suffering is the concept of power. Everyone wants to be more powerful and rich. This is part of human nature, and no religion or worldly institution can suffocate the want of the individual to excel over his station. This creates suffering, because for every winner there will be a loser who will suffer.

The conclusion is that suffering belongs to human nature, and even though one day physical suffering, diseases, and death will be eliminated, suffering of the soul will never end. There are no remedies to cure the soul, and the so-called psychotropic drugs only help the symptoms of the disease. They cannot cure the malaise of the soul.

Anyway, the first lesson I learned while I was working with those severely ill people was that instinct is born with living beings and no force can suppress it. Instinct can be kept under control, not suppressed.

Now I want to break a lance in defense of love.

There was a man at the center around seventy-five years old. One day he asked me to push his wheelchair to take him to the supermarket to buy some oranges and tissues. It was a pleasure for me to do that. His name was James and he was a man of robust build. His hair was crew cut and showed no signs of grayness, despite his old age. He still had the look of the worker, and for sure, he had been a strenuous, strong worker in his younger years.

When we arrived at the supermarket, he asked me to pick up a ten pack of tissues and a basket of oranges. At the counter he gave me his wallet to pay for his items. I paid for him and put the wallet back into his pocket.

After we got back to the center, we sat down in the lounge area for a while. I saw that he was trying hard to take his wallet out of the pocket of his trousers.

"What are you doing, James?" I asked.

"I want to show you my wife's picture, but I cannot take out my wallet. It is stuck to my trousers."

"Don't worry, James. You can show me your wife's picture another time."

James had only one leg; the other had been amputated due to complications deriving from his diabetes. His diabetes was so acute that he had to get insulin many times during the day.

He told me that when he was in good health, he had worked in shipbuilding. Two years ago his wife had passed away from cancer. Thinking of his wife, James's eyes stared into the void, and then he strove again to get her picture.

"Don't worry about the picture," I said again. "Instead, tell me how long you were married."

"Fifty years!" he answered with a lump in his throat.

"Did you love her?"

"Of course I loved my wife. More than my life."

"Now who looks after you?"

"My daughter. We are a very close family." My conversation with James made me think twice about the non-existence of love on Earth.

Another day, I was asked by the manager of the center to take a disabled person to the shopping center. "What is your name?" he asked.

"My name is Vincenzino. And what about yours?"

"My name is Gabriele. It is an Italian name because my mother was Italian and my father was English. I can speak both English and Italian. My parents met during the Second World War. My father served in the British Army in the south of Italy in a region called Calabria. During the breaks between heavy fighting he met my mother. Their love rose like the sun in the haze of the battles. When the war was over, my father returned to his country, but he couldn't stand being apart from his loved one for long. So he went to Italy often to see her. Finally, after a year or so, they got married."

"Was it a loving marriage?" I asked.

"Yes, my parents loved each other for more than fifty years. I remember every year when we went to Italy to spend our holidays with my grandparents, my father wanted to give some money to my relatives. They would have been offended if my father had done so, so we always arrived in Italy with a mountain of presents for them. I always had a good time there, surrounded by the warmth of my grandparents, my cousins, and my uncles. I still have an uncle in Calabria.

"When I was born, the delivery was very difficult and my mother almost died. She had lost too much blood. The doctors fought strenuously to save my mother and my life faded into the background. As the year passed, my parents noticed that I couldn't stand up. In fact, my brain was not able to give the muscles of my arms and legs the proper commands. I could neither walk nor use my arms. Neither my parents nor the doctors in Glasgow could understand which disease I was suffering from. They thought it might be a psychological issue.

"At the age of two, my parents took me to a specialist in London, who analyzed the situation and made the diagnosis of brain damage caused by the difficult labor. The specialist prescribed therapy and told my parents to purchase a pair of crutches for me. Thanks to the therapy I made progress, and for a while I was able to walk on crutches. However, I was very shaky on my legs and fell down continuously. It was a battle lost from the beginning.

"Sometimes a mother's love is more effective than medicine though. She encouraged me and spurred me to keep going. Day by day, with constant training, I was able to hold my crutches firmly, and pivoting on them I was able to stand up and finally walk. So, I attained my independence."

"Did you go to school, Gabriele?" I asked.

"Yes, I went to a special school where every student had a different kind of handicap. Some were blind, some deaf, some morons. Can you imagine what happened there? Nobody could be taught well. I was not able to read, even after five years of attending that school. My mother was very worried. She was convinced that I would never learn to read.

"After a few years, my parents enrolled me in a boarding school. I stayed there for five years and finally learned to read. As for writing, at first it was more difficult than reading, because my brain couldn't properly control the movements of my hand, but I finally succeeded.

"Now my parents are both dead. I have one brother. When I am home, I have a caretaker who looks after me."

"Have you ever driven a car, Gabriele?" I asked.

"Yes, but my life can be compared to the ascent of a high mountain and the following descent. I had good mobility for around forty years, but then it started diminishing little by little, and now I am completely paralyzed and in need of a person that can feed me."

"Have you ever worked, Gabriele? What I mean to say is, have you ever had a job?"

"Yes, I am still working! I have worked at a special factory my whole life where disabled people like me are taken on."

"What kind of work do they do?"

"In our factory we mostly print, but there are also people who make things by assembling pieces."

"What is your job there?"

"I am a switchboard operator. As you see, my English is very clear. I am also quite talkative. The telephone in the factory rings continuously, and I answer the phone and give the information that the customers or the suppliers need, or I just put them through to the manager."

The stories told by James and Gabriele about the love that reigned in their families proved to me that love is the driving force of life on Earth. Nevertheless, we humans have a duty to see beyond appearances. By digging deeply into human feelings, we'll discover that what we call love is indeed an instinct that is present in the entire animal kingdom.

When I lived with Sebastiano on the estate in Pollicarini, the farmhand took care of the she-asses that he co-owned with my family. We didn't have to worry about the condition of the animals, and the farmer looked after them as if they were his family members. He curried them often. You could see their good health from the brilliance of their coats. Whenever he took one of the she-asses out from the stable, they both brayed, pawed the ground, and got restless. They couldn't endure being parted. Later on, after they were reunited, they showed their happiness by smelling each other.

Was that love? Why shouldn't it be considered love? Love for friends or partners belongs to the nature of all creatures. It can be considered a gift of nature. There is no difference between animals and human beings when it comes to love.

In some species love is stronger than humans. There are many animals that are monogamous. The pre-eminent monogamous species is the emperor penguin, but there are many other birds and a few mammals with strong dispositions to love. The mandarin ducks, also called loving birds, have only one union in their life. When one of the mates dies, the other won't accept another partner and remains alone for the rest of its life.

The logical corollary of what I expounded on above is that the love we have for our children, our friends, and our relatives doesn't add any merit to our being, because the feelings we express don't depend upon our free will and heart. We just instinctively express a kind of love that is not dissimilar to that of animals.

Real love is different—it is unconditional and universal. It goes beyond a couple's love. It has nothing to do with the group, family, or clan one belongs to. Human love is usually on mutual terms: "I'll love you if you love me." Even parental love, which is the strongest, is subject to reciprocity. If a child is disrespectful or aggressive against their parents, they stop loving their child to the point that they can throw their child out of their home. The same happens in the animal kingdom, where the mother loves her cubs until they start competing with her. In that case, separation is inevitable.

What I learned in the center for disabled people is that for love to be authentic it must be unconditional. When you love, you have to give without expecting anything in return. Only a limited number of people have shown themselves to be examples of real unconditional and universal love over the centuries. One of those few noble figures is Saint Francis of Assisi.

Only now can I understand the three cornerstones of the Franciscan rule, which are poverty, chastity, and obedience. In fact, to fully love your neighbor, you must get rid of your sexual urges, covetousness, and desire to take the lead. Only when you free yourself from these three hindrances can you start loving. The Franciscan habit has not changed today, and it differs from that of other monastic orders. As it was at the time of Saint Francis, the frock is girdled with a cord with three knots to symbolize the three main vows of a Franciscan friar.

My ex-friend would object, "Don't censure sex, because life is born by sex. If everybody followed your recommendation to practice abstinence, humanity would become extinct. Saint Francis's rule is just as absurd and utopian as the new humanism that I dream of. In fact, not only is chastity nonsense, but obedience is also impossible. Think for a minute about what it would be like if everybody practiced obedience. There would be no leaders to obey!"

"The giver of life is God and not sex!" I would answer. "Life was born before sex. God's love and the vibrations of his voice created the universe, human beings included. As for obedience, I say to you that leaders also obey, just not their subordinates. It all depends on what your idea of leadership is. Kings and subjects are not different in the way they obey. If you consider leadership not as an arbitrary act but a service to others, you will see that leaders also cannot shirk their duty of obedience."

One evening I was sitting in the lounge along with the disabled people to watch a singer who was putting on a show. I suddenly had the sensation that that singer didn't recognize me as a normal person. Since I was in mixed with all the ill people, she thought that I was one of them. I was about to get up and walk to show her that I was normal, but then I realized that I was really stupid to think that way.

I am not different from the disabled people. If I observe them closely, I realize that they have a soul not different from mine, and they are even more sensitive and more clever than me. Thinking like that, I learned my second lesson at this center: souls are all same, and in paradise there will be no difference as to physical form or cerebral abilities.

I have to say that sometimes I had a feeling of repulsion when I saw the condition of some of the guests. Most of them had a hosepipe inserted in their stomach, and their urine flowed away into a bag that we quite often had to empty. Some guests had a hole in their stomach and their excrement passed through the hole and flowed into a plastic bag. Every morning, with the help of a staff member who removed the bag full of excrement, I had to clean the area around the hole to eliminate any traces of feces.

One day I had to look after a young man who was spastic. Sitting in his wheelchair, he was able to move all around the center by pushing the ground with the tip of the only foot that he was able to use.

In the evenings, we all gathered in the lounge where a musician or a singer came to cheer up the night. I noticed that all the guests had some kind of reaction to the music. The vibrations contained in human voice and instruments didn't leave them indifferent, even though their bodies seemed insensitive to external stimuli.

The lessons I learned from disabled people that I attended to for two weeks were extraordinary. They were weak but showed attachment to life. They didn't wish to die, nor did they give in to despair. They seemed to live normal lives and showed smiling faces, while many volunteers, including I, sometimes were in the grip of anxiety.

They taught me the meaning of unconditional, universal love.

Chapter Fourteen
My Meditation

Saint Francis's words resounded in my mind quite often. "Purify your heart, mind, body, and actions, and then you'll see God inside you!"

I thought that meditation would be a good way to purify my heart, mind, and body. I started to research the topic to uncover the path. Most people today focus their attention outward instead of inward. Their main interests are to become rich, famous, have a beautiful partner, and so on. I'm not saying that all these desires are sins. It is normal and plays a prominent role in human society, but if you don't want to act like a machine and strive to become a spiritual being, it is necessary to focus your attention inward as well.

Meditation means to look inside yourself and see who really you are. Many meditators say that when you find your real nature, all your worries and longings disappear like snow under the sun. Your mind becomes empty and you are an organic whole with the universe. Contrary to what many people think, meditation is not escaping from the world. On the contrary, by mediating we can live a better ordinary life and succeed socially.

Meditation, alertness, and consciousness are nearly synonymous. True meditative people meditate not only within the walls of their home, but also while they are working, playing, eating, dancing, or doing just about anything. In this case, meditation consists of watching oneself performing any action. By watching ourselves while we are living our lives, our actions cease to be automatic or unconscious. We behave as fully conscious people, always aware of what we are doing.

We humans tend to live according to the patterns and paradigms we learned during childhood. Our family and society funnel us towards fixed tracks, which we then follow automatically without ever asking ourselves whether those tracks lead us in the right direction. However, if we want to know more about ourselves, we need to drop conditioning given to us as children. When we meditate we set spirituality before worldly ambitions. In doing so, we go beyond the behavioral models that we were schooled in. We follow a new, authentic way—the way to God.

In India and many other parts of the world, meditation is a good way to find "enlightenment." Once a person is enlightened, they see things as they really are and not as they appear to our deluded minds.

I read many books about meditation and visited a few places and monasteries where I could study meditation techniques, but now I needed to practice it by myself instead of studying it theoretically. One of the techniques I learned is called Vipassana. It is one of the most ancient methods of meditation, and it consists of watching your breathing and watching yourself.

At first I was doubtful about it. How is it possible that just watching one's breathing can get a person to enlightenment? By deepening my studies, I learned that our minds are like monkeys, always jumping from one thought to another. By meditating, we get free from a host of useless thoughts and focus our attention on the search of our real nature.

Ramana Maharshi, one of the greatest Indian masters, says that when you meditate you have to focus your attention on the question "Who am I?" He claims that if you meditate on that single thought, all other thoughts will be chased away from your mind and in the end it will be empty.

One day I sat down on a chair, closed my eyes, and focused my attention on breathing in and out. I was only able to do it for a few minutes, because I couldn't prevent thoughts from entering my mind. Then I tried to meditate, asking myself "Who am I?", but by doing so I mixed breathing meditation with Ramana Maharshi's method and worsened the situation as I jumped from one technique to the other.

A doubt entered my mind. Maybe I feared to meditate and look inside myself. Every time I was about to get my mind free from thoughts I saw my identity disappear and saw that I am nothing but energy. I've got a name, a family, friends, and good social standing. What would have happened to me if I had discovered that my name, wealth, and prestige were just veils that masked my real being?

There was another hindrance to my meditation. I was concerned about discovering who I really was. Maybe I was not the good and considerate person that I appeared to be. Perhaps I was basically a dirty soul that had been modelled into a good man by my family and society.

Despite that, I decided to continue my endeavors. Whenever a thought arose, instead of blaming myself for not being able to avoid thinking, I just observed my thoughts as an external watcher. Then, after the disturbing thought disappeared, I came back to watching my breathing. Little by little, I was more able to watch myself and my breathing without being distracted by thoughts, and my mind became quieter. It was a good start, but so far I had discovered nothing about the hereafter, which was the main subject of my quest.

While I meditated, I looked inside myself to try to see who really I was. I actually didn't think that my body moved and acted automatically. There had to be an energy that was independent from the body. The problem was to understand whether that energy dies with the death of the body or if it survives.

To deepen my study, I decided to go to India to a renowned city called Rishikesh, said to be the best place in the world for meditation. I asked my wife to join me in my spiritual quest. She accepted and we decided to go to India after the winter holidays.

Chapter Fifteen

Goa

Rishikesh is located in northern India, 500 meters above sea level. It is not far from the Himalayas, and it is quite cold in the winter. My wife hates the cold and had no intention of going to that cold city in the winter months. She insisted that we could find other warmer places where I could satisfy my desire to meditate.

"You can even meditate in our room or in the street," she said. "You don't need to go to a secluded place to have good meditation."

One of the reasons why I preferred to be alone when I travelled to deepen my spiritual search was that tastes and dispositions vary from person to person, and that difference wound up limiting my freedom of movement. When I was younger and I happened to travel with a friend of mine, his views quite often clashed with mine. I liked to visit certain kinds of places, while my friend had different tastes. What to do? You can choose to be alone in your life and have complete freedom of choice, or you can interact with others and have your freedom limited. As for me, I prefer interacting with others even if it means losing part of my freedom.

I reached a compromise with my wife. We would spend the month of January in Goa, a state by the Indian Ocean where the weather is mild and it's possible to swim in the ocean, and then we would move to Rishikesh in February when the weather was supposed to be a little warmer.

We decided to meet in Mumbai after our winter holidays spent respectively in Scotland and Athens. The plan was that I would arrive at the airport first and then wait about three hours for her flight. Unfortunately her flight was delayed, and the route was also changed, so I didn't know which Mumbai airport she would land at. On the other hand, I couldn't collect my baggage because my airline had mislaid it.

I had a few instants of worry, but then I recalled an old saying from Enna: "There is a solution for everything except for death." Furthermore, Saint Francis had taught me that life's worries are a trifle in comparison with the search for God. Losing my baggage and the twelve-hour delay of my wife's flight to Mumbai was nothing by comparison.

While I was waiting for my wife, I decided to find accommodations in a hotel near the airport. Then I strolled along the Mumbai streets near my hotel. I saw people whose condition was much worse than mine. I was anxious because I couldn't find my wife and my baggage, while homeless people in this metropolis had the sidewalk as their home. I happened to see a young child covered with a thin blanket; only its feet were visible. It wasn't possible to tell if that child was dead or sleeping. A few starving dogs lay down on the same sidewalk. Some dogs were markedly scabby. Apparently there was not much difference between them and the homeless people who shared the same place. Both dogs and people begged for food to stay alive.

In the streets there was bustle of cars, rickshaws, buses, and motorbikes that polluted the air. I had no doubt that the homeless who lived alongside the road would not live long. Besides their lack of hygiene and proper feeding, they had to breathe air poisoned by the exhaust fumes.

The owner of the hotel suggested I go to the domestic airport to meet my wife, because the airline she was travelling on used to land there. I did so, and after a few hours of waiting, I finally spotted my wife at a distance and we both ran to hug each other with joy. As for my luggage, it still wasn't there the following day, so I took advantage of the opportunity to renew my suitcase and wardrobe.

Finally, everything came out right; my mishaps were solved and my wife and I could plan our journey to Goa. What couldn't be solved was the problem of the many homeless people sleeping on the sidewalks and begging for a piece of bread. According to the Hindu, the miserable condition of the outcasts is the consequence of the many sins they have committed in their previous lives. There is no hope for them to improve the quality of their living in this life. In fact, they have to make amends for their negative karma until the end of their lives.

We decided to take a night bus from Mumbai to Goa. The coach was drafty, and some of the passengers got a cold. Moreover, there was the big problem of going to the toilet. The bus didn't stop often, and when it did we passengers, both men and women, had to relieve ourselves along the side of the road, as the coach stopped only for a few minutes.

We arrived in the town of Mapusa around nine in the morning, and from there we took another overcrowded bus to Arambol, one of Goa's beaches. A picture on the upper part of the bus's windshield showed Jesus, Mary, and another figure, who seemed to be Mary, holding the baby Jesus on her arm. As soon as we set off, the driver lit a stick of incense and put a garland of flowers around the icon. Apparently he was Catholic.

Goa had been a Portuguese colony, and as happens to every territory conquered by invaders, the new masters brought not only their armies with them to subjugate the new country, but also their culture and religious traditions. Catholic churches were widespread in Goa. I spotted two churches built in a fashion similar to those I had seen in Mexico.

On the other hand, the same happened in Sicily at the time of the Arab conquest. The Arabs remained in Sicily for two centuries and brought with them good culture in the fields of art and literature. They also improved the agricultural irrigation systems. Likewise, they also brought the new Islamic religion, so that Sicily swarmed with mosques. According to some authors, at the time of the Arab occupation there were more mosques in Palermo than in Istanbul. There were also many mosques in Enna, but they were all converted into Catholic churches after the Normans took the Arabs' place in Sicily. One of these converted churches in Enna is that of Saint Michael, whose Moresque features are still visible.

The sandy beach is the highlight of Arambol. It is quite broad and surrounded by coconut palms and other tropical trees. A few fishing boats are alongside the seashore. Judging from the tiny fish the fishermen extricated from their nets, I inferred that that sea must not be teeming with many fish.

All along the beach people walked, ran, played ball, did yoga, and played badminton. I even noticed a man playing his saxophone facing the sea in the early morning. It was not possible to hear the sound of that instrument because of the noise of the breakers. I couldn't understand what meaning there could be to playing the saxophone at the water's edge. There probably was no meaning, just someone who enjoyed playing his instrument.

Maybe meditation and prayer are different according to the place where they happen. So praying by Saint Francis's tomb, for instance, is not the same as praying within a church. This time I wanted to try a kind of meditation that a Sufi from England had recommended to me. Here, facing the Indian Ocean with the sound of the waves breaking on the waterline, my meditation would be different.

The Sufi had advised me to sit cross-legged with my spine straight and inhale deeply through my nose and exhale through my mouth. He said, "When you inhale, expand your stomach. Confine yourself to watching your breathing. If a thought comes to your mind, expel it through your mouth when you exhale. Then stand up, spread your legs a little bit wider than your shoulders, with your feet parallel, stretch your arms to the side, count to thirty, and then relax. Stretch and relax your arms in that way five times."

I planned on practicing his Sufi meditation every morning in Goa. Even though I didn't get any spiritual enlightenment by doing so, it would definitely be beneficial and help me separate my mundane worries from the aim I was looking for, which was to find that drop of God that is inside every human being.

Many people lay down to get a tan or chatted in the bars in the afternoon. Most tourists were Westerners, many of them from Russia. It seemed to me that they were all leading an existence devoid of goals. They chatted, played on the beach, swam, and took pictures. There were two ladies who enjoyed being photographed close to a bull lying on the beach. Sometimes I asked myself if it was me who was the real outcast, someone who persisted in searching for a goal in life, while life actually has no end. All those people seemed to be devoid of spirituality, but they all had their inner lives. Some looked quite strange. I saw a man take off his swimming suit and rinse it in the sea. He remained naked for a few minutes. Nobody cared about him, and he cared about no one.

Over the days, I noticed that not everyone who spent their holiday in Goa was devoid of inner content. In the yoga class there were youngsters who looked very learned in the spiritual field. At the break of day the shore swarmed with people doing meditation, yoga, and other spiritual activities. Some played the flute, others the drum. Others did walking meditation, which is a kind of meditation based on watching one's own steps. Others did laughing meditation, which is obviously based on laughing. From this I inferred that no one on Earth is devoid of spirituality. Everybody has his or her inner world, but it is different from one another.

The same went for my wife. Even though we had been married for a long time, our inner landscapes differed. My wife had the good habit of keeping a diary since her school days. She writes down everything she sees and what happens to her every day. When we compared our writings about Goa, we discovered that we had written and portrayed different things and situations. I had written about human behavior, while she had focused her attention on love. She had noted down the inscriptions that many lovers drew on the moist sand. There were a lot of details in her diary that I hadn't noticed.

"I am sure," I said to my wife, "that if we ask each person in Goa to write their impressions, everyone will note down something different. Some will focus their attention on the sun that dives into the ocean, marking the end of the day. Others will talk about the evening star that gleams a few minutes after the sun has set, or they will describe the ebbs and flows and the small fish that come near the shoreline and then dart towards the ocean. Some will focus their attention on the hang gliders that depart from the hill, or about the sky lanterns that fly across the beach at night, while others will tell of the many stray dogs on the beach that seem to be familiar with tourists.

"Why there is such a difference in the way people see places and situations?"

"It happens because we are all different from one another," my wife answered. "There is a difference, a veil of incommunicability that separates all living creatures. Love and understanding are the bridge that makes communication and dialog possible."

As for my wife, she noticed a detail that many people, including I, would have overlooked. A man was sitting near the water's edge and playing the flute. Four stray dogs were sitting placidly by him. Apparently they loved the sound of the flute.

"I heard," I said to my wife, "that cows in some farms are made to listen to good music and the sound of the melodies helps them produce more milk."

"Every living creature has a soul and loves music," added my wife. "Even plants are sensitive to music and good words. If you say 'I love you' to a plant, it will grow better and produce more flowers and fruit."

I remember talking once about an existential subject with one of the workers at my father's company, who looked well-educated. "What is the goal of your life?" I asked.

"I have given up trying to find a goal in life, otherwise I get lost," he answered. "I pursue small goals like planning an enjoyable vacation, or saving money to buy a gift for my girlfriend. These are my little aims, and have nothing to do with metaphysical speculations."

Who knows if the worker was right! As for me, I cannot live without asking myself the why of things. It is probably because of my conditioning from my philosophy teacher. I didn't excel in philosophy in high school. It appeared too abstract to my empiric mind. The teacher was not pleased with my progress at school. He was convinced that I was a very shallow student, and one day threatened to fail me.

"I'll fail you, Vincenzino, unless you start to ask yourself why everything exists and happens. You have to ask yourself why the earth is round, why the moon orbits the earth, and why the planets orbit the sun. If you are on the bus, you have to ask yourself why it is moving. In other words, you have to find an answer to everything that happens."

That teacher conditioned me to such an extent that I now cannot live my life as it happens. I search for the meaning and the why of every thing and situation I come across. My wife was convinced that my search for answers to the many questions that life presents was useless.

"You have to just enjoy your life, without asking what happens after death," she said. "The only people who can learn that are those who have already died. You will know the truth when you die. For the moment, confine yourself to enjoying life in the best way you can."

Goa is a place where yoga teachers thrive. Yoga schools vary according to the kind of yoga that is practiced. My wife and I enrolled in a Hata yoga school. It lasted for two hours and started at 8:30 in the morning. So, after our Sufi meditation was over, we walked along the shore for a while and then moved to the yoga class, which was held on a rooftop terrace of an unpretentious building behind the beach. It didn't shine for cleanliness, but the shade of the trees and the view of the ocean compensated for the dusty floor.

The teacher was from New Delhi. He didn't look like a teacher; rather, he looked like a beggar, and his clothes were not very clean. Nevertheless, his yoga was very good. I had the impression that he believed in his work and was eager to lead the class. Over the days, I noticed that our teacher expressed philosophical truths in simple ways while leading the class. "Everybody is different. No competition, no comparison. Do according to your comfort level. No hurry, no worry. Something is better than nothing." He repeated these words every day, as if they came from a tape recorder.

We started by doing some breathing exercises called *pranayama*. Then we performed several *asana*, which are body positions. Most *asana* look like stretching exercises, but the stretching involves the entire body. According to our teacher, we should perform the *asana* like a meditation, as they affect both body and mind.

After two hours of yoga, all the muscles of the body were tuned up, due to both the breathing exercises and the stretching. I felt very relaxed after practicing yoga in an environment surrounded by trees on one side and the ocean on the other. Yoga stretches out all body muscles, which are often contracted due to the sedentary lifestyle one leads, or mental ailments like anxiety, which stiffen the body as a side effect.

I had the sensation that by doing meditation, yoga, and swimming in the warm waters of the Indian Ocean, my body condition improved. I was slowly purifying my body and mind, which would take me closer to God as Saint Francis had taught me.

While I was performing the *asana*, I recalled a friend of mine who wanted to solve all his health problems by taking medicines. Whenever he had a slight ailment he went to the doctor, who prescribed a medication for him. Even when he started to feel anxious or depressed, he thought to quench the feeling through anxiolytic agents. He trusted his doctor blindly. His absolute faith in taking medicines made it seem as though he was taking Holy Communion.

Even though Enna is a very small town, he refused to walk the short distance from his home to his workplace. As for eating, he was never short of hot and tasty food. Even though he had some health problems due to lack of motion and an unhealthy diet, his doctor would resolve the problem by prescribing him the right medicine.

Another friend of mine was fond of thermal baths and springs. He thought that by drinking spring water and taking thermal baths his health would improve. They are probably both helpful, but without a proper lifestyle to go along with them, there is no need to go there.

Both of them died before their time.

In my opinion, the best medicine is living in touch with nature, breathing pure air, jogging in the forest, or swimming in the ocean. Also, yoga and other holistic disciplines are useful in keeping the body and mind in good health.

Every time I went to my doctor's office in Enna to ask for a medical certificate to go to the gym or the swimming pool, I found the waiting room packed with people waiting to have prescriptions filled. If all those patients practiced some sport in the open air, the doctor's waiting room would be less crowded and the National Health Service would save a lot of money!

Sadly, I, the one who wanted to hand people the right remedy to live a long life, got a fever. Apparently swimming and doing yoga were not enough to keep me in shape.

"It serves you right!" said my wife. "You had the self-importance to criticize your friends who didn't follow your advice for keeping well, and now your elixir of life is not working for you. You boast about knowing everything. You should be more humble. Remember your Aunt Marietta?"

"Yes, of course. I loved my dear aunt."

"Well, she lived to the venerable age of one hundred years. She was a housewife. She never practiced yoga or other physical activities."

"I also remember her husband," I remarked. "He was a good shooter and walked in the forest often. He was crazy about hygiene. He always washed his hands before eating, but he dried them naturally. He thought the towel might contain germs. Nevertheless, he ended his life early by killing himself."

"Remember your Aunt Agata?" continued my wife. "She was from Catania and a rich businesswoman with many servants and cooks at her service. She didn't move much, nor did she play any sports or do yoga. In the morning her chauffeur drove her to her firm. Then she stayed in the control room all day long, before finally going back home where a tasty meal made by her cook was waiting for her. Well, she lived to be ninety-six and was able to manage her business until a month before she died.

"Therefore," continued my wife, "everybody has the right to lead their life according to their own wishes. Forcing people to do yoga or jogging in the open air is like condemning them to a lifestyle that doesn't suit them."

"The cases you have quoted are just exceptions," I retorted. "Every rule has its exceptions. You cannot deny that if you maintain your car well it lasts longer. The same can be said about the human body. A good lifestyle, which is comparable to good car maintenance, makes human life last longer.

"On the other hand, only God knows when our last day comes. So placing one's trust in a physician, or following my suggestions about eating good food, doing moderate physical exercise, and yoga, cannot solve the problem that all humans are doomed to die."

In Goa, I wanted to try Ramana Maharshi's method of meditation again. I couldn't succeed in meditating more than a few minutes in Enna, probably because I was too distracted by work worries, but here the environment was more suited to meditation, especially at sunset when there was an unusual atmosphere of peace at the beach. Many people sat on the sand to watch the sun disappear.

I sat down on the sand, closed my eyes, and while I asked myself who I was, I tried to go deep inside to see my real nature. I realized that my body had undergone many changes since I was a little boy. It had become bigger. Over time my teeth had rotted and had been replaced with manmade ones, and my hair had thinned, but something inside me had not changed. In fact, the little child who ran in the streets of Enna and dried his nose with his hand was still me. The sensation that I had of myself then and now was still same.

There is something unchangeable inside every human being. What I wanted to know was the nature of that invisible changeless entity. Maybe only mystics and saints can know that. As a common human being, I cannot reach lofty truths. An old proverb of Enna says "God helps donkeys and children," which is equivalent to the Italian saying "Fortune smiles on beginners." Who knows, maybe someday fortune will smile on me and I'll get enlightenment.

A few days later, I changed my routine. I dropped my daily meditation and replaced it with jogging on the seashore and watching nature and the people around me. In fact, when a person looks for enlightenment there are no fixed rules. It is possible to look inside oneself, as in meditation, or outside as well. Watching the ocean, the sun, the moon, or the people around us is like watching God's painting.

One morning I was watching the ocean when I had the feeling that Jesus was suggesting a new kind of meditation to me. "Open your heart to everybody. That is the best meditation!" he seemed to say.

I tried this new meditation as the days passed, and I can say that it was very powerful. I sat silently on the beach and focused my attention on opening my heart to all living beings, both friends and those unknown to me. After a while, I felt my body and mind purifying. I talked with my wife about this discovery.

"Yes, I agree with you," she said. "Focusing our attention on opening our heart to everybody makes us realize that God is within every person. It is no coincidence that the Indians use the word *Namaste* as a greeting, which means 'the godliness inside me greets the godliness inside you.'"

"I will name this discovery open-heart meditation," I said with my eyes beaming with joy.

The Arambol beach has a different look in the morning than it does in the evening. Usually my wife and I went to the beach at daybreak. The sun had not risen yet behind the hills, and the fishermen strained to beach their heavy boats. Sometimes I helped some of them with that hard effort. Some people enjoyed jogging, while others did Tai Chi. I noticed that a great many had themselves tattooed. An old man even had a tattoo on his face, while other tattoos on his body depicted barbed wire and scenes of violence.

Each person seemed a separate world. It happened that a man who brought his chessboard to the beach invited me to play with him under the scorching sun. I didn't feel like playing chess at the time and kindly declined his invitation, but I later saw him playing with someone else.

What struck me was the solitude of many people in Arambol. I observed the solitary souls in the early morning at the beach and in the evening at the restaurant.

"I would not be able to spend my holidays alone at a beach resort," my wife said.

"Me either!" I answered.

Indeed, during my youth it was quite unusual to see a person walking alone in the streets; a lonely person was considered mad. In the summer when I wanted to go to the beach, I was careful not to leave Enna alone. I feared that if someone from the town saw me alone they would have pity and say, "Look at poor Vincenzino. He is alone like a madman."

Therefore, I was never alone, and it didn't matter if my fellow traveler was smart or cheerful. The important thing was that I had a companion. One year I went on holiday at a seaside resort with a companion who wasn't very intelligent, just so that I wasn't alone.

In Goa, I had the opportunity to see the absurdity of my previous behavior. There is a basic distinction between solitude and loneliness. The former is free choice, while the latter is feeling, usually linked with melancholy or sadness. You can be in solitude without feeling sad. Many people in Arambol were living in their freely chosen solitude, but I didn't get the feeling that they felt alone.

Walking along the beach, I saw a lady that danced before the sea, a man playing the flute, and a group of Indian young men who played cricket. As for us, my wife suggested saluting the rising sun and imagining that its golden light pervaded our entire bodies, healing and purifying them.

In the evening, the atmosphere was completely different. Many people walked along the beach. It was like being at Belvedere in Enna during the summer, where people enjoyed strolling on the crammed public walk.

Little by little daylight gave its place to night, and every now and then the disgusting smell of marijuana wafted in the air. It happened that some drug peddlers approached to try to sell us marijuana. I was looking for natural paradise, not an artificial and transient pleasure like that given by drugs, so I refused.

It was still cold in Rishikesh. We had stayed in Arambol for ten days, so we decided to visit other places in the south of India before going north. It was said that there were many enlightened gurus and holy places in India. I wanted to visit those areas. I thought that I might be able to feel the same energy that emanated from Saint Francis's tomb in the Indian holy places.

Chapter Sixteen

Puttaparthi

I wanted to meet an enlightened person, hoping that he or she would give me some more insight into my spiritual path. I had heard that an exceptional guru named Sai Baba lived in the city of Puttaparthi in southern India. It was said that he was the reincarnation of a former Indian saint of the same name.

We took a night bus from Goa and arrived near the village of Hampi in the early morning. From there we took a rickshaw, which drove us into the heart of the old city. The alleyways seemed to all be the same, and if it had not been for my wife's sense of direction, I would have had difficulty finding the way to our guesthouse.

The remains of that ancient capital were spread over a wide area. What caught my attention was the large number of monkeys that lived in town and around the old temples. They were ready to snatch bags containing food away from unaware tourists. I noticed a policeman who had a long stick on his desk, which he used just to chase away the monkeys.

A river runs through the town, and in the evening we took a seat in one of the bars along its banks just to enjoy the peace of the place.

We stayed in Hampi for two days, visiting the historical places. The day before our departure, while we were inside an ancient temple, I noticed a couple of people who seemed to be homeless close to a gate that was very dirty with excrement. I asked them if we could get through the gate and they answered yes. My wife didn't want to pass through that dirty gate, but she finally gave in.

To our surprise, once we had passed the gate a wide, sloping rocky space unfolded before us. The color of the rock verged on light pink. We walked uphill up to a small temple. When we reached the top of the slope, an incomparable sunset and a view of an extensive valley below, dotted with villages and houses, unfolded before us.

"Sometimes," said my wife, "we should take the narrow alley that leads to bliss, while the wide and cozy way often takes us to a dead end. If I had not passed through that filthy gate I would not have seen this unequalled scenery."

On the way home, my wife unexpectedly came across a lady from her country. She said that she had been in a cold city in the north of India where she had attended a Vipassana meditation course for a month.

"How did you manage to attend a meditation course for so long? I cannot do Vipassana for more than ten minutes," I said.

"You have to start gradually," she answered. "For the first three days, you have to confine yourself to watching the air that passes through your nostrils and hits your upper lip. Then you have to watch your entire body from the crown of your head to your feet. Meditation starts at 4:30 in the morning and ends at nine in the evening. Little by little, as you meditate you have the sensation that your mind is being purified."

"What is the sense of watching yourself for so long a time?" I asked.

"If you watch yourself, you can learn who you are. Through Vipassana, you observe yourself completely," said my wife.

The Greek lady was a lonely traveler. She was short with black curly hair, and was bubbling over with joy. She was dying to talk with us, as if she had not seen a human being for years.

"Let me introduce myself," she said. "My name is Maria. I have been visiting India for a long time. One of my most adventurous travels was the one I took from Lumbini to Lee. Actually, Lumbini is located in Nepal, but it is very near the Indian border. It is the town where Buddha is from, and many monasteries have been built around the palace where he was supposed to have been born.

"From Lumbini," she continued, "I moved to Varanasi. It is a holy, fantastic city, which the Ganges runs through. Of course, I bathed in that holy river."

"I thought it was very dirty," said my wife.

"Yes, it is," answered the lady, "but it is said that *sadhus* keep the water of the river clean so that nothing happens to the devout person who lowers themselves into it.

"At Varanasi I took a bus to Haridwar, which is another holy city, and from there to Manali at the foot of the Himalayas. I then took a minibus to cross the mountain range and went to Lee, where I planned to stay for a while."

"I didn't know that it was possible to cross the Himalayas by bus," said my wife.

"Actually," she replied, "there is a mountain pass from Manali to Lee. It is the highest pass in the world at 5,500 meters above sea level. It is difficult to breathe at that altitude. You have to drink a lot of water. There are also no toilets on the road, so the bus stops from time to time along the way.

"Our bus broke down, and we were given the option of spending the night in a marquee at an altitude of around four thousand meters or continuing our way with another bus that had a few vacant seats. I opted for continuing my journey, because I couldn't endure the altitude. I was very dizzy and had the feeling that I would collapse at any moment.

"The bus travelled on a vast plateau. No roads or paths were visible, but the driver seemed to know the way very well. I never imagined that there were such vast tablelands in the Himalayas. It was almost like a lunar landscape. The soil was dry, and needles and rocks emerged from the ground here and there—no trees, not a blade of grass. I had the sensation of having landed on another deserted planet in our solar system. Apparently, the monsoons can't overcome the mountain range. Nevertheless, now and then I spotted some isolated green areas."

"How is it possible that there are only patches that are green with trees? I asked a person sitting next to me."

"It is like an oasis in the desert. Somehow there is water underneath the ground. The city of Lee is just an oasis. It doesn't rain there much, but the area is rich in underground water, he answered."

"We reached the maximum altitude of the pass and I felt relieved," the woman continued. "From then on the bus would go downhill. The worst had passed, and I gradually started breathing normally."

The Greek lady's account sounded fascinating, but it was late. We were tired and sleepy, and we had to wake up early in the morning. I told her that we couldn't stay and talk any longer.

"May I know your next destination?" she asked.

"Yes, of course," my wife answered. "We're going to Puttaparthi to meet Sai Baba."

"I know him," she answered. "He is a holy man, but you cannot leave India without seeing Amma."

"Who is Amma?" I asked.

"She is a holy woman, and her ashram is in Kerala, which is a state in the extreme south of India."

We took a bus to Bangalore, and from there another bus to Puttaparthi. As soon as we arrived in town we headed for Sai Baba's ashram. I had never seen such a large and well-maintained ashram. Furthermore, it was the cheapest place I had visited so far. We could have a good meal on ten rupees, the equivalent of a few cents.

People say that Sai Baba is an uncommon man. He has the power to make golden rings and necklaces out of thin air. It was said he was able to create a special holy powder in the same way. At the entrance, a lady who said she was from Switzerland directed us to our room. She asked us not to have sex while we were staying in the ashram. Moreover, she asked me to buy a traditional Indian dress for my wife. In fact, it was not possible for ladies to stay in that holy place in casual Western clothes.

The meeting place with Sai Baba was a large hall that could hold 10,000 or more people. The meeting happened in the evening. Men and women were not allowed to stay together in the hall, so my wife took a seat on the right, while I sat down on the left side of the hall. Sai Baba was sitting in a wheelchair. I couldn't see him because I was far away, but my wife spotted him and got the sensation of seeing a very weak man.

Later, at lunch I exchanged a few words with an Italian guy whose wife was a devotee of Sai Baba. "I've come here for twenty-five years!" he said. "I have seen Sai Baba's materializations many times. He gave my wife a golden ring, which she keeps at home in Italy."

Before leaving the ashram, my wife bought a booklet that described Sai Baba's teachings. *Food is God* was the title of the small book. The first line said, "You are what you eat." By reading that booklet, I learned how to purify my body and mind just by eating natural, sound food, which obviously doesn't include meat.

Chapter Seventeen

Amma

The Greek lady's words resounded in our minds. "You cannot leave India without seeing Amma. She is a holy woman!"

We were not far from Kerala. Furthermore, the journey to Amma's ashram looked alluring, because to go there we had to cross the Back Waters by boat.

We headed for the town of Alleppey, the starting point for the boats bound for the Back Waters. The boat was wooden and ploughed the waters very slowly. Now and then it stopped to take aboard or land people. An Italian lady took pictures with her camera the entire way. Sometimes I compare this crossing to one that I had years ago when I sailed up the Mekong River in Laos on a slow boat like this. At the time, the sailing lasted two days; now it would take around seven hours.

I couldn't tell if we were sailing fresh water or seawater. In fact, sometimes the course narrowed and took the shape of a river, while right after the levees were so broad that they looked like seashores. Vegetation was green and luxuriant, but I couldn't spot any waterfowl. Before arriving at our destination, the water became so vast that it was evident that we were sailing the sea.

We landed at a small wooden dock. To go to the ashram, we crossed an arched bridge built to modern standards, but it was so narrow that only pedestrians could walk on it. Amma was not in the ashram. She used to move around India, and often visited other countries as well, but this time we were lucky and were told that Amma would return in three days.

We had been led to this place because we trusted the Greek lady we had met in Hampi, but we didn't know anything about Amma.

"What does she do?" my wife asked a Scottish man who was having dinner by us.

"She doesn't do anything special. She confines herself to hugging people. So when she comes here you will be hugged by her. While she hugs she whispers something in your ear."

"What is the meaning of her hugging?" I asked.

"She hugs you and transmits good energy and her love to you and to all beings. I could perceive her love message," answered the Scottish man.

"Did you come here just to meet Amma, or there is some other special reason?" asked my wife.

"When I am at the ashram I go to the Ayurveda Hospital, which is nearby. There, I have a treatment called panchakarma to purify my body."

"Can we get this therapy as well while we are waiting for Amma?" asked my wife.

"Yes, you can come with me and I'll show you the hospital, but the complete treatment takes several days. How long are you going to stay here?"

"Just three days," I answered. "After hugging Amma we will leave."

We spent three days waiting in the ashram. I noticed that schools and hospitals had sprung up around the area. Apparently, Amma had been beneficial to local people. There was also a temple where she used to pray. It was open to everybody. The guests in the ashram usually gathered there in the evening. A statue of the goddess Kali stood out from the central wall of the temple. She is the goddess of all-consuming time.

We were asked to do volunteer work while we stayed in the ashram. So, for a few hours a day we cleaned the staircases and statues at the entrance to the temple.

In the evening while I was in the temple, I took a seat and tried to practice my open-heart meditation. I closed my eyes, and for just a few minutes watched my breathing. Then I focused my attention on my heart, imagining opening it to all human beings, even to my enemies.

"What is the difference between good and evil?" I once asked a friend of mine.

"Good is opening, while evil is the closure of your heart," he had answered.

Now I understood his saying. Closing oneself to the world turns into acting badly. On the contrary, an open heart can only bring good to oneself and others.

Some time ago, a cousin of mine gave me the nickname "Hedgehog." In hindsight, I can say that he was right on. For the greater part of my life, I had acted as if I wore armor made of thorns to protect myself from other people and the happenings of life. Only now, by practicing my open-heart meditation, can I understand how difficult it is for me to open my heart, which had been locked for so many years.

On the third day, Amma arrived at the ashram. I spotted her in the temple from a distance in the evening. The following day she would hug everybody.

The line was quite long, but the long-awaited moment finally arrived. First, Amma hugged my wife and then me. The hug lasted just a few seconds, because the guard that regulated the line hastened us to be quick.

"What did Amma whisper in your ear?" I asked my wife.

"She said 'You can do, you can do!' And what about you?"

"She whispered 'Oh my dear, oh my dear,'" I answered.

We left the ashram by bus. Our next destination was Auroville.

Chapter Eighteen
Auroville

In the minds of the founders, Auroville would be an international city open to people from every country and all walks of life to come together and live their lives with full freedom of speech, thinking, religion, and political opinions. With the passing days, I noticed that there was no discrimination based on someone's place of origin. As for trade, there was no currency. In fact, all visitors had to purchase a special card called an Aurocard, by which purchasing could be done.

Auroville is near Pondicherry, which had been a French colony. The French name, Auroville, means the city of Sri Aurobindo, who is the founder of the community along with a French lady called Mirra Alfassa, and also known as "The Mother."

Sri Aurobindo invented a kind of yoga called "Integral." When my wife and I visited his ashram in Pondicherry, we bought a booklet about it. But after having read it, I couldn't find a method to practice it; in fact, I couldn't understand what it was. The book talked about the creation of a super mind. Maybe, according to Aurobindo's Integral yoga, the super mind is intended to transcend materiality and be one with the universe.

When years ago I visited Tanzania, I noticed that many tourists and volunteers came from Germany. In my opinion, it was due to the fact that Tanzania, previously called Tanganyika, had been a German colony.

The same goes for Auroville. Many visitors and residents are French, because Pondicherry had been a French colony. I don't think this is an accident. Both the French and the Germans are still fond of their ex-colonies. Despite the proclaimed universalism, nationalism is still strong in people's minds, and many individuals are still proud of their nation's past glories. It was possible to become a citizen of Auroville, but it took quite a long bureaucratic procedure.

I don't know exactly what the residents did to make a living. I heard that they had some kind of job. Some are teachers, other farmers, and so on. A Korean lady, who now is an Auroville dweller, invented a job to get by. She made and sold kimchi, a traditional fermented Korean health food.

There were neither temples nor churches in the area. Apparently, the founders had intended to prevent the erection of any place of worship that might discriminate against the residents on the basis of their creed. To carry out the ecumenical end, a round gilt building called the Matrimandir had been erected that encompassed all religions. People who are both from Auroville and the outside are allowed to enter just to meditate. But while residents can go in anytime, non-residents need to make a reservation.

My wife and I were admitted two days after our booking, on the condition that we watch a video about Auroville before entering the Matrimandir. The wide, gilded dome stands on a large lawn. At the entrance of the area is a big banyan tree. It is reputed to be sacred. In the evening, people light candles and meditate around the big tree.

We entered the building and followed a circular walkway. I didn't see any statues or religious symbols. We were told that we would see a prismatic crystal on the top floor of the Matrimandir that emanated special energy. When we at last reached the top floor, people were meditating facing the crystal. It was dark inside. I didn't see the prismatic crystal; my wife spotted it, but said she didn't feel that it emanated any special energy.

The city of Auroville extends along the countryside. The buildings are not very tall, in an effort not to spoil the environment. The community centers, like the city hall, schools, swimming pools, cinema, yoga centers, and restaurants, are so widespread that to move from one place to another, you needed a motorbike, or at least a moped. Despite the fact that I had not ridden a moped for a long time, I was forced to rent one. The roads were made of packed earth and not busy, so it was easy to move from one place to another.

We usually had our meals at the restaurant, but in the morning our breakfast was served in the guesthouse kitchen. It was a good opportunity to meet other guests and chat. We sat at the same round table with a French couple. Both of them had been married previously, but have now been married to each other for twenty-five years and have one daughter. They both had other children from their previous marriages.

"What a big mess," my wife said to me later. "Children from three different unions!"

"What matters now is that they love each other," I replied— and they actually do.

The husband was a good painter. He showed us some pictures of his paintings. They were amazing.

"Are they oil painted?" asked my wife.

"Unfortunately not," he said, sighing deeply.

"Why do you say unfortunately?" I asked.

"I have been painting in pastels my whole life. Over time, my body has been absorbing the pastel powder and that has most likely been the cause of my cancer."

I grimaced with sorrow. Indeed, every time I heard the word cancer, I always diverted my attention to different topics. But this time I couldn't, because every morning we met in the kitchen to have our breakfast and sat together at the same table. A natural feeling of friendship arose between us. His wife was very talkative and witty. I noticed that Jacques would spread butter and jam on a slice of bread and hand it to his wife. He remained sitting at the round table without eating anything.

One day he solved the mystery of his fasting. "I have to fast for twenty-one days. If I don't eat anything the carcinogenic cells die, but they will form again later. There is a very good Tibetan doctor that comes here from time to time. When he comes he sees me."

I wanted to ask him how it was possible to fast for twenty-one days and still keep fit. In fact, except for his paleness, he seemed to be in good health and was plump. However, I refrained from saying anything that might invade his privacy.

One evening he organized a full moon tea party on the roof terrace. Only six were present at the party: Jacques, his wife, two French ladies, and my wife and me. A tablecloth had been laid on the floor with cakes and beverages, while soft music radiated in the air. The food and cakes were delicious, but Jacques didn't eat anything because he still had to fast for ten more days. It was a unique party. I had never seen a person that couldn't eat food organize a party for his friends. We ate cakes and many other delicacies. There was neither beer nor wine, because they don't sell alcohol in Auroville.

"How long are you going to stay in Auroville?" asked Jacques.

"One week more and we'll move to Thiruvannamalai," answered my wife.

"It is a holy place. I know that area very well!" Jacques said.

"When you go to Thiruvannamalai," he continued, "don't miss doing three things. First, you must climb Arunachala Mountain. It is not difficult, but you have to get up early in the morning or the sun will be scorching. You'd better go alone and leave your wife in the cave to meditate. It is an arduous climb.

"Secondly, you must take part in the Full Moon Festival. Every month on the full moon, people from many parts of India come together and walk round Arunachala Mountain.

"Third, not far from the ashram is the house of a lady with special powers. Around ten in the morning people gather in the hall of her house. She passes amid them silently. She confines herself to passing amid the people. Now and then she stares at somebody. Even though she doesn't talk, she transmits energy. She is very powerful!"

The party went on for around three hours. We enjoyed the full moon night, talking music, art, and spirituality. After a while, the two French ladies left and we chatted with Jacques and his wife a little longer. I have to say that it was a party that I would never forget.

Next to Auroville is Sadhana Forest. The word *sadhana* means spiritual practice. According to the founder, who was an ex-philosophy professor from Israel, the forest should be a place where people spend their time in total contact with nature, far from everything that sounds modern, like electricity, running water, and stone houses.

There were almost 200 volunteers from all over the world in Sadhana Forest, who had come just to spend some time plunged into a primitive environment. Their task consisted of planting trees and preserving the forest from fires, which can break out due to the dryness of the area.

We arrived in the forest by bus in the afternoon. The Israeli professor gave a speech about life in the forest. He said that many families lived there. One of the visitors asked, "What about your children? Do they go to school? Who gives them an education?"

"Our children," the professor answered, "have home schooling. Then, if they want to go to school they can, but if they don't want to go we don't force them to have compulsory education."

The professor led us around the forest and their tiny village, which was built on pilings. The dormitories for the volunteers were just over the pilings. There was neither running water nor electricity, except in one or two pilings. They produced power by a bicycle and solar panels.

They offered us a vegan meal and showed a film about life in the forest. We also saw how mercilessly they grow chickens and pigs in developed countries, which are fed inside very narrow cages until they are killed.

In the evening, when we got off the bus, a young man gave us a flier. Once at home we read it. The young man complained about having been expelled unjustly from Sadhana. Apparently, despite human endeavors, it is not possible to create a perfect society where everybody can live happily and without conflict, even in the forest.

Before leaving Auroville, we visited an ancient city called Mamallapuram. It is not far from Pondicherry, so in the morning we went there and returned to Auroville in the late afternoon. What attracted me was Krishna's Butterball, a huge, rounded boulder that stands on a slope and looks as if it is about to roll down at any moment.

A new spiritual stage was waiting for us. It was the holy mountain called Arunachala.

Chapter Nineteen
Arunachala Mountain

The city of Thiruvannamalai is where the master Ramana Maharshi spent almost all his life.

One day, when he was still a teenager, he was seized by an irrational fear of death. He had the sensation of being about to die, even though he didn't suffer from any disease. From that moment on his life changed radically. He started meditating about his real nature. His main question was "Who am I?" After meditating for a long time, he realized that he was not his body. His real nature and identity would survive after death. In fact, only his body was subject to annihilation, while his real self wouldn't die. At the age of sixteen when he started meditating, he moved to Thiruvannamalai, a town at the foothills of the holy mountain of Arunachala.

One day, while my wife and I were visiting the biggest temple in Thiruvannamalai called Arunachaleswara, we noticed an underground room where Ramana Maharshi withdrew to meditate. He remained in that small room for many days without caring that insects and rodents were ravaging his body.

Later, a *sadhu* saw him and was so enchanted by Ramana Maharshi's figure that he started serving him and became his personal attendant for the rest of his life. Ramana lived inside a cave called Virupaksha in Arunachala for nearly seventeen years. His attendant begged for alms, cooked, and took care of him. Ramana's holiness spread all around India and foreign countries as well.

As time went on, more and more people came to see him. After seventeen years in the small cave, Ramana moved to another cave called Skandashram, where he lived for five years. Then he moved to the ashram that had developed around his mother's tomb.

As soon as we arrived in Thiruvannamalai, my wife and I headed for Ramana's ashram with the intention of remaining there for a few days. At the front desk, a person dressed in white, who looked like a monk, accommodated us in a wide, clean room outside the ashram. As for meals, we would eat at the refectory inside the ashram. We ate there three times a day. The food was delicious, but we had to eat with our hands. Cutlery was not available at all.

After three days at the ashram, I went to reception to check out and pay for our lodging, but the same person that had welcomed us three days before said, "You don't have to pay. It is free!"

It was the first time in my life that I had been given free accommodation. I considered it a gift from Ramana Maharshi.

We could move to Rishikesh soon, because it was late in February and the weather should be warmer, but we wanted to stay in Thiruvannamalai a little longer to learn more about the places where the great guru spent his life. Moreover, Jacques had given us three pieces of advice, and we wanted to follow them. Finally, we found accommodations in a guesthouse not far from the ashram.

Jacques had said we needed to climb Arunachala Mountain. Looking up from the bottom, it seemed to be quite a challenge. The hill was quite high. Furthermore, somebody had told us that it was dangerous to venture out in that place without a guide. It was impossible to climb the mountain in the daytime because the sun was too strong. Therefore, we had to set off when it was still dark and come down no later than nine o'clock.

Where to find a guide? Fortunately, the owner of our guesthouse knew the track well and offered to lead us. We set off at five o' clock in the morning. It was dark, but it was possible to see people in the street. Apparently, life in India never stops. There were four of us: our guide, a girl from Korea who was also staying in our guesthouse, my wife, and me.

We followed our guide in the darkness and I asked, "Why is this mountain considered holy?"

Our guide answered, "The Hindu trinity is formed by three gods: Brahma the creator, Vishnu the preserver, and Shiva the destroyer. One day a dispute arose between Brahma and Vishnu. Both of them claimed to be superior. To settle the dispute, Shiva manifested himself as an infinite column of light so dazzling that it was impossible to look at. Brahma and Vishnu prayed to Shiva to take a less dazzling form, so he took the form of Arunachala Mountain. This place is sacred to Lord Shiva, and represents the element of fire."

To go to the mountain we crossed Ramana's ashram and followed a path to Skandashram Cave. Jacques had advised that my wife wait in the cave, but she wanted to climb to the top of the mountain. So, we all walked to the top of the hill. Our guide told us to be quick because the sun would soon rise and it would be impossible to stay on the mountain.

"How high is the mountain?" I asked.

"It is eight hundred thirteen meters above sea level," our guide answered.

While we walked, the magnificent temple of Arunachaleswara appeared in the distance. "What a grand temple! It is one of the five temples associated with the five basic elements: water, air, earth, fire, and sky," said our guide.

From time to time we stopped for a few minutes. The Korean girl had brought some eggs, oranges, and bananas, which she shared with all of us. Monkeys and dogs waited at a distance to eat some of our leftovers.

We got to the hilltop at daybreak. I felt as happy as a mountaineer that had climbed the highest peak in the world. The sun appeared faintly on the horizon, and I was a little bit cold. The top was exposed to the wind, but from there I saw a vast landscape that stretched to the horizon. Our guide showed us two footprints that had been impressed by Shiva. There was also a trident to symbolize that the mountain was sacred to Lord Shiva.

After we climbed down the mountain, we expected to have leg pain, but mysteriously we didn't have any, even though we were a little bit tired.

The second thing Jacques had advised us to do was take part in the Full Moon Festival. There were three days to the full moon, and we didn't intend to miss the event. We stayed in Thiruvannamalai, postponing our journey to Rishikesh.

In the mornings we went to meditate in the same places where Ramana used to. Sometimes we meditated in Virupaksha Cave, sometimes in Skandashram Cave, which were not far from each other, and sometimes in Ramana's ashram. I wanted to meditate as Ramana had advised. So I sat in a cross-legged position and focused my attention on who I was. I stayed in that position for an hour, but unfortunately I was unable to meditate for more than five continuative minutes because my mind was too distracted and I had the tendency not to live in the present. My mind was always thinking about the past or the future. Meditation was impossible.

One day while we were hanging about on the streets nearby the ashram, we stumbled across the house that belonged to the lady that Jacques had recommended we see. She lived in a three-story building. The ground floor was just a wide hall where visitors gathered every morning around 9:30 to wait for her arrival at ten o'clock.

My wife and I sat on the floor and waited. There was an armchair opposite us. At ten sharp, a lady with an olive complexion and wearing a sari entered the hall. Her hair was covered with a veil. She stepped slowly towards the armchair and sat down. Her features were still striking, despite that fact that she was probably over fifty.

She sat on the armchair motionless; only her eyes moved. She fixed her eyes and shifted her gaze from one person to another. Then she stood up and walked along the rug that separated her from the visitors. She kept staring at the people, and then stepped to the exit as slowly as she had entered.

People said that they had felt some energy when she stared at them. As for us, neither my wife nor I felt anything. Nevertheless, that doesn't mean that the lady was not a powerful, enlightened person. Many times, when visiting places like that, people report having been overwhelmed with energy. When I visited those same places, I felt nothing.

I have only felt energy three times so far. It had happened at Saint Francis's tomb, another time while I was visiting a lady in Italy with stigmata named Natuzza Evolo, and a third time in the nearby town of Calascibetta where a young man named Rosario, who claimed to see Our Lady, lived.

At last, the long-awaited full moon day arrived. People flocked to Thiruvannamalai all afternoon. Under the full moon, which enhanced the splendor of the contours of Arunachala Mountain, the human river seemed to flow as if it was about to burst its banks. Millions of people looked like a huge snake that sinuously slithered around the holy mountain. I couldn't believe my eyes.

The walk is fourteen kilometers. Most Indians cover the distance barefoot. A few foreigners tried to do the same, but the consequences were often unfortunate. I spotted a white man with his feet bleeding. He was forced to give up the walk.

The street was surrounded with stalls selling many kinds of goods, above all refreshments, but also Ayurvedic medicines and toys. Here and there people lined up for free food provided inside the temples that were scattered along the street. We too were invited to eat, and we entered an open square close to a temple and enjoyed a wonderful free meal.

It was an experience that I would never forget. I didn't want to leave Thiruvannamalai and the places where Ramana used to meditate, but now it was time to move on. We had to reach our main destination—Rishikesh.

From Thiruvannamalai, we went to Chennai and took a flight to Delhi. Once at the airport, we went to the Kashmiri Gate and took a night bus to Rishikesh.

Chapter Twenty
Rishikesh

We arrived in Rishikesh around five in the morning. It was still dark and cold. We took a rickshaw, which directed us to a guesthouse. On the way I spotted four or five homeless people sleeping under a small porch. Each of them was covered with a blanket; it was definitely not enough to protect them from the coldness of the night.

The rickshaw man got us a drafty room in an area of Rishikesh called Tapovan. The blanket was not thick enough to warm us up, but I was still grateful to God for being in a much better situation than the homeless people I had seen, who were shivering.

At daybreak I heard rolls of thunder. The sky clouded over, a strong wind blew, and the windowpanes rattled. The draft in the room flapped the curtains, and then it started raining, and I suddenly missed the days spent on the beach in Arambol when my wife and I jogged happily across the seashore. Why didn't I remain in the warm south of India? I felt guilty about my wife, who feels the cold, but our spiritual quest had to go on. Being in a place that was seemingly hostile would be a good lesson for us.

There are two ways to live our lives. One is to be content with little, remain confined to one's own birthplace, and lead a peaceful life. The other is to get out of one's friendly environment and venture into the unknown for the sake of knowledge and exploration. Opting for one way instead of the other doesn't depend on one's merit, but on the inner psychological makeup. As for me, if I didn't suffer from a pathological anxiety and fear of death, I would never have started my journey around the world in search of a solution to the issue.

My mother always used to repeat that neither bad weather nor good weather lasts long. It was a good lesson, and now the bad weather in Rishikesh seemed to be an allegory of life, which passes through sunshine and storms. Sometimes it flows smoothly and sometimes stormy, but it is worth living to the fullest.

Around noon the sky was less clouded, and now and then the sun peeped out from behind the clouds. My wife and I took advantage of the fair weather to have a walk around the area. We spotted a stretch of the Ganges River. The water looked green and clean. It was different from what I had seen in Varanasi many years ago. There the riverbed was broader and the water flowed quietly. Here the channel was narrower and the river was choppy.

Rishikesh is considered a holy city. They don't sell alcohol in the shops, and you cannot find meat in the restaurants. The Ganges is a sacred river for the Hindus. At the sight of the green color that covered the river like an emerald blanket, I too felt a certain air of sacredness in it.

We walked downhill along a street flanked with shops, restaurants, and temples. There were many yoga and meditation schools. Then we turned onto a narrow staircase that led us to the bank of the holy river. Actually, the river didn't look as rough and narrow as it had appeared to be up high. In some stretches it was broad and calm, similar to what I had seen in Varanasi, but its waters were much cleaner and it had an olive-green hue.

We went to the bank and dipped our feet into those holy waters. Then I scooped up some water with my hand to see its color; it was colorless. Apparently, the olive-green hue was the reflection of the trees that covered the surrounding hills.

That night I couldn't sleep well. I was seized with the fear of death once again. My wife was sleeping close to me, and I wondered if she had made a good choice in getting married to such an anxious man.

Just like my Uncle Vincenzo, I was assailed by the doubt that all the cells in our body die at the same time. Actually, there are body functions that continue after death. For instance, hair and nails keep growing. I have always been terrified of being buried when my mind is still conscious, even though my body has died.

Finally, I realized that my anxiety and continuous fear of death wouldn't help my spiritual search. Being terrified beyond measure would only confuse my ideas and mind, preventing me from living my life.

Here in the holy city of Rishikesh, I wanted to try my open-heart meditation again. As soon as we woke up, after having a cup of coffee and eating some bananas, we meditated for fifteen minutes. My wife did her breathing meditation, while I watched my breathing for a few minutes and then tried my open-heart technique. While I was watching my heart, imagining that it was open to everybody, I recalled a statue of Jesus that I'd kept in my room since I was a baby. The statue is around one meter tall. Jesus is portrayed as a master with a white robe and a red tunic, and his heart sticks out of his chest.

Not only is the heart fundamental for Christians, but Buddhists also believe that the mind is located in the heart. They think that the mind is a mental continuum without beginning or end. The Buddhist "mind" may be considered the equivalent of what Christians call the soul. Obviously, when I say that the house of the mind or soul is in the heart, I don't refer to the physical heart, which can even be implanted from one person to another, but to the spiritual heart, whose house lies close to the physical heart.

While I was meditating on opening my heart to life, people, and every living being, I had the sensation of having a stone instead of a heart. It was as if I had my heart locked in a safe that was impossible to open. However, I was sure that continued meditation would open my heart to life sooner or later.

"Meditation is useless if you don't put your resolution into practice," my wife said. "In fact, you must open your heart to everybody in real life, not only in meditation."

I actually found it quite difficult to open my heart to certain people with whom I had had some disagreement or I didn't like, but I had to do it or my open-heart meditation would be just nonsense.

The weather in Rishikesh changed radically the following day. The sun was shining and it became much hotter. We walked along the same lane as the day before and arrived at a narrow bridge. Only pedestrians and motorbikes could use it. Monkeys stood along the handrails, hoping to get some food.

We crossed the bridge and walked along the other bank of the river, which was also full of shops and restaurants. While we walked on the bridge, I admired the river in all its majesty, and noticed that the olive-green color was constant, even in stretches where the banks were surrounded by houses, when the trees were far away and the sky was cloudy. Its wonderful green color remained even at twilight. Obviously, the constant hue depended on some phenomenon that I didn't know about, but there had to be something mysterious in the amazing Ganges. It could be considered sacred not only by Hindus, but by everybody. It cannot be ruled out that God, who is the same for all people, regardless of the race, becomes manifest in different ways so that He can show Himself through those holy waters.

Cows wandered freely in the narrow streets, while donkeys and mules were used to carry river sand, gravel, and red bricks to building sites. I hadn't seen this kind of transportation for at least seventy years, when long lines of donkeys, mules, and horses carried goods and people from the countryside into Enna.

One of the peculiar features of Rishikesh was the many *satsangs* that were held all over the city. *Satsang* is a Sanskrit word that means gathering together with a master for the truth.

One day my wife and I entered a hall where a *satsang* was to be given. At one end there was an armchair, and about a hundred people sat in the hall facing the empty chair. Then one lady who was about fifty years old came in and sat down on it. Before she could open her mouth, one person in the hall raised his arm and asked to talk. He was given a microphone, and he then asked the lady a question. Other people then asked questions and the lady answered each of them. This happened for almost two hours. Most of the questions were about how one should live his or her life, and what a person can do to self-inquire and know their real nature.

Most people were young. One of the young men who had asked to speak caught my attention. "If I don't judge people," he had said, "how can I know which person is right for me and who would do me harm? Obviously, in my daily life I need to judge and weigh people and situations. Do I act correctly when I judge people?"

The master in the armchair answered without hesitation. "You will know better if you don't judge. In fact, you don't need to judge, because you can learn what to do just by using your heart."

A lady of about forty was given the microphone and then asked her question. "Every morning my mind spins with thoughts. I strive to be still but I cannot stop the whirl of thoughts. What can I do to be still?"

"You don't need to strive to be still," answered the master. "What you can do is just watch your thoughts. Yes, confine yourself to watching and watching, and then you'll see that your thoughts will melt and become like water. Only then will you be still."

The following day we went to attend another *satsang*. This time the master was a man from Jamaica. The venue was not in Tapovan, but near the marketplace in Rishikesh. The hall was quite wide and could hold more than a thousand people. On the wall behind the platform, two portraits were hung; one of Ramana Maharshi and one of Papaji. Other portraits on the walls portrayed Amma, the former Sai Baba, and the Jamaican master.

The *satsang* was not dissimilar from the one we had attended the day before. Most of the questions and answers were on the same topics as the previous day.

When the *satsang* was almost at an end, the master invited the person who was questioning him to come to the platform. Then the master asked, "Can you tell me something impermanent that is the same on Monday, Tuesday, Wednesday, and the days to come? According to you, there is a certain starting point or a universal, unchangeable truth? What does ultimate truth mean?"

The young man strayed from the topic and was unable to give the right answer. Then the guru addressed the audience for an answer. A lady raised her arm and said, "The real truth is that now I am awake, while when I sleep I am not awake."

"That is not a universal truth," answered the master. "The consciousness of being awake or asleep depends on subjective perception!"

Nobody in the hall could give the right answer.

Another *satsang* was given by a guru who came from a Portuguese-speaking country. From his complexion, I inferred he was Brazilian. He spoke only Portuguese; a girl sitting close to him translated his words into English. This time, the *satsang* didn't start with questions and answers unlike the previous ones. The guru, who had a long white beard and a pigtail, gave a long opening speech.

"The path to self-realization," he said, "passes through the heart. There cannot be spiritual life if the person builds walls around them. I can say that spirituality is synonymous with love. A human being has to open his heart to everybody and pull down all the walls he has been building to protect himself from the outside. A spiritual search means creating harmony inside and outside oneself."

When we left the hall, my wife, even though she appreciated the goodness of the master, made a clarification. "The three masters we have seen so far talk of love and the opening of one's heart. If we keep attending *satsangs*, I am sure that we'll find other gurus that speak in the same way.

"The most difficult thing to do," she added, "is to put the opening of one's heart towards everybody into practice. In daily life, instead of opening our heart, we lock it. Whether we like it or not, we raise walls all around it to protect ourselves from life's dangers."

However, we kept attending *satsangs*. I thought that we might find a guru who would teach us something we didn't know.

In the morning, we usually meditated for about fifteen minutes—my wife in her way, while I used my open-heart technique. Watching my heart, I could see the walls that surrounded it. They were the walls that I had erected during the course of my life to protect myself from disappointments. With those walls, I avoided being hurt.

Most of the disappointments came from being refused or left by the women I liked. I often felt unbearable pain from a fallen dream. Whenever a girl said to me, "Sorry, but you are not my kind of lover," or worse, "We can be friends because you are a good boy, but I will never be your girlfriend," my self-pride was so wounded that I had to somehow find a way to protect myself from such pain.

Every time I had to cope with a challenge like an aptitude test or a job application, I was more worried about the potential wound my heart might suffer in the case of failure than about the situation itself. Over time, the fear of failure led me to avoid situations that would create problems for me. As a result, my mind was always projecting into the future or the past, instead of being present in real life.

There are two main kinds of visual acuity. A far-sighted person can see very well far away but cannot see nearby; he cannot even read a line without using glasses. The near-sighted person cannot see far off but is quite able to see things close. As for me, I was continuously projecting into the future or the past and was unable to live in the now. It was as if I needed glasses to live my life.

Here in this mystic city of Rishikesh, I at long last decided to live not only in the future or the past, but also in the present so my field of vision would be complete. Whenever I perceived that my mind wasn't living in the present, I told myself, "Put on your glasses and you will enjoy the now."

In the morning, whenever I did my open-heart meditation, I also focused my attention on opening my heart to life and the joys that it brings us. It may seem a banal meditation, but in my case it was not so obvious. In fact, I was unable to live my life fully and joyfully.

There was a distant episode that was at the root of my tendency not to live in the present and enjoy my life. When I was eighteen years old, I got my driving license. At that time, I was in a relationship with a girl named Giuseppina from Palermo. Her father was the prefect of Enna. Although she belonged to a high-class family, her parents would not allow her to come in my car with me. It would have aroused scandal in a small town like Enna.

She was a typical Sicilian girl. She had black hair and eyes with Arab features. I had noticed her one day while she was crossing the gate of the prefecture, and was bewitched by her majestic gait. She looked like the most polished girl in the world. After that, whenever I saw her my heart leapt.

I didn't know how to approach her. She didn't have many friends, and had a preference for going to church. She went to the Church of San Giuseppe, which stood across from the prefecture palace, every evening. So I started attending Mass as well. In the evening, I chose a pew not far from hers, but instead of following the Mass, my mind wandered elsewhere, dreaming of endless love with Giuseppina.

My first contact with her happened naturally. I smiled at her whenever she turned her head towards my pew in the church. Then, once the Mass was over, I waited for her outside the church and kept smiling at her—but I didn't dare make an approach. One day after Mass, we happened to be close to each other while following the stream of people heading for the exit. Being side by side, it was quite natural to me to ask her name.

"My name is Giuseppina," she answered.

"My name is Vincenzino," I said.

"What a beautiful name! It is very uncommon," she said.

"Yes, it is. My parents named me that as a sign of respect for my mother's younger brother who died before his time. Giuseppina is also a beautiful name. It is the woman's version of the name Giuseppe, who was Jesus's putative father. Now I know why you always come to the Church of San Giuseppe."

"How can you know that?"

"Because you are Giuseppina, you come to San Giuseppe Church."

She burst out laughing. Meanwhile, we had arrived at the entrance of the prefecture, which was a stone's throw from the church. "See you tomorrow at the exit of the church!" she said, still smiling.

I kept watching her until she disappeared beyond the forecourt of the palace. At that moment, I was the happiest person in the world. Giuseppina had smiled at me and walked with me. And above all she had said, "See you tomorrow!"

In the passing days, we saw each other over and over again. Our strolls became longer. We didn't confine our walks to just going from the church to the prefecture. We sometimes walked Via Roma or Belvedere, or to the Castle of Lombardia, and we even walked in the park that surrounds the tower of Frederick the Second.

After a year of walking along the streets of Enna, I tried to convince her to ride in my car. Actually, I used my father's car. However, all my endeavors to convince her failed. She was unshakable.

"If we were in a great city like Palermo," she said, "I would. But here in this small town, I cannot get in your car because my father would find out. I cannot disobey him. If he knew that I was in the car with you, he would be very disappointed." I loved her so much that I respected her decision.

Later, her father was transferred to Palermo to become the city prefect. It was a great blow to me, but we exchanged letters and talked quite often on the phone. An old song says that being away is like the wind that puts out small flames and sets blaze to bigger fires. My love for her was a really big fire and I couldn't stay far from her for long.

One day, I asked my father permission to go to Palermo in his car. At first he was reluctant, but since he knew that I wanted to go to meet Giuseppina, a girl of high rank, he gave in.

"Don't drive fast!" he said. "Palermo is a big city. Be careful at intersections!"

"Don't worry, Father. I am a good driver."

I drove from Enna to Palermo in three hours. I arrived half an hour early at the Piazza Politeama, the place where we had fixed the appointment. At noon sharp, Giuseppina appeared in the distance. She wore a black skirt and a red silk blouse. She looked like a fairy. We drank an orange juice at a refreshment booth. Then she proposed we take a walk on Via Libertà.

"You promised," I said, "that when we were in Palermo you would get in my car. Do you remember?"

"Yes I do, but I have a terrible fear that my father will find out."

"Don't worry! Palermo is a big city and your father will never know."

"Okay, I'll do as you ask, but we had better go to Monte Pellegrino so nobody can see us and report back to my father."

To go to Monte Pellegrino, I drove towards Mondello and took the panoramic road that leads to the top of the mountain. The road was full of sharp U-bends.

"I feel dizzy if I look down," Giuseppina said.

At the end of the winding road we arrived at a square. From there, a flight of steps led to the Sanctuary of Santa Rosalia, also called the Santuzza, who is the patron saint of Palermo.

It is said that in 1624, when the plague was causing many deaths in Palermo, Rosalia appeared to a shooter and led him to the cave on Mount Pellegrino, where her bones could be found. Then she asked him to take her bones to Palermo to be carried in a procession along the streets. The hunter did what Santa Rosalia wished and, after her remains were carried in procession three times, the plague ended. From then on, Santa Rosalia has been the patron saint of Palermo.

The sanctuary was inside the cave where Santa Rosalia's remains were found. Entering the cave, I was enchanted by the silent atmosphere. The German writer Wolfgang Goethe, who visited the place, described Monte Pellegrino as the most beautiful promontory in the world.

Not far from the entrance of the cave were some votive offerings from people who had been granted a blessing. Going forward, my attention was attracted by the drops that came from the top of the cave. The drops were canalized on thin silvery metal sheets to a basin, and were used to fill the holy water stoup at the entrance of the church. I don't know why, but I had the sensation that the dripping water was teardrops, as if that holy cave were shedding tears for me.

At the end of the cave was a marble statue portraying the Immaculate Conception. I genuflected and, watching Mary's statue, asked her to lead us in the best way according to her will. Unfortunately, Giuseppina and I couldn't escape our fate! Before long, a thunderbolt would fall on us.

At that moment, I recalled one of my mother's poems that I had read when I had found Vincenzo's diary.

LIFE

We were sitting on our stone staircase.

What is life? I asked my siblings.

"Life is breathing," answered Biagio. "Even trees breathe."

"Life is a tiny bird on a small branch," said Vincenzo.

"Unexpectedly the sprig snaps,

and the little bird flies away."

"As for me," replied Carolina, "life is a dream,

sometimes beautiful and often nightmarish."

"Life is destiny!" I ended off. "It is a beautiful drawing on the sand,

and the drawer already knows when the tide will erase it."

Once we left the sanctuary, I drove off the road and looked for a secluded space. I found a clear space from where we could see the beach of Mondello and the sea that stretched to the horizon. While we were admiring that amazing scenery, our eyes met, and as if by magic our lips also met. We closed our eyes and kept kissing each other, as if the world had disappeared and only we remained on the surface of the earth.

We were so enraptured that we didn't notice that the car was slowly moving towards the precipice. In fact, to get closer to her, I had unwittingly slipped the gear into neutral. Moreover, the hand brake was not in working order. As soon as the car hit a big rock, I realized what was going to happen, but now it was too late as the car had gained speed and it was impossible to keep it under control. The ground was too uneven and steep. I applied the foot brake, but the car kept skidding.

"Get out of the car!" I cried out.

I opened the door and got out, while Giuseppina was not quick enough to do the same. Inevitably, the car fell from the cliff nearly 300 meters high. I was numbed by grief. From paradise, I had fallen into hell. Giuseppina lost her life, while I kept living with that tragic event engraved in my heart and mind.

Fifty years had passed since then, and now while I was in Rishikesh, I again tried to open the doors of my heart that I had kept locked for half a century. I wanted to smile again at life.

Every morning I meditated as soon as I woke up. First, I watched my breathing for a few minutes in order to calm myself, and then I watched my heart. I could see a heart so tiny that it seemed impossible to open. It looked like a little mouse shut inside a mousetrap. It had been imprisoned for too long, but now I wanted to open it to life, as it was fifty years ago before that appalling, fatal accident.

Sometimes I thought that my resolve to start living a normal life again was just ridiculous. In fact, I was now seventy years old and had exhausted the greatest part of my life. It was too late now. It was as though I wanted to poke up fire on burnt wood. However, something is better than nothing, and life is worth being lived all the way.

By practicing my open-heart meditation, I saw nature in a different way. Now, the Ganges, the green hills, the moon, and all people seemed to smile at me.

"I am convinced," I told my wife, "that God is within everything and in every creature. We should open our heart to everybody. The only way to know God is through His creatures. If we open our hearts to all beings, we'll see God inside them."

"I don't think so," answered my wife. "Do you think that God is also inside a serial killer? Or a robber? Or a rapist? If God were inside those despicable beings, they would not act in such a bad way."

Before answering my wife, I took a few moments to reflect. I recalled that while I was in Goa watching the ocean, I had the sensation that Jesus was suggesting the open-heart meditation to me. No one is able to open his heart to all human beings as Jesus did. His love was unconditional and all-encompassing. He didn't make discriminations based on one's deeds. He loved without considering the good or bad actions done by humans. He was even able to love his executioners.

"If Jesus loved everybody, criminals included," I answered, "it means that also serial killers, robbers, and rapists have God inside them. We cannot judge anybody, as we don't know the ultimate reality of things, people, and phenomena. In fact, reality can be different from appearance. We don't have the right to separate the good from the evil, because we don't know either of them. I can say that all criminals suffer because of their ignorance and distorted minds. Behind wickedness there are delusions, which are wrong representations of life and human relationships."

However, while I was meditating on opening my heart to life, a question arose in my mind—how to live life. In fact, there are many ways of living. On this point, a conversation that I had a long time ago with a politician friend of mine came to my mind. His career in politics had been so successful that in just a few years he became a mayor.

"In life, you opt to either be a tractor or be towed. You can be either a leader or a follower, a proactive or a submissive person. As for me, I have chosen to be a tractor that is a leader.

"There are two main characters in human life," he continued. "Those who take the initiative and those who are subjected to others' initiatives. Only the former makes history, as the latter just follows other people's will. If you want to go on in your life, be a leader!"

At that time I was puzzled by my friend's words, and I am still not convinced of the soundness of his thesis. By opening my heart to everybody, I could realize that it doesn't matter whether you are a leader or a follower, a winner or a loser. What matters is having a pure heart open to life, and then you will naturally find your position and role in society. The basic rule is to live with a spirit of service, and we will find that there are neither leaders nor followers, because everyone is subject to the first principle of serving and being in communion with others. In this case, the one who wields power with a spirit of service doesn't exercise it to get personal prestige and gratification; he acts to serve his or her subjects.

Our stay in the mystic city of Rishikesh was coming to an end. Before leaving, we went to see the River Ganges one more time. For two days, the water had turned a yellowish color because it had rained much in the mountains and the flood had raised mud from the riverbed, but now the olive-green water was again as shining as ever.

We went to the bank and sat down on a rock. From that position we could admire the suspension bridge that connected the two opposite banks of the river. In some stretches, the river is flanked with black cliffs that alternate with green hills. If I had been a painter, I would have set up an easel and painted that unique scenery.

We were admiring the river when a little girl came close to us. She wore a torn gown, but her black eyes showed liveliness. She wanted to sell us a little round-shaped boat made of dry leaves with flowers, a tiny candle, and an incense stick inside.

"What is this?" my wife asked.

"It is a *diya.*"

"What is it for?"

The little girl, despite her young age, looked like an expert seller. "The *diya*," she said, "is made just to make wishes. You light the candle and entrust the *diya* to the River Ganges."

"Okay, you convinced me. I'll buy it," I said.

The little girl lit the candle and the incense stick and put the *diya* on the river. Then she dipped her little hand into the water and waved it to drive the *diya* towards the river's current.

"Now you can express your wish!" she said before going off, skipping gaily.

The *diya* floated, driven by the current. We followed our small boat and made our wishes. As soon as I closed my eyes, I saw my car somersaulting in the air fifty years ago on Mount Pellegrino before falling straight down into the crag. I opened my eyes for an instant and watched the *diya* disappear in the distance. The small candle was still lit.

"Deliver my wishes, oh little boat! May I meet Giuseppina someday in another life to express my regret for what happened that day. May we all be born again in a new star or on a new planet rich in spirituality, a new earth free from diseases, old age, and death—a new earth where people don't live mechanically but are aware of whatever they do; a new earth free from ignorance and error, where people don't turn to suicide to resolve their unbearable sufferings; a new world without violence, free from the poor, beggars, homeless, maladjusted people, and social malaise."

I would have continued my wish list, but all day would not be enough to finish it. Before reopening my eyes, a thought went to my disabled friends and a friend of mine who was suffering from a congenital disease called thalassemia. To be kept alive, he needed regular blood transfusions. I expressed the wish that congenital diseases would be eradicated someday, as well as the physical disabilities like those that struck my British and Italian friends for whom I volunteered on several occasions.

The *diya* loaded with my wishes had gone far off, and along with it my dreamed new earth had faded away. Harsh reality is another thing. We said goodbye to the holy River Ganges and the mystic city of Rishikesh.

Chapter Twenty-One
The Marian Sanctuaries

My natural desire to meet the supernatural and allay my fear of death had, over time, been leading me to the places where it was said that the Virgin Mary appeared to human beings. In my life, I had visited quite a few Marian sanctuaries, a few of them by chance, others of my own free will.

A constant of all the sanctuaries I visited was that Our Lady had appeared to children or plain folk. This made me think about my way of searching for God. I read hundreds of books about enlightenment, meditation, religion, Holy Scripture, and so on. I don't want to say that my work has turned out to be useless. Learning is better than ignorance, but definitely it is not enough to get close to God, because the path to God can only be covered by the soul and not the intellect. The soul doesn't need learning, only purity of heart.

Syracuse

The first experience I had regarding the apparitions of Our Lady happened in Syracuse a long time ago. I didn't go to Syracuse of my own will. In fact, I was just twelve years old. Nevertheless, as if it were yesterday, I remember when my family went to Syracuse to see a plaster plaque of Our Blessed Lady weeping.

In 1953, a bride and a groom had been presented with a plaster plaque portraying the Immaculate Heart of Mary. The newlyweds were very poor and went to live with the husband's parents for some time. The plaque was hung on the wall over the headboard of the bed.

The wife, Antonia, had a difficult pregnancy and suffered with convulsions and clouded vision. One day, after a seizure and a bout of temporary blindness, Antonia opened her eyes and noticed that the plaster plaque portraying the Virgin Mary was weeping. When she called out to her relatives and told them that the effigy was weeping, nobody believed her. But later, everyone saw that the small statue really was in tears.

Tears kept flowing from the statue's eyes for a few days and were seen by the people that flocked around Antonia's house. Filmed sequences of the plaque showed the phenomenon. The tears were collected and sent to laboratory to be analyzed. The tests showed that they were human tears. The Catholic Church declared the lacrimation a miracle. Now a church has been built in the area, where more than sixty years ago there were an unsurfaced square and a cluster of low houses.

I remember as soon as we arrived in Syracuse and parked our car at the end of the square, there were so many people in the square and around the house where the miracle happened that it was impossible for us to move on. As I wanted to see what was going on, my father, who was taller than average, picked me up so that I could see the happenings.

I noticed a line of detached one-story houses on the opposite side of the square and people standing and looking at those houses. Suddenly, I heard a voice that sounded like stammering.

"What happened?" I asked my father. "Why is that person stammering?"

"That man has been cured miraculously. He couldn't walk, but now he has left his wheelchair and is walking."

When I returned to the same place many years later, the square and the low houses didn't exist anymore. The plaster plaque portraying Our Lady had been moved inside the new church to be exposed to the believers.

Lourdes

The cult of the Virgin of Lourdes is followed by many in Enna, and every year in May a train loaded with pilgrims, volunteers, and seriously ill people travels to Lourdes. It is called the White Train. Lourdes is a place for pilgrimages for Catholics from all over the world, and every year around five million visit the cave where the apparitions happened.

In 1858, Our Lady appeared to a little girl named Bernadette Soubirous in a cave called Massabielle in Lourdes. The apparitions occurred for five months, and were initially seen with skepticism by the Catholic Church, but when the apparition revealed herself to be the Immaculate Conception, all doubts were removed. In fact, the little girl couldn't understand a deep theological concept like that of the Virgin Mary.

The journey from Enna to Lourdes takes forty-eight hours, as the White Train stops continuously to give precedence to regular trains. The volunteer's main task is serving meals in the train and pushing the wheelchairs once arriving in Lourdes. Only the most expert volunteers look after people with serious disabilities.

One year after Giuseppina's death, I still acted like an automaton and a dark fog separated me from the rest of the world. The police had investigated the incident for a few months, but I was eventually acquitted. My mother was very worried about me. She had no idea what to do, and confined herself to praying for me. Moreover, every week she used to go to the Convent of Saint Marc to ask the nuns to pray for me as well. She hoped that all those prayers would sooner or later rid me of my heavy depression.

"What about going to Lourdes?" she said one day.

I was so clouded that I didn't have the strength and will to answer her. But she insisted. "Do you want to go to Lourdes on the White Train? It leaves from Enna in ten days. It is a good opportunity to take your mind off your idea you are guilty of Giuseppina's death."

"I don't want to go," I said curtly.

"But it is a good opportunity to help the sick!" my mother said.

I actually considered myself a social waste, but the thought that I could be helpful to somebody in need made me feel less despicable. Moreover, I couldn't remain in a state of inactivity forever. I had stayed at home like a prisoner for a year, but sooner or later I had to come down from my ivory tower.

"Okay, I'll go," I said, and a feeble ray of hope revived in my heart. Maybe someday I would come back to life as a normal human being.

After twelve months spent in my room reading books, magazines, and listening to the radio, my eyes were not accustomed to daylight. My mother had arranged everything for my journey, including packing my luggage and providing my volunteer uniform, which was brown, while the ladies wore white skirts, white stockings, blue cloaks, and veils similar to those of nuns.

My parents came to see me off at the station and entrusted me to the priest who was the spiritual guide of the pilgrimage. He was from a town near Enna called Valguarnera Caropepe. Father Guido was a red-haired man who, despite the reformation of the Second Vatican Council that had given priests the freedom of dressing, still wore a cassock.

The train was very old, and two special cars dating back to the Second World War had been arranged to accommodate disabled people on stretchers. The two cars still bore the huge red crosses from the war. We didn't have any hoist, so we had to lift the people on stretchers into the cars by hand. It wasn't that hard a task, since we had many volunteers to do the work.

We had finished lifting stretchers when I saw a stretcher on wheels coming from the side entrance of the station. On it was a young man who had to weigh nearly 200 kilos. I couldn't imagine how we were going to get him on the train. It took six of us to lift the stretcher. My arms and legs were still weak after a year of inaction, but through our joint efforts we finally set him on the train.

It was the late afternoon when the train finally left the station. The sun was setting beyond the mountains, and in a few hours we would serve dinner to the pilgrims and invalids. Meanwhile, I went to my compartment and watched the green countryside and the wheat that waved under the breeze through the window. My eyes were looking outside, but my mind still saw the car plunging down into the ravine with its human load. Apparently, going out of my house had changed nothing. I was as absentminded and depressed as I was when secluded in my room. The environment had changed, but my heart was still shut to life.

Before entering the ferry from Messina to mainland Italy, the train stopped many times to take on more sick people, pilgrims, and volunteers. There were four volunteers in our compartment, but from time to time Father Guido came and sat down to chat with us.

When the train left the station in Catania we started serving dinner. The train was very long, and every volunteer was given the task of serving a certain car. I was told to serve dinner in the car with the people who were the most seriously ill.

I was doing just that when I heard someone call out my name. I turned back, thinking that another volunteer from Enna was calling me, but I didn't see anybody.

"Vincenzino, Vincenzino!" the voice kept calling.

I stopped serving and saw that it was the fat young man that we had lifted on the car that was calling me. "How do you know my name?" I asked.

"It is written on your badge!" he answered.

I was so absentminded that I hadn't paid attention to the badge on my uniform. "What is your name?" I asked.

"My name is Carmelo, and I want to thank you for the great effort you made in lifting me. As you see, my body is all out of proportion. My weight keeps increasing more and more, and all I can move are my head, eyes, and lips. All the rest is paralyzed like dead flesh. I can see that you are not peaceful but, believe me, your adverse fortune is nothing compared to mine."

Tears streamed down his big cheeks. "Can you see the moon and the stars out of the window?" he asked.

I bent my head and Carmelo also slowly turned his head to watch the full moon. "Ask the moon and the stars if it is right that my body lies on a stretcher from my birth to my death, while my mind is clear and realizes the uselessness of my life."

His words dumbfounded me. I had thought that only my problems existed and other people were immune from them. After Giuseppina's death, I had isolated myself in my room, thinking that I was the most unlucky person in the world. But now, Carmelo was opening my eyes to real life; his condition was far worse than mine!

"Tell me," continued Carmelo, "why there are half-men like me? I have done nothing to deserve such miserable luck. Do you think that my harrowing life derives from God or from a different malicious being? I am completely useless. While you may be helpful to others, Vincenzino, I am just human waste who is kept alive by a moral and criminal code that doesn't allow society to kill the heap of flesh I am."

It was as if I had been catapulted to life again. After a long time of seclusion, now in front of me was someone who was talking to me and wanted me to answer him, but I actually didn't know what to say. I looked around to see if the meals had all been served, and noticed that the other volunteers had done the work in my place. As for Carmelo, he had been fed in advance by a qualified nurse.

As for the second of his questions, my answer sprang from my heart naturally. "You are not a useless person, Carmelo. Thanks to you, I am coming back to life. I have been living like a vegetable for a year, except for speaking with my mother in monosyllables. Now, talking with you has been as if a thunderbolt has fallen on me. You have shocked me! Now I can see and watch you, while I saw no one before so immersed in my thoughts as I was."

"What happened to you?" asked Carmelo.

"It is an old love story that ended tragically, but now I can see that there are people like you who have no hope to live a normal life, while I am in a better condition. You have been like a mirror for me. Through you, I have looked inside myself and realized the uselessness of continuing to torture myself."

"What about my first question?" asked Carmelo.

During my year of insulation, I read many books and magazines. One of the most significant was the Book of Job in the Bible.

"Do you know the story of Job, Carmelo?"

"I have heard something about him. Job was renowned because of his patience, right?"

"Job was a rich, pious man," I answered, "who later lost all his riches, his children, and even his body became purulent. 'What have I done to deserve such bad luck?' Job asked God one day. The answer was that man cannot know what God's plans for us are. Therefore, Carmelo, accept your situation and do your best to live your life fully, even under such bad conditions."

The forty-eight hours spent on the train seemed never-ending, but the other volunteers in our compartment were cheerful. From time to time, Father Guido also joined us to say the rosary. When we arrived at the station in Lourdes, we had to offload the baggage and take the invalids to the hospitals. Then we volunteers went to the hotel.

My task was to carry the invalids from one place to another. The wheelchairs in Lourdes had a handle in the front, while some disabled people had their own personal wheelchairs that could be pushed.

Every day, in the morning and the afternoon, the disabled in their wheelchairs were lined up in the hospital courtyard and the volunteers took them wherever they liked to go. The disabled usually wanted to go to the Massabielle Cave to pray before the statues of Our Lady and Saint Bernadette, or to the baths, which stand in the place where Saint Bernadette found a spring by digging in the ground with her hands. This water was supposed to be miraculous, and several miracles have actually been recorded and corroborated by the Catholic Church. People who wanted to have a bath were just dipped into the water for a few seconds. They got dressed while they were still wet, but the water had the properties of drying immediately, so towels were not needed.

There were frequent Masses both in the cave and in the churches and basilicas. In the late afternoon, the sick and disabled were lined up in the vast square in front of the basilica and Holy Communion was given to them.

One afternoon while I was in the square looking after a sick old man, I lost my faith. I had the sensation that God was just a human creation. I saw the earth and the universe like matter with no spirit inside and no God that could vivify it. It was a real paradox that I had come to Lourdes to strengthen my faith in God and in life, but instead I had become an atheist. I remained in this condition as a disbeliever for several months, but with the passing time I felt that my life was completely empty without Jesus. After the terrible accident with Giuseppina, my only anchor was Jesus. Therefore, my atheism didn't last long, and for the rest of my life Jesus has been my only safe harbor.

During my staying in Lourdes, I wanted to do my very best to serve the sick people that I looked after. One afternoon I took a sick lady from the hospital courtyard. She was around sixty years old and dressed in black.

"Where would you like me to take you?" I asked.

"I want to go shopping!" she answered. In Lourdes, there are so many shops that sell holy images, rosary beads, small statues, and every kind of holy item, that sometimes I had the impression that big business gravitated around the cult of Our Lady.

The sick lady wanted to buy a small golden medal, so we went around many shops to find the item she liked. After two hours of shopping, she found the one she wanted. Afterwards, she wanted me to take her to the top of the hill, as she wanted to cover the Stations of the Cross. At last, after a long day of walking, I took her back to the hospital.

As soon as we arrived at the hospital courtyard, the sick lady got up from the wheelchair and walked at a brisk pace. I looked at her with a slight annoyance. Why had she asked me to carry her around when she was able to walk by herself? But suddenly the lady started crying out, "It is a miracle! A miracle! I couldn't walk before. That volunteer can testify to it," she said, pointing to me.

A few people gathered around me. "Is it true?" one of them asked.

"What?"

"It was really a miracle?" he insisted.

"I don't know," I answered. "I can only say that the lady was already sitting in the wheelchair when I took her out to the shops. Then I took her to the hill where the Stations of the Cross are, but I cannot say if she was able to walk before I met her."

"Okay, thank you," said the man who had questioned me, and soon the small crowd of onlookers dispersed.

The following day I heard from the volunteers, whom I used to meet at lunchtime, of a miracle that had happened in Lourdes. I didn't ask what kind of miracle they were talking about. It possibly referred to the lady that had regained her ability to walk. At the time I had fallen into my feelings of atheism, so I wasn't interested in the subject.

Many years went by, and that episode seemed to have fallen into oblivion, but one day it came to mind for some reason. I wondered why that sick lady would have deceived me, pretending to have been miraculously cured when she was already in good health. What was the point?

That afternoon in Lourdes was still vivid in my mind. I relived seeing the lady dressed in black sitting in the wheelchair waiting for a volunteer. When I arrived at the hospital, as soon as I saw her I headed for her and grasped the handle of the wheelchair without uttering a word. Once we were in the street, I asked her where to go. Then we went shopping and then to the hill. At last I took her back to the hospital.

I decided that there had to be a rational explanation. Maybe the old lady was lazy and didn't want to walk by herself. Perhaps she took advantage of me to stroll around Lourdes while sitting comfortably in the wheelchair. Nevertheless, my conjecture collided with the fact that the lady had been admitted to the hospital in Lourdes.

If my memory serves me right, there were two hospitals for sick people at that time in Lourdes, one bigger and one smaller. Neither of them admitted patients that were not disabled. There should be medical records certifying her disability. Being wise after the event, at that time I was very shallow. I should have investigated the matter in depth. However, if she is still in my mind after so many years, perhaps something supernatural really did happen that afternoon in Lourdes.

La Salette

The Carmelite monks of Sicily and Veneto organized a pilgrimage to Lisieux, a town in the north of France where the Carmelite nun, Saint Therese of the Child Jesus, had lived in a convent. The pilgrimage started from Verona, a city in the north of Italy, where the group coming from Sicily joined the other from Veneto.

I could never imagine going on a pilgrimage to the north of France, and I hadn't even heard of Saint Therese of the Child Jesus. It was a girl named Margherita, who attended Saint Joseph Church in Enna, who proposed I take part in the pilgrimage with her. Despite her young age, she had a degree in classic literature and taught ancient Greek at Enna's high school.

"It is not just a pilgrimage," she said to me. "It is also a sightseeing tour. We will visit Paris, a few castles by the Loire River, and Versailles."

I had fallen in love with Margherita, and the chance to go on a trip together thrilled me. So I accepted with enthusiasm. Unfortunately, people's minds and hearts are changeable, and a few days before the start of the trip she told me that she had changed her mind and wouldn't come. What to do? I could cancel my booking, but I didn't, despite the fact that travelling with a group of people who I didn't know didn't thrill me at all.

At that time, I feared of travelling by airplane, and that was not my only phobia. I also feared being isolated from other people. What would I do alone on the trip? All the other participants knew one another, while I didn't know anyone. I resigned myself to being alone for the duration of the trip, but I felt very ill at ease.

After I arrived at the station in Verona, I walked to the meeting place, which was not far away. A girl was waiting there for the rest of the group. As soon as I arrived I seized the opportunity not to be alone.

"My name is Vincenzino. What is your name?"

"My name is Lucia," she answered. She was tall and lean and had shadows under her eyes.

"Do you want to sit together on the bus?" I asked.

She looked at me with her broad eyes full of surprise. Certainty she would have preferred saying no, but she was too polite to refuse my request. "Okay," she answered, "you can sit close to me."

I was relieved because I had solved my problem of being alone, but over time I realized that I had behaved stupidly. In fact, I had compelled that well-mannered girl to stay with me while she might have preferred to travel with her friends whose company was more enjoyable than mine. I had treated her not as a human being but as a tool to solve my problem.

The trip leader was a Carmelite monk from northern Italy. His name was Father Leo, and he was a very learned person who knew Saint Therese's life to perfection. He gladdened our trip on the bus by telling biblical stories and, above all, talking about Saint Therese.

"Saint Therese of the Child Jesus was declared a Doctor of the Church by Pope John Paul II. She is the youngest person, and the third woman, to be so honored in the history of the Catholic Church. She died from tuberculosis when she was just twenty-four years old."

"What did she do to be declared a Doctor of the Church?" asked one of the pilgrims.

"She pointed out the 'Little Way' to humans. It does not take vast learning to know God, but it does take humility and simplicity of heart," answered Father Leo.

We had just visited the Palace of Versailles, and on the bus Father Leo kept telling the humble life story of Saint Therese. As for me, I couldn't help comparing a nobleman's life in the Palace of Versailles to life in a convent. They were two opposite ways of living. I concluded that everyone follows his or her own path according to their destiny and tendencies, but in the end paradise has its gates open to all, because God is inside every human being.

What made an impression on me was when Father Leo told us the story of Saint Therese's miraculous recovery.

"At the end of 1882, Saint Therese was seized by a persistent headache that lasted until Easter of the following year. She was just nine years old. Afterwards, she got worse and the doctor diagnosed a serious rare disease, unusual for a little girl. She was bound to die, but one day while she was praying before a statue portraying Our Lady, she saw the Virgin Mary smiling at her. Suddenly big tears welled in the little girl's eyes. From then on she started recovering, and five years later she entered the Carmelite convent as a cloistered nun."

"How is it possible," I asked Father Leo, "that a teenager is allowed to take the vows?"

"You are right to ask this question," he answered, "but Saint Therese got a dispensation from the bishop. Indeed, canon law is not as strict as civil law, thanks to the institution of dispensation. Obviously, if the bishop allowed Saint Therese to enter the convent at a very young age, he did so after due consideration."

On the way back when we were near the sanctuary of La Salette, I took a seat near another pilgrim. At that moment I saw Lucia laughing for the first time. Now she was sitting near a nun, with whom she was at ease. As for me, I had overcome my stupid fear of being alone.

On the way, Father Leo told us the story of the apparition of Our Lady of La Salette. "One hundred fifty years ago, La Salette was a small village in Southern France. There were less than one thousand people living there. One day, two children who had been minding the cows on Mount Sous-Les Baisses came back to the village and reported that they had seen a weeping beautiful lady.

"According to the children's account, the apparition, who spoke their dialect, was weeping because people didn't respect God anymore. The lady gave the children a few messages, which were all based on her wish that human hearts are converted to God."

Our bus took us up to the top of the mount where the apparition had happened. At that moment, thin mist alternated with clear sky. I had the sensation that the whole area was enveloped in mystery, as if Our Lady had left the imprint of her apparition on the mountain.

When I returned home from the pilgrimage, I saw Margherita with another man. I thought maybe they were just friends, but unfortunately they were already engaged, and six months later they got married.

I had lost Margherita, but I had gained much more. In fact, the pilgrimage to Lisieux and La Salette strengthened my personality. Now I had the sensation of being stronger and less picky. Apparently, the teachings of Saint Therese about keeping a simple and pure heart had worked.

Fatima

I came in touch with Our Lady of Fatima when I was around sixteen years old. At the time, the crowned statue of the Virgin of Fatima was taken across Italy. The statue arrived in Enna by helicopter and was then taken to the monastery of Montesalvo, where it remained for a few hours. I followed the statue all the way to the playground where the helicopter had landed and then took off.

The following day at school, I talked about Our Lady of Fatima with my schoolmates, who didn't seem as enthusiastic as me about the coming of the statue.

"Have you ever heard about the three secrets of Fatima?" asked Carlo, one of my schoolmates. He was a priest's nephew. His uncle, besides being a priest, was also a teacher of Latin at our school.

"No, I haven't. I don't even know about Our Lady of Fatima," I answered.

"Okay, I'll tell you what happened on May 13, 1917. That day, Our Lady appeared to three children, named Lucia, Francisco, and Giacinta, in a place called Cova da Iria, and asked them to come to the same place on the thirteenth of each month for five consecutive months at the same time.

"The civil and religious authorities didn't believe the three young shepherds, and Lucia's mother accused her of lying. On August thirteenth, the three children were arrested and forced to confess that they hadn't told the truth, but they were unshakable and kept their side of the story. The children couldn't go to Cova de Iria that day because they were in prison, but Our Lady appeared again to them on August nineteenth, and this time she promised that on October thirteenth, which would be the day of the last apparition, she would give them evidence of the authenticity of the apparition so that everybody would believe them.

"On the appointed day, people from all over Portugal came to Cova de Iria to be present at the miraculous event that had been predicted by Our Lady. There were believers and non-believers there, as well as civil and religious authorities and many anticlerical journalists.

"It was a rainy day. After noon it stopped raining and a cloud enveloped the three children. Our Lady asked Lucia to build a chapel in that place, and announced that the war would be over soon. Then the miracle happened. The sun started twirling in the sky. It was visible to the naked eye. It suddenly seemed that it was falling down toward the crowd. Then it halted before going up again in the sky."

I listened to Carlo with my mouth wide open. I was really mesmerized by his account, but my mind was turned to the secrets. "What about the secrets?" I asked.

"Oh, they are terrible! You should know that the third secret of Fatima has not been revealed yet. It was given to the Pope by one of the three children to whom the Virgin Mary appeared. In fact, of the three young shepherds, two died very young while the third, Lucia, is still living."

"Do you know the contents of the first two secrets?" I asked.

"Yes. In the first secret, Lucia, Giacinta, and Francisco were shown hell. In the second secret, Our Lady said that after the First World War, another would burst forth that would be worse. Furthermore, she said that someday Russia would be converted and the world would enjoy a time of peace."

"Does your uncle the priest know anything about the third secret?" I asked.

"No, he doesn't. Nobody knows the third secret except the Pope. In my opinion," said Carlo, "there must be something catastrophic in the message. Otherwise, the Pope would have revealed it. Maybe the message talks about the end of the world."

At Carlo's words, a shudder of fear ran throughout my body as I linked the end of the world to the end of my life.

More than fifty years had gone by since my conversation with Carlo. Meanwhile, the third secret, which had been kept in the Vatican archives for fifty-six years, was revealed by Pope John Paul II, who said that the secret was related to him.

The text of the third secret was also reported in our local newspaper on June 27, 2000. I read the article, cut it out, and put it into the drawer of my bedside table, where still I keep it. The article tells the secret and contains a theological comment by Cardinal Joseph Ratzinger, who later would become Pope. Not one catastrophic prediction was contained in the third secret. The real meaning of the message, according to Vatican, is that one can change his or her destiny through prayer and penance.

I had believed that every human being has his or her destiny already assigned and cannot do anything to change it. Now the third secret of Fatima had turned my way of thinking upside down. On the other hand, it is unthinkable that God, who is the giver of life and the creator of all things, is not able to change destiny.

Here is the unabridged text of the third secret:

After the two parts which I have already explained, at the left of Our Lady and a little above, we saw an Angel with a flaming sword in his left hand; flashing, it gave out flames that looked as though they would set the world on fire; but they died out in contact with the splendor that Our Lady radiated towards him from her right hand: pointing to the earth with his right hand, the Angel cried out in a loud voice: 'Penance, Penance, Penance!' And we saw in an immense light that is God: 'something similar to how people appear in a mirror when they pass in front of it' a Bishop dressed in White 'we had the impression that it was the Holy Father.' Other Bishops, Priests, men and women Religious going up a steep mountain, at the top of which there was a big Cross of rough-hewn trunks as of a cork-tree with the bark; before reaching there the Holy Father passed through a big city half in ruins and half trembling with halting step, afflicted with pain and sorrow, he prayed for the souls of the corpses he met on his way; having reached the top of the mountain, on his knees at the foot of the big Cross he was killed by a group of soldiers who fired bullets and arrows at him, and in the same way there died one after another the other Bishops, Priests, men and women Religious, and various lay people of different ranks and positions. Beneath the two arms of the Cross there were two Angels each with a crystal aspersorium in his hand, in which they gathered up the blood of the Martyrs and with it sprinkled the souls that were making their way to God.

Tuy, January 3, 1944

My wife and I were flying from Rome to Lisbon when I told her, who is not a believer, what happened on May 13, 1981, at Saint Peter's Square in Rome.

"It was a peaceful afternoon at Saint Peter's Square when Pope John Paul II was passing through the crowd. Suddenly a Turkish man, who was a professional killer, fired two bullets at the Pope. The Pope was taken to the hospital unconscious and was about to die, while the attempted assassin tried to run away, but was blocked by a nun named Sister Lucia. Don't you think that these are singular coincidences?"

"What coincidences?" asked my wife.

"The first coincidence is the date of the event. Both the first apparition to the shepherd children and the attempt on the Pope's life happened on the same day, May thirteenth. Furthermore, the person that caught the killer was called Lucia, like the young shepherdess of Fatima."

"Yes, they are astonishing coincidences. Did the Pope survive?"

"Yes, he survived, and he had no doubt that it had been Our Lady who had deflected the bullets, which otherwise would have been fatal. The Pope was bound to die, and the prophecy contained in the third secret of Fatima would have been carried out if not for the intercession of the Virgin Mary. Hence, the future and prophecies can be changed if it is God's will."

We landed at the airport in Lisbon and remained in the city for a few days before going to Fatima. While in Portugal, we visited Cabo da Roca, which is the extreme western tip of Europe. It is the place where the land ends and the ocean begins. Watching the immense ocean from the top of the headland, I revived the dreams of the great navigators of the past who had left the safety of the land to sail the unknown. Seen from an altitude of 140 meters above sea level, the ocean gave me a sense of immensity and infinity. It was like watching the firmament from above rather than from below.

We arrived at Fatima in the early afternoon and found accommodations in a very good hotel near the sanctuary. A few steps further was a square wider than I had ever seen, and at the opposite end was the sanctuary of Our Lady of Fatima. What impressed me was the view of the tombs of the three shepherd children; two were close to each other, while Francisco's was detached. Near the sanctuary is a museum where the crown of Our Lady is kept. Set in the crown is the bullet that had crossed Pope John Paul II's body without damaging vital organs. Not far from the square there was a small train that took tourists to the houses where the three children had lived and the hillock where the angel had appeared to them.

We left Fatima bound for another holy place called Santiago de Compostela in Spain.

Banneux

One day my wife said, "There's another important sanctuary that you have not seen yet called Banneux in Belgium."

I really didn't know about Our Lady of Banneux, even though I was always looking for holy places. "We should go there," I said. "And we'll take the opportunity to visit Belgium, which is a small country, but rich in traditions."

When we arrived in Brussels we found accommodations near downtown. What left me speechless was the view of the Grand Place, which is an architectural jewel. We visited all the tourist attractions in Brussels, and then we moved to Banneux by bus. It is a small village near the city of Liege.

Mariette was the first-born child of seven children. She went to school and catechism, but she didn't make much progress because she didn't have time to devote to study, as she had to help her mother in the daily chores. On the evening of January 15, 1933, she was looking out of the window, waiting for her brother who had not yet come home, when she saw a young, beautiful, shining lady in the garden.

"Mom!" she called. "I see a lady in the garden. She is the Holy Virgin."

The apparition appeared eight times. The Virgin called herself "The Virgin of the Poor." During the second sighting, Our Lady led Mariette to a spring, saying that it should be reserved for Herself and for all nations. As it had happened in other places where the Holy Mother appeared, she also recommended praying, and asked that a chapel should be built in the place where she appeared.

When we arrived in Banneux, the bus stopped next to a square. At the end of the square there was a street that led to the sanctuary. The atmosphere in Banneux was different from other Marian sanctuaries. It was much simpler and there weren't many shops. We walked towards the chapel and found a water basin on the right, which was where little Mariette had dipped her hands. We too dipped our hands and drank some of the water.

After visiting the chapel, we walked through the woods that bound the water basin. While we were walking, I realized why Our Lady had called herself The Virgin of the Poor. We well-to-do people tend to underestimate the issue of poverty. It is one of the most serious social problems. Here amid the woods of Banneux, in my mind I saw all the jobless, poor Sicilians that had migrated to Belgium to work in the coal mines after the end of the Second World War. Many of them died trapped underground, while those who survived contracted an illness called silicosis, which was a progressive disease caused by the inhalation of dust in mines. My mind went to the immigrants that try to reach the Sicilian coast packed in precarious boats, which sometimes wrecked, causing the deaths of hundreds of people, whose only fault is to be poor and searching for a better place to live.

I recalled a butcher in Enna who had a large family. My father used to go to his shop to buy lamb at Easter. Over time, many butcher shops sprang up in Enna, so that butcher couldn't match the competition and became poor. He took on debts to feed his family, hoping he would be able to pay them, but things didn't go well. He fell into despair and couldn't find a way out. One night he left his home and told his wife that he had to cut a few lambs' throats, but things went differently. He pulled down the shutters in his shop, and instead of cutting lambs' throats, he cut his own. The following day his blood still leaked through the chink of the shutter, flowing into the street.

There are many tragedies caused by poverty that we don't know about. Sometimes, even when we know about them we ignore them instead of doing something to try to overcome the scourge of poverty.

Here, where Our Lady of the Poor appeared, I saw in my mind's eye how many conflicts were sparked off by poverty.

Indigence gives rise to social malaise, and then to a Mafia, terrorism, and war. It is not by chance that terrorists and members of the Mafia are recruited from the poorest classes.

We left Banneux and headed for Amsterdam. My wife wanted to visit the Van Gogh Museum, which contains an ample collection of his paintings. He was a genius, but also a very unlucky man who suffered from mental disorders. He was found dead at the age of thirty-seven from a gunshot wound that he likely fired himself.

Our Lady of Guadalupe

My search for God led me first to Australia and then to Mexico. I wanted to learn if religion was just an invention by priests or if it was an innate idea. If a newborn baby is taken away from their mother and grows up alone without meeting anyone that can teach them religion, will they ever develop the idea of God? I wanted to study ancient civilizations that had had no contact with people from foreign countries to see if they had ever practiced a form of religion.

To study the native Australians, I flew to the city of Darwin in northern Australia, as I knew that many Aborigines lived in that part of the country. My aim was to live for a while in an Aboriginal village, but it was not as easy as I had supposed. In fact, I needed special permission from the Australian government to stay with the natives. I remained in Darwin for a few days, hesitant about what to do.

One day while I was walking in the street, a young man gave me a flyer that advertised his religion. We chatted for a while, and he then invited me to his church, which was Christian. I went there, and I have to say that I was at ease, but they asked me to be baptized with them. I couldn't do that, because if I had accepted I would be giving up my Catholic faith, which I had no intention of doing. Therefore, I kindly declined and we parted ways.

I saw many of the Aboriginal natives in the streets, but they looked as though they were pariahs. Many were homeless and beggars. I asked one of them, who looked a little bit less impoverished, what his religion was.

"Christian!" he answered, to my surprise.

"Don't you have a traditional religion?"

"Nowadays most of us are Christian. There are some of us who practice strange rites, but it is not right to follow them."

I remained in Australia for a week and learned, by talking with a member of a group of Aboriginal dancers, that they have an old, traditional religion that is completely original.

"We believe in a spiritual force," he said, "that permeates everything: trees, creeks, mountains, and so on. There was a primordial era before the formation of the world. We call this *dreamtime*. The world was undifferentiated and populated by gigantic creatures that left the imprint of their passage, which are the mountains, rivers, trees, and so on. Therefore, nature is sacred. Dreaming is fundamental for us, because through dreaming we can communicate with the spirits."

I left Australia firmly convinced of the originality of their traditional religion. Now it was time to move on in my spiritual quest.

I wanted to gather information about the Mayan culture and religion. Until the discovery of America, the Mayans had been isolated from the rest of the world. Because of that, their religion, cults, and rites had to be unique. I flew from Catania to Cancun and found accommodations with a host family in the city of Merida in Yucatan, the area where the Mayan civilization had thrived.

Fortunately, the same family also lodged a lady from Texas named Melanie, who was a Spanish teacher and knew the Mexican culture very well. She was at least ten centimeters taller than me. Her father was from Portugal and her mother from Ukraine, but she was born in the United States. As soon as she knew that I was interested in the Mayan religion, she led me to an archeological site called Uxmal, where there was a wide pyramid.

"Pyramids," she said, "have a religious meaning. Let's go up to the top through the staircase and I'll show you why."

We climbed the steep staircase and reached the top of the pyramid, where there was a temple.

"The pyramid," she said, "symbolizes the mountain, and as you know, according to many traditions, the gods live on the top of the mountains. Think of Mount Olympus, which was the house of the Greek gods. Think of Mount Sinai where God appeared to Moses, or Mount Tabor where Jesus's transfiguration happened.

"The weak spot of the Mayan religion," she continued, "is the many human sacrifices they performed to placate their gods."

"The Mayans were not the only ones who performed human sacrifices," I said. "Many civilizations did the same. Even the Greeks, who were very civilized people, performed human sacrifices. Agamemnon sacrificed his daughter, Iphigenia, to the goddess Artemis to placate her, who didn't allow the Achaean fleet to sail to Troy. The Druids performed human sacrifices as well."

"Yes, you are right, but the Mayans' cruelty was unique." she replied. "They sacrificed children and prisoners of war. A missionary friar described human sacrifices that he witnessed in detail. According to his report, the victim had been kept in prison without food for a few days so that he couldn't offer resistance. Then he was brought to the temple and held down by four men. A man got close to the victim with a sharp flint in his hand. With great expertise, he suddenly made an incision in the chest and pulled out the victim's heart with his hand. Then he put the heart, which was still throbbing, on a tray and handed it to the priest, who smeared the statues of the gods with the blood that was dripping from the heart."

"The cruelties practiced by the Catholic Church were no less appalling," I countered.

"Did Catholics sacrifice their victims by ripping their heart out?"

"If you come to Rome someday, I'll show you the statue of the philosopher Giordano Bruno who was burnt alive by the Catholics. That kind of death is cruel as well."

"Yes, I agree," she answered. "Wickedness is innate in the human heart, regardless of country or race. But now, let's forget human sacrifices for a while and go swim."

"Swim? Where? We are a long way from the sea, and there are no swimming pools in this archeological site."

"We can go to a *cenote!*" she answered.

"What is a *cenote?*"

"*Cenotes* are sinkholes, but some of them are quite wide so swimming is possible. You can find those kinds of wells only in Mexico, due to the softness and porosity of the limestone. In ancient times, the Mayans performed rituals in the *cenotes*, as they believed that the sinkholes were a meeting point between the worlds of humans and gods. Archeologists have found many human skeletons in the *cenotes.*"

We visited a few *cenotes* that day. Some were wide and it was possible to enjoy swimming, while others were smaller, but no less amazing. In one of them, we had to step down three upright ladders before reaching the water. It was a thrilling experience.

The next day Melanie took me to another archeological site called Chichen Itza. The area, which was once a large, thriving city, was very vast. There is a pyramid with a temple on the top as well. We saw a building that looked like an observatory. There is also an area called the Great Ball Court, which according to Melanie is the widest in Mesoamerica.

"Have you ever visited the sanctuary of Our Lady of Guadalupe?" I asked.

"No, I haven't. It is in Mexico City. I am leaving in two days, so unfortunately I cannot take you there."

"It doesn't matter. I'll go there by myself," I answered. I couldn't leave Mexico without visiting one of the most venerated Marian sanctuaries.

I arranged a flight from Merida. Once I arrived in Mexico City, I took the subway and got off the train after a few minutes and walked along a street that led to the basilica of the Virgin of Guadalupe. The place where the basilica stands is called La Villa de Guadalupe.

It was early in the morning, but the street already swarmed with people and food vendors. After ten minutes of walking, I arrived at the side entrance of the basilica. There was a large square before the main church. Actually, there were a few churches in the area besides the basilica that houses the original cloak on which the image of Our Lady is imprinted. The place where the basilica now stands was a holy place long before the Spanish conquered Mexico. It is called the Hill of Tepeyac. At the site there was a temple devoted to the mother goddess called Tonantzin. Later, the Spanish destroyed the temple and built a nearby chapel. But the destruction of the temple couldn't prevent the natives from pouring into the site.

Ten years after the Spanish conquered Mexico, a local peasant named Juan Diego, who had recently converted to Christianity, had a vision said to be Our Lady in the same area, who asked for a chapel to be built in the place. Diego reported what Our Lady had requested to the Franciscan bishop, but his account left the bishop doubtful. In fact, he required proof to corroborate what the native had reported.

Juan Diego went back to the hill where the vision had happened, and asked Our Lady to give him proof that she was really the Virgin Mary. This time, Our Lady asked Juan Diego to pluck some flowers and take them to the bishop. This would prove the truthfulness of the vision.

He did as Our Lady required; he picked some roses and wrapped them with his cloak. Then he hastened away to the bishop. When he was in the presence of the bishop, he unfolded his cloak. The roses fell onto the floor, and the image of the Virgin Mary was shining on the cloak. From then on, Juan Diego's cloak was guarded with care by the Franciscan friars, and a chapel was built in the place of the apparition.

People from all over Mexico rallied to the chapel to worship the shrine, and it is reported that many miracles occurred. Nevertheless, the natives kept calling Our Lady by the name of Tonantzin, the ancient mother goddess revered by the native population. This gave rise to the doubts of the Franciscan friars, who were convinced that the veneration of the holy image was a pagan cult.

Something similar also happened in Enna. In fact, Our Lady, who is the patron saint of Enna, replaced the ancient cult of Demeter, who was the town's mother goddess. The celebration in honor of Our Lady happens on July second every year, the same time when the old pagan cult of Demeter was celebrated. People of Enna today still invoke the name Kore, who was Demeter's daughter.

In my opinion, it doesn't matter the name you give to God; what matters is the spiritual feeling that radiates from the worshipper. So you can call God Allah, Brahma, Vishnu, or Shiva without losing the purity of your heart. Jesus and the Virgin Mary are beyond time, as they existed before time, long before coming into human history. They also existed in the pagan era and were worshipped differently.

The Virgin Mary appeared to Juan Diego in the form of a crossbreed maiden, and in the same place where the Spanish had destroyed the temple dedicated to the goddess Tonantzin. That means that nobody is allowed to destroy others' temples, even if they are considered pagan. In fact, religion and spirituality are not related to a particular cult. Over the years people have given various names to God and worshiped Him in different ways, but it doesn't entitle anybody to resort to violence to make one religion prevail over another.

As for the holy image imprinted on Juan Diego's cloak, it was kept for some time by the Franciscan friars until it passed under the custody of the diocesan priests. With the passing of time, possibly in good faith, the original image was retouched in some spots. For instance, the crescent on which the Virgin Mary stands was painted with silver. Apparently, nowadays the retouches have discolored naturally, while the original image is still unaltered.

Pilgrims and visitors flocked into the square in front of the new basilica. I saw people, who from their olive complexion seemed to be natives or crossbreeds, carrying litters full of flowers. Some of them laid the litters on the floor and staged devotional songs and dances. I have to say that few times in my life have I seen such beautiful scenery. After having danced and sung, the pilgrims went into the basilica with their litters covered with flowers. I followed them and entered the basilica from one of the gates. It was a round church with an altar opposite the many rows of pews, and the holy image of the Virgin Mary was over it.

I sat on one of the pews and watched the shrine from a distance. Meanwhile, other groups continued to arrive in the basilica and headed for the back of the altar. I followed them and arrived at a moving walkway below the shrine. I admired the holy image for a few seconds while the walkaway moved. Then I went out of the new basilica. I spent all day at the Villa de Guadalupe and visited the churches and buildings scattered in the area.

The old basilica housed Juan Diego's cloak until 1974. A museum stands not far from the small old chapel erected on the same spot where the apparition happened. There were many exhibits in the museum. I lingered in a room full of many paintings that portrayed the Virgin of Guadalupe. The painters had tried to make a copy of the original image, but none of them had been able to reproduce it perfectly. Then I stood in front of a photograph, which was an exact copy of the original and had been approved by the ecclesiastic organs. While I was admiring the copy, I heard a voice behind me.

"Who knows what the number eight symbolizes?" asked a man who was leading a group and had the air of being a professor.

Nobody in his group answered his question. "The number eight symbolizes the infinite," I answered.

"Exactly!" said the professor. "Now look at Mary's pink robe. There are eight four-leaf clovers on it."

Yes, I thought, *the Virgin Mary is infinite, beyond space and time. She always has been and always will be. That means that she was on the Hill of Tepeyac long before the Spanish came to Mexico, even though she was worshipped under a different name.*

I left Mexico City and returned to Merida, where I stayed for a few days. Then I returned to Enna.

Chapter Twenty-Two

The Forum

Once I finished acting the most salient episodes of my life, our director Paolo went on stage.

"Now is the time for our debate," he said, addressing the audience. "Usually when we go to the theatre or the cinema, or when we watch a TV forum, we are passive onlookers. I recognize that mass media, movies, and theatrical performances are a good source of information. In particular, theatre has a cathartic function, as it purifies our mind and soul, but I want the members of the audience to be part of the play in my theatre, not just passive onlookers. For this reason, whenever I direct a play, there is always a debate in the end. Now, any of you who want to say something can speak up."

There were a few minutes of absolute silence. It seemed that the play had left the members of the audience indifferent, but someone sitting in the last row raised his arm and asked permission to talk. Paolo nodded to him.

I knew that man. He had been my first playmate. His father, Michele Macaluso, had run a shoe repair workshop in a room that my father had rented to him. He was known as the packsaddle repairer, because besides repairing shoes he also fixed packsaddles for donkeys and mules. He was a stout man, despite the fact he led a sedentary life. He always wore a cap. In fact, I had never seen him without one. His mustache was so thick that you couldn't see his lips.

There was just an inner door to separate his workplace from my home. I used to cross that door and talk with him. He was kind to me, despite the lawsuit he had against my father, who had given him notice to vacate. On one of the walls of the room stood a large portrait of a mustachioed man. On the opposite wall were pinned smaller posters that portrayed people holding red flags.

"Who is that man?" I asked one day when I opened the door.

"You don't know him? He is the most powerful man in the world. His name is Joseph Stalin. He is my idol."

"The Americans are much more powerful," I replied. "They have the atomic bomb, which can wipe out your Stalin at any moment."

"The Soviet Union has nuclear weapons as well. Furthermore, Stalin's scientists have invented a lethal ray that can bring down enemy jet aircrafts. One day," he continued, "communism will also triumph in Italy and social injustice will come to an end. Everybody will be given a house and land to use. There will no longer be private property, because everything will belong to the state."

I was just a child and couldn't understand politics, but his words and enthusiasm enchanted me. So whenever I could, I went to his workshop and listened to him.

"When the working class takes power in Italy, the churches will be confiscated and converted into public offices," he said one day.

"There are no churches in communist countries?" I asked.

"Not many, as Stalin has converted many of them into swimming pools, gyms, and public offices. A few churches have been razed to the ground, like the Cathedral of Christ the Savior in Moscow. Stalin will build the Palace of the Soviets on that site, which will be the tallest building in the world."

Undoubtedly, that shoe repairer was an ardent communist, but also a good person. After he was evicted and I couldn't meet him anymore, I appreciated his good heart, because despite the lawsuit against my father, he never mentioned it whenever I chatted with him, nor did he speak badly of my father.

When he died, the priest denied permission for his body to be taken into the church. At that time, communists were excommunicated and excluded from the sacraments. He couldn't receive Holy Communion, Extreme Unction, or a Catholic funeral. It came as a great blow to his family members, because his wife and children were Catholic. His body was taken stealthily from his home to the graveyard. Only a few relatives, comrades, and family members were present at his burial.

Now, in the small Church of Santa Croce, his son Gino was questioning me. His frame was similar to his father's. He also wore a mustache and a cap. He stood up and started off his speech by attacking my quest.

"I want to know what you have discovered after travelling across the world for so long. You have just wasted your money, or more accurately, the money that your grandfather left to you. You had better give alms instead of inquiring into life after death. There is nothing after death! You are just a stupid man!"

Hearing his fiery words, I flushed with embarrassment. I wanted to interrupt him, but Paolo shook his finger.

Then Gino went on with his tirade. "Religion," he said, "is just the fruit of alienation. It is not God that creates man; it is man that creates God! Therefore, God as an independent reality doesn't exist. In the course of history, the priestly class has always enjoyed privileges. Many priests are billionaires, and the Vatican is the richest state in the world. Over the years, civil power has been allied with ecclesiastic power. During Fascism, the Catholic Church, instead of fighting dictatorship, supported it. And now, even in our little Enna, the party in power is just the Christians, while our glorious Communist Party is relegated to being the opposition. I want to know what politics and religion have to share!"

There were a few members of the audience who belonged to the Christian Party. They quivered with rage, grumbled, and wanted to intervene, but Paolo managed to calm the audience down. There were also a few priests who knew that it was not true that the Catholic Church had backed Nazi-Fascism, and raised their arm to intervene, but Paolo also asked them to hold on a few minutes.

"Thank you for your contribution to the discussion, Gino," Paolo said. "I have appreciated your speech, because it has pointed out a few real issues. As for me, I believe in God just by faith. My faith is not blind, but reasoned and based on the Holy Scriptures. I cannot imagine that those who wrote the Holy Scriptures were gullible. Certainly, the Evangelists gathered accurate information before writing their Gospels. Matthew, Mark, Luke, and John actually reported that Jesus died and was resurrected, and this is proof that we human beings are made not just of material flesh, but also of some kind of energy different from the body, which is subject to deterioration. However, this is just my opinion.

"Now, before going on, let Vincenzino answer Gino's questions."

"Thank you," I said, turning to Paolo who, waving his hand, reminded me not to argue. "Every now and then I have the sensation of having lived a previous life in an Eastern country. In the winter, when I get up from my bed in the morning, I go to the bathroom to wash my face with warm water. In that moment, I feel as if I have done a similar action in another life between the eighteenth and nineteenth century while I was in a hotel or guesthouse room in a country, which might be Russia. I see myself dressed in the clothes in fashion at that time. Russia has always had a special attraction for me."

"There is no other life!" interrupted Gino, raising his voice and getting worked up. "Many religions," he continued, "believe in reincarnation, but this is a groundless assumption. Can you give me proof that we are reincarnated into another body after our death?"

His question bewildered me, and I didn't know what to answer, then I answered Gino with another question. "Do you think that at the time of our birth we come from nothingness?"

"Don't be ridiculous, Vincenzino! We come from the zygote, which is the organism resulting from the union of your mother's egg and your father's sperm. Both egg and sperm have their own energy and DNA that transmits the hereditary characteristics from your parents to you. There is no soul, no previous life! When we die, our energy comes to an end and we disappear into the same thin air from where we came."

Gino's words were so crude that they made the saliva dry up in my mouth. I was seized by the doubt that he might be right. Actually, believing in life after death could be considered an escape from reality. I didn't know what to answer. Then I pulled myself together and tried to digress.

"Before answering your question, Gino, I want you to listen to my travel to Moscow, which is the capital of what once was the Soviet Union, of which you are so nostalgic."

"Okay," said Gino, "I am curious to know something about Russian culture."

Chapter Twenty-Three

Moscow

Some time ago, I got close to the Buddhist religion, specifically to a branch of it that makes reference to the teachings of a great monk who lived in the north of India around the tenth century AD. A Tibetan monk, who belonged to this Buddhist branch, wanted to export these traditional teachings to Western countries, and for that purpose he created a center in Southern Ireland.

From that tiny seed, in the span of twenty-five years, the center had grown to become 800 scattered throughout the world. A real surprising growth! The Tibetan Buddhist monk had not established a center in Russia yet, but he made contact with a Muscovite who wanted to spread Buddhism in his country.

I had already visited Buddhist centers in Ireland and America, and now I was eager to get in touch with that Russian man. What attracted me to Russia was not only my passion for travel and the desire to spy out new countries, but also my want to collect data to understand whether religions are just opium for people, or if they are genuine.

I succeeded in getting the name and address of the Russian man that was training to become a Buddhist teacher, and I immediately sent him a letter manifesting my wish to visit his city for a month between December and January. I received his answer nearly immediately.

"You are welcome in Russia!" he wrote in his letter. "My name is Igor. Attached, I send you the Cyrillic alphabet. The knowledge of Cyrillic characters will be particularly useful to you, as in Moscow we don't have signs written in Latin letters. You can come to Moscow anytime, whenever you wish. You will be my guest. You don't have to pay anything for your accommodations."

"Thank you, but I don't want to impose on your kindness," I replied in a letter. "I would be glad if you could find a small apartment for me where I can stay for a month. Please let me know what I need to do to get a visa from the Russian Embassy."

He sent me a formal invitation to go to Russia. I then went to the Russian Consulate in Palermo and got my visa easily.

A few days before my departure I received another letter from Igor:

Dear Vincenzino,

I got good accommodations for you. During your stay in Moscow, you will live in an apartment that belongs to a friend of mine. The apartment is very comfortable and is located in a Soviet-style building. From there you will enjoy an amazing view of Moscow.

I arrived at the airport in Moscow at five o'clock in the morning. Igor was waiting for me at the exit. He was a man around fifty years old and was as tall as me. His hair was darker than mine, and his dark eyes gave him a look of wildness. Our meeting was warm. We stepped into his car and drove towards the apartment that I was going to occupy. Along the way, Igor got lost several times, but we arrived in the apartment a few hours later.

It was located near Sheremescaya Street, on the fourteenth floor of a building the stamp of which was markedly communist. The entrance, elevators, and rooms had a Spartan air.

That same day in the evening, Igor picked me up and we went to visit a friend of his named Arkion. "Once Arkion was a great violinist," Igor said. "He underwent a surgical procedure on his left hand, and can no longer play his violin very well. Now he is meeting with many difficulties in his life."

"What does he do to make a living?" I asked.

"From time to time, someone calls him to play in a band. He also gives a few violin lessons. He is a good teacher indeed!"

Then we moved to another area of Moscow to meet one of Arkion's friends. She was a French woman named Caroline, who had lived in Moscow for fifteen years. The building was quite old, but Caroline's apartment had recently been remodeled. The wooden parquet floor was scattered with toys for her three pets that lived with her: two cats and a small dog, named Julienne.

"Julienne belongs to that breed of dogs best loved by Tsarina Caterina," Caroline said. "Then, due to the size, breeding has been reduced. Julienne is smaller than my cats, but he is very smart and sensitive. He looks like a human being."

We took a seat in the living room. Many musical instruments were hung on the walls. Some of them were rare and typical of Russia. Arkion took something similar to a mandolin in his hands.

"This is not an Italian mandolin," he said, "this is Russian! It is less convex than the Italian one."

There was another instrument similar to a harmonium, but it had a crank on one end and a small keyboard in the middle.

Now and then, Arkion stroked Julienne and played with him, or tried some other instrument. Igor and Caroline chatted in Russian.

"We're talking about Cossack music," said Caroline, turning to me.

"I adore Cossacks!" said Igor. "They have traditions, myths, and chants that go back to the dim and distant past. Their music is very deep and their traditions uncontaminated. Their task is to protect the Russian borders. You can even find

Cossacks in Vladivostok! At the time of the Bolshevik Revolution, half of them sided with the Tsar. Over time, many Cossacks have been killed off because they didn't want to give up their traditions."

Before we parted, she and I exchanged telephone numbers. Then she drew a map that I could use to reach her house without getting lost.

The next day, I set off from my apartment and, using my map, I easily located her apartment. We only stayed a few minutes at her home, just long enough to drink a cup of tea. Then we walked to her friend's house. It was a painter's studio; two painters shared the same room.

That evening, only one of the painters was in the room. His name was Oleg. He had a flowing reddish beard, was blue-eyed, and not very tall. Overall, he gave the impression of being a man who wants to live his life without having problems or straining himself to get ahead. The room was cluttered with colored tubes and paintbrushes. We sat around a small table.

After a few minutes, a lady taller than Oleg appeared. She was his wife and a painter as well. She cleared away the brushes and paint colors, and laid two trays down on the table. On one she had put some salmon and another kind of fish, which was a lake fish typical of Russia. On the other tray she'd put a cabbage, a vegetable pie, some bread, pistachios, and chocolate candies.

Another French lady, with her Russian husband and an Orthodox priest, joined us. Oleg showed everybody his paintings. One of them portrayed many people who were busy in a kitchen.

"We are three families that live in the same house and share the kitchen. In Russia, it is normal for families to live together. Is it the same in Italy?"

"I don't think so," I answered.

Meanwhile, the Orthodox priest reminded Caroline to come to church on Christmas Eve. "We'll go together!" Caroline said, turning to me.

"I think Christmas has gone," I said. "Today is January third."

"Orthodox Christmas happens on a different day. In Russia, we celebrate Christmas on January seventh, exactly nine months after the Archangel Gabriel told Mary that she would conceive Jesus. It is the most important holiday in Russia."

I thought it strange that while Communism wanted to suppress religion, Christmas was the most important holiday in Russia. Apparently Karl Marx failed in trying to convince people that religion is just opium for the masses.

Caroline and I went to a large Orthodox church on Christmas Eve. I noticed that there were no pews. There were just a few benches around the walls for people with disabilities.

The Mass lasted around three hours, and the congregation stood the entire time. Orthodox rites are completely different than the ones in the Latin Church. When the Mass was over, the priest invited Caroline and me to have dinner at his home. Starting on November 27, the members of the Orthodox Church had been fasting for forty days, and now it was the time to break the long period of fasting.

The priest's house was close by the church, and a table had been set for a few intimate friends. Caroline was one of the priest's closest friends. We ate every kind of food throughout the night: meat, cakes, salad, fruit, and above all we drank a lot of vodka. It was an unforgettable night.

Meanwhile, I started to get used to living in Moscow, and decided to visit the monuments and places of that fantastic city by myself. By taking the subway, which was not far from my apartment, I got off near Red Square. It was a place that I had seen many times on TV during the Soviet Union's parades.

I entered the square by passing through an archway. On the opposite side of the square, I saw the breathtaking view of Saint Basil's Cathedral. It had been built by order of Tsar Ivan Vasilyevich, also known as Ivan the Terrible, to commemorate the conquest of Kazan and Astrakhan. It is the symbol of Russian art and culture. Legend says that when the Ivan the Terrible saw the masterpiece, he was so impressed with its beauty that he ordered that the architects who had designed it should be blinded, so they could not build something similar again.

The entire Kremlin area is full of masterpieces. Even the walls and towers of the Kremlin are works of art. Not far from there is the Cathedral of Christ the Savior, which is the tallest Orthodox church in the world. It stands by the bank of the Moskva River. It was rebuilt after the fall of the Berlin Wall. It had been razed to the ground by Stalin, who had planned to build the Palace of the Soviets on its site.

Stalin couldn't carry out his plan, and now the Cathedral of Christ the Savior stands to signify that it is impossible to suppress religion, which is rooted in the human heart.

Chapter Twenty-Four
The Ending of the Play

The atmosphere in Santa Croce Church warmed up. Now there were two opposing parties: the spiritualists and the materialists.

A young man from the spiritualist party raised his hand and asked to talk. Paolo nodded and asked him to introduce himself. He was a player on Enna's rugby team. He was curly-haired, tall, and stout. As soon as he got up, the girls in the audience turned towards him, mesmerized by his figure.

"My name is Giuliano, and I have something to say about the subject matter."

"You are allowed to talk as long as you like!" answered Paolo.

"Whenever I want to discover something new and never unveiled before, I picture a man who is wandering in the desert," the young man said. "He is thirsty and walks along the dunes. He needs some water to survive, and hopes to find an oasis. Suddenly, he sees a pond in the distance. He quickens his pace to get to the oasis as soon as possible, but once he gets close, it disappears because it was just a mirage and not a real oasis.

"He sees more mirages as he continues walking. What to do? He is tempted to give up and surrender to his ill luck, but he is a man of faith. He has faith in good luck, and is sure that sooner or later he will find real water not just a mirage. He walks and walks, dune after dune, until, in the end, he finds a real oasis. His faith has saved him."

That young man in his twenties, besides being a handsome boy, was endowed with intelligence as well. In spite of his young age, he'd expressed ideas worthy of a theologian.

"What is the meaning of what you are saying?" said one of the materialists, who wanted to contradict him.

"The meaning," answered the rugby player, "is that everything is a projection of our inner being. If we really want to achieve an end, we must have faith in ourselves and in God. Without faith you will be a loser. As for if there is life after death, there are two possible answers: either be an agnostic or act as a person of faith. The latter, as happened to the man who wandered across the desert, has the real possibilities to discover the oasis, which is God."

After the young man finished talking, I had the impression that the conversation was about to become a political argument, which I wanted to prevent. In fact, the theme of the forum was about life after death; politics had nothing to do with the issue. However, Paolo was the director, and it belonged to him to steer the direction of the debate.

A member of the Christian Party turned to Gino. "The communists have been persecuting the opponents of the regime and sending them to concentration camps in Siberia. Only Christians have shown tolerance through the years."

"That is not true!" answered a member of the left-wing party. "Christians have been persecutors as well. After Emperor Constantine liberalized their religion, Christians became intolerant of pagans. They persecuted the heathens and killed them. The classic example of pagan persecution is Hypatia, a Greek scientist in Egypt, who was killed by Christian monks."

"That episode belongs to the distant past. We don't know how things really happened," answered one of the Christians.

"I can quote more recent instances of intolerance from the Catholics," retorted a member of the Socialist Party. "They persecuted the heretics, whose only fault was thinking differently from the Catholic Orthodoxy. They were burnt at the stake and even tortured to wring confessions out of them."

"Nowadays," said a priest who was sitting in the audience, "the Catholic Church is tolerant and deeply respectful of religious freedom. What matters is the now, not the past. Yes, the Catholic Church has made many mistakes in the course of its long history, but that doesn't mean that it is not a sound institution."

The discussion went on for hours. The main political parties in Enna argued about things that had nothing to do with the theme of our play.

Gino raised his arm and asked to talk. "I want to know," he said turning to me, "what is your opinion, Vincenzino. You have been researching for all your life. What have you found? Tell me something about the hereafter."

"I cannot give you the answer, Gino, because I don't know how to respond. Maybe saints, yogis, or mystics know the truth, but not me."

The mayor of Enna was in the audience and asked to show the new city plans. He got on stage, followed by a few city planners.

"As you can see from the relief map," said the mayor, "many churches are doomed to be demolished. Actually, we have sixty-four churches in Enna, but a good half of them is useless because there are no priests to take care of them. Therefore, they will be razed. Where there were churches, new squares, greens, and broad streets will be built. I will turn Enna into a modern city!"

I turned to the mayor, dumbfounded. Apparently, there was not much difference between what had been done by Stalin in Soviet Union and our rulers. I looked at the map and couldn't spot the Church of Santa Croce.

"What about our church?" I asked in a feeble voice.

"It will be demolished!" answered the mayor in a harsh tone.

The news gave rise to grumbling in the audience and the actors, but there was nothing to do to save our small church. A resolution for demolition had been taken by the city council. A new large street would be built where our glorious old tiny Church of Santa Croce once stood.

The loss of our cultural heritage is the toll that must be paid for progress, I thought.

As soon as Paolo heard the bad news, his face turned pale. He had spent most of his life taking care of the Church of Santa Croce, and now the news that it would be razed distressed him as if he lost a member of his family.

Four more actors should have performed after me, but Paolo didn't have the strength to go on with the play. He came on stage, and his eyes were misty and he couldn't contain his emotion, but in the end he addressed the audience.

"I thank you all for attending our play. After Vincenzino, a few more actors should have gone on, but the news that our meeting place will be wiped out doesn't give me enough strength to keep directing the play."

Little by little, the members of the audience left. They all had a hangdog look. An usher put out the candles that had formed the number eight. The two musicians got up and left the stage, carrying their instruments. The actors also headed for the exit. Paolo left the church last and closed the front gate behind him.

I don't know how it happened, but I didn't have enough strength to get out and they left me inside the church. They'd forgotten about me! I remained alone in the darkness. I had the feeling of being paralyzed.

How is it possible that the scenery changed all of a sudden? Up to a few minutes ago, I was acting on stage, and the church was full of light and the atmosphere cheerful. Now everything had disappeared: the church, the stage, the actors, our director, the audience, and the candle-lit number eight that symbolized the infinite in Paolo's mind. Now everything was over.

I suddenly thought that the change from life to death is sudden and unexpected—but I had discovered nothing about the hereafter.

I could not see anything in the darkness. I heard hammering outside. I had the impression that someone was sealing the front door from the outside. I wanted to cry and tell the hammerer that I was still alive and inside the church, but nobody could hear my voice. The church had turned into a coffin for me. I could not breathe or see anything. For a moment, I was seized by the terror that the materialists might be right: there is nothing after death.

Then I recalled the rugby player's speech. The only way for me to survive was through my faith.

Though I was sinking down, I continued to hold out to the last. I was sure that the infinite universal love energy which permeates all living beings on Earth would not forsake me.

"Always remember, Vincenzino, that the universe is ruled by an immense source of love which cherishes even the tiniest creatures. You must conform to it in your life!" once Sebastiano told me while we were admiring the starry sky from the terrace of our house in Pollicarini.

"Yes, I have to trust the universal love energy which is so powerful that it can get my soul out of this goddam coffin. And now I can realize that my soul always guided my life to the right direction like a lantern in the dark night." I thought.

By having this faith, I saw a faint glimmer of light coming from the street door. It was not a mirage! It was a real trail of light. I followed it to see what would happen.

Review Requested:
If you loved this book, would you please provide a review at Amazon.com?
Thank You

Lightning Source UK Ltd.
Milton Keynes UK
UKOW03f0337190517
301419UK00001B/90/P